Shanghai
Shadows

Shanghai Shadows

LOIS RUBY

HOLIDAY HOUSE / NEW YORK

for
Hannah Miriam Ruby,
who has brought it
all full circle

Library of Congress Cataloging-in-Publication Data
Ruby, Lois.
Shanghai shadows / Lois Ruby.—1st ed.
p. cm.
Summary: From 1939 to 1945, a Jewish family struggles to survive in occupied China;
young Ilse by remaining optimistic, her older brother by joining a resistance movement,
her mother by maintaining connections to the past, and her father by playing the violin
that had been his livelihood.
Includes bibliographical references.
ISBN-10: 0-8234-1960-6 (hardcover)
ISBN-13: 978-0-8234-1960-9 (hardcover)
1. Jews—China—Shanghai—Juvenile fiction. 2. World War, 1939–1945—
China—Juvenile fiction. 3. China—History—1937–1945—Juvenile fiction.
[1. Jews—China—Shanghai—Fiction. 2. World War, 1939–1945—China—Fiction.
3. Family life—China—Fiction. 4. Austrians—China—Fiction. 5. China—History—
1937–1945—Fiction.] I. Title.

PZ7.R8314Sha 2006
[Fic]—dc22
2005050342

Prologue

There's a lot to learn from a lying, cheating, knife-wielding pickpocket like Liu, and believe me, I soaked up all that he had to teach me. My brother, Erich, *should* have been my guide to this mysterious country, since he's two years older; but the truth is, he always expected the worst possible thing to happen, and he was never disappointed. He got me into a lot of trouble, while Liu rescued me more times than I could count. Liu had a talent for conning his way through the streets. If survival was an art here, he was the Michelangelo of Shanghai.

I was just his apprentice. I came to China as a proper Austrian girl, with all my pleases and thank-yous in place. Such a good girl, I'd never have dared steal so much as an orange from our own pantry. Now I wouldn't recognize myself if I met me in Vienna. Besides barely casting a shadow, with sunken cheeks and sandpaper skin, I've bribed, stolen, cheated, sabotaged, sneaked, and lied. Liu's been a terrific teacher.

He might have been my age, or as old as Erich. It was hard to tell because he was small and wiry but with the smarts of somebody who'd been around forever. Living on the streets your whole life will do that for you.

I didn't live on the streets. I lived in a proper house when we first got to Shanghai. Well, not so proper compared to our beautiful home in Vienna. But we were Jews, and Hitler was . . . Hitler. What choice did we have? We could leave our home or die, which was no choice at all if you have half a brain. There were hushed rumors that our borders would be closed, that we'd be trapped like rabbits in a cage, that the Nazis were rounding up our people and sending them to labor camps in Germany, where they worked themselves into the grave. So Father got our family out of Austria while we could still escape.

Of course, I wanted to go to America. Mother had lived in America years before. Dreamily she'd tell us, "There, oranges hang so low that you can pluck them off a tree while lying on the grass." Better yet, in America people went to the cinema every day.

Well, America didn't want us. Shanghai was the only port that would take us in, thousands of us. Who would have dreamed that I'd have my eleventh birthday in China?

Naturally, I was sad to leave Vienna and my friends, especially my best friend, Grete, and our dog, Pookie. But I was a hopeless optimist, so I told them all, "Be happy for me. We're not just leaving Austria. We're sailing to the Far East. To Shanghai, China!" Grete and my other friends gave me sympathetic looks—*Poor Ilse, going to a place where people didn't even use knives and forks!*

But I was an adventurer—or at least I could be if I ever wriggled out of Mother's clutches. Leaving Vienna, I believed that anything was possible in a huge, bustling, exotic place like China. Anything.

CHAPTER ONE
August 1939

"I'm boiled alive," I complained as we filed off the ship that had carried us from Genoa, Italy. Everyone was grumbling in a dozen languages. My hair whipped my head in the fierce, hot wind off the sea. "Erich, aren't you dying in that wool suit?"

"No, I'm comfortable." My brother jammed his hat down to keep it from flying off, but I saw the band of sweat around it.

"You're just too stubborn to admit it." Or to admit that he was nervous about our first steps in China.

He tapped my shoulder. "I'm as cool as that man," he said, pointing to a half-naked rickshaw puller.

Mother poked Father's arm. "Oh, Jakob, what have we come to, men pulling carts as if they were beasts of burden?"

"The man's called a coolie," Erich explained.

Mother gave him half her attention while toggling on her toes to read signs. None were in German, but Mother read English, since she'd lived in America for a time.

"It's how he feeds his family." Erich glanced nervously at Father. We all wondered how Father would feed *us*. He looked away, hugging The Violin's case upright like a dance partner. His hands were stained with the black dye that was bleeding off the leather case. Erich and I thought of The Violin as the fifth member of our family. Father loved it more than he loved the rest of us put together.

I held my skirt at my knees so it wouldn't balloon around me like a parachute. Not that I'd have cared, but Mother whispered, "Remember at all times, Ilse, you are a Viennese lady."

Erich and I snickered, and he doffed his hat behind Mother's back.

A lady, ha! In Vienna I'd preferred climbing our tree to sitting in the parlor with my knees clamped together, balancing a teacup, with Mother and her deadly dull lady friends.

Now my dress was soaked and sticking to my back and chafing at my neck and wrists. How could sun be so unforgiving? At home and all through the sea voyage of the *Conte Verde* Mother had kept me out of sunlight, since I'm a redhead and freckle something terrible. Two weeks here, and I'd be as spotted as a giraffe.

The man just ahead of us in the processing line used his shirtsleeve to mop up the sweat rolling down his face. That's when I first noticed a small Chinese boy zigzagging through the crowd as if he were tracking down something he'd lost. Spotting the man with the coat flung over his shoulder, the boy grinned and went into action.

"Shoeshine, boss?" He dropped to one knee, whipped a rag out of his pocket and jerked it back and forth across the man's shoes.

Erich pointed to an angry-looking red scar on the boy's leg. "Looks like someone carved an *X* into his leg."

The boy looked up and raised one eyebrow like a tailor measuring me for a new coat, then seemed to dismiss me and returned to the man's shoes.

"Poor thing," I whispered to Erich. "He looks like he hasn't eaten in a week!"

"Poor thing? Look what he's doing."

He'd tied the man's shoelaces together and then jumped to his feet in one quick move. When the man stooped to untie the laces, the boy lifted the man's wallet and backed away into the crowd.

"The little crook," I cried, though I have to admit to a heart-fluttering. Only twenty minutes in China, and something daring, something criminal, had happened right before my eyes.

Still, I was a law-respecting Austrian, so I said, "Mother, did you see what happened?"

"Shhh," Mother replied. "Your father is next in line."

"Well, I'm telling that policeman over there." Erich tried to stop me, but I'm as stubborn as he is. Since I didn't know a word of Chinese, I pantomimed the whole thing. Nodding with understanding, the policeman chased the boy and grabbed him by the scruff of the neck and barked something to him.

The boy immediately slipped a bill out of the stolen wallet, stuffed it into the policeman's pocket, and disappeared back into the crowd.

"Did you see that, Erich?"

"He's a professional," Erich said with admiration. "The police are in on it. That's how people do business here, with bribes."

"That's terrible," I muttered.

"So? Is it any worse than how we got out of Austria?" Leave it to my brother—so serious, so wise. In Vienna he'd run around with a group of schoolboys who gathered in our front parlor and boasted like big shots. They were going to cross over into Germany, and steal into Hitler's headquarters while all the guards were snoring or wooing, and do unspeakable things, murderous things. They'd be national heroes and save us all. How they talked and talked! Father thought it was healthy for young men to have such ideas. "Not good to be so helpless," he said, which is how he and Mother felt while waiting for our exit papers.

After all the Jewish schools were closed down and the Nazis began boarding up our shops one by one, Erich and his friends had long hours to fritter away. The boys sat on their haunches, ready to spring into action. But there was no action, just talk, and now the rest of those boys were still in Vienna, while we stood in line in far-off China. Were we lucky, or were they?

Mother seemed unaware of the spectacle all around us as she peered over Father's shoulder. He was presenting our papers to the immigration man and pressing The Violin case to his chest so as not to get separated from it in the crowd.

"Shpann family?" an Austrian resettlement man barked. We elbowed our way toward him, bundles and all, and he led us from the dock through the clogged streets to a more civilized neighborhood. Such a long walk! Halfway, Mother took off her shoes and padded along in her stockings, with her pointy heels hooked through the straps of her pocketbook. I glanced behind me to gauge how far we'd come and saw the pickpocket following us. Why? Because we looked prosperous? I hung my pocketbook around my neck for safekeeping and gave him a half smile to say, *I know what you did.*

"Get away!" our guide yelled, clapping his hands. The boy scurried off. "Watch out for these bandits," the guide warned us. "This one, Liu, he's the worst of the lot. Come along, people."

We stopped abruptly in front of a beautiful three-story building. "It looks like our house at home," I whispered to Mother. She pressed her gloves to her heart, and I saw her mind arranging furniture, setting a vase of flowers in the front window, replacing the brocade drapes with white sheers. The front door was painted a shiny red, with a brass pineapple knocker at its center.

"Lovely," Mother said, "and so big."

The refugee man cleared his throat. "Yes, well, seven families share this house. One kitchen," he added quietly. "Your rooms are in the back, third floor. Very sunny. Southern exposure."

"Home," Erich said grimly as Mother's face fell.

Not mine. I squared my shoulders and scuttled up the steps to give that brass pineapple a resounding thunk. We waited for someone to open the door. And waited. I glanced at Mother's watch. It had been her mother's, a piece of Swiss workmanship so elegant that it hummed softly and never lost a minute. But already moisture beaded under the glass, and Mother had to shake the watch to clear the fog. One thirty. It was still yesterday in Austria, or was it tomorrow?

Mother opened the red door and put her shoes back on. We four huffed up the stairs, pushing and pulling our bundles and The Violin. The whole trip would have been lots easier if The Violin had sprouted its own legs. At the second landing a door was opened by a girl around my age, holding a white winter muff of a cat. The cat narrowed its eyes and swished its tail across the girl's face.

"Don't mind Moishe," the girl said. "He's nervous around strangers." She spoke in Yiddish, but it was enough like German that I could understand her. She looked our family over and whispered something to the white fur. If the cat didn't like the looks of us, would we have to find another house?

There were cartons stacked to the ceiling beside her door. Mother wrinkled her nose in disgust when a cockroach skittered out from under the boxes.

"*Voden?*" the girl said over the top of Moishe's fur, meaning, "What else would you expect in a place like this?" The cat made a snarling sound and leaped out of her arms in pursuit of the gigantic bug. Lunch?

This was not a promising greeting! But then the girl smiled and said, "*Bruchim haboim*, welcome to you all. I am Tanya Mogelevsky. Here I live with my mother, only we two."

I said in German, "My name's Ilse Shpann. We're new here."

"I think she can tell," Erich said, nudging me up the stairs with his satchel.

"Shall I knock on your door after we get settled?" I called back to Tanya, and she nodded.

On the third floor I snapped the key out of Mother's palm and unlocked the door to our apartment. Before us spread a large, sunny room, rounded at one end like a wedding cake, with carved cherubs framing the ceiling.

Mother held her gloves to her cheek. "Oh, Jakob, it's lovely, no?"

Father nodded, not convincingly. There wasn't a stick of furniture in the airless room. Father and Erich opened all the windows, which helped a little.

Three doors were spaced evenly along the wall, the one opposite the wedding cake. "Many doors, a good sign," Mother said. Her heels clacked across the shiny hardwood floor until she reached the first door, which led to a closet. "Very good, we shall have where to hang our clothes." Mother hurried to the next door, which opened into another closet, a little bigger. The third door, the same. "So many closets? Where are the other rooms?" Mother asked.

I liked the closet with the small octagon window that let in a lacy pattern of light. But Erich tossed his hat into that room. Spreading his arms from wall to wall, he announced, "I hereby claim this space as mine because I'm the oldest."

Hah! He was thirteen, with just a hint of orange fuzz above his lip, and those two years over me gave him privileges. Anyway, the space wasn't large enough for Mother and Father's bed; none of the closets were. And now it seemed clear that my room was to be a stuffy shoe box without so much as a square of a window for daylight.

"Moth-*er*," I wailed.

Father's hand weighed heavily on my shoulder. "We shall make this our home until we can find more commodious quarters." He set The Violin down in the third cubicle, his studio. Such a fancy name for a windowless wardrobe no bigger than one of our water closets in Vienna.

Erich unbuckled his satchel and began piling clothes and books on the floor of his room. "This is the best we can expect as stateless refugees."

Mother snapped, "We are not refugees, and we are not stateless. We are Austrians temporarily living in China."

"Yes, yes, my dear." Father humored her, but he added under his breath, "We left our home, our work, our photographs, our savings—"

"And Pookie. I'm lonesome for Pookie, aren't you?"

Erich snarled, "Did you really think we could take her on the train through the Brenner Pass and trot her halfway across Italy to the harbor? A *dog*? We barely got past the checkpoints ourselves."

"But I love Pookie!"

"Children, please," Mother said. She waved her arms to encompass our home, with its windows that stretched from floor to ceiling and our three impressive closets. "Tell me, is this not a splendid, sun-filled apartment? Three beds, a nice little table, a few chairs, that's all we'll need." I saw her mind churning with possibilities, and then she said sternly, "Remember, children, we left Austria of our own free will."

"Ach." Father slapped his thigh. "Free will, indeed. What else could we do with Hitler's bloodhounds right behind us?"

Mother was riled. I knew because she was telling Erich and me the things she meant for Father's ears. "We *chose* this city, children."

"This is the only place in the world that would let us in without a visa," Erich reminded her.

Mother looked as though she might flick his chin with her fingernails—her favorite means of letting us know who was boss—but instead, she shed her suit jacket and ran a gloved finger over the dusty windowsill. "We must always choose the country that is our home. What is important, children, is that we have a solid roof over our heads, and we are all together."

"What is important," Father said quietly, "is that we're alive."

CHAPTER TWO
1939

Father bartered for mattresses, a table and chairs, and a two-burner cookstove, while Mother dusted every inch of our apartment and washed the walls and floors with lukewarm water, since there hadn't been time to buy soap, and anyway, the house had no hot-water heater.

I unpacked my clothes and a few pots and dishes, some books and sheet music, Grandmother's kiddush cup, a clock—the sum total of our treasures from Vienna. Erich went to scout out places to buy food and such necessities as toilet paper, soap, and tooth powder, plus a bamboo basket to carry all our supplies back and forth to the water closet—a community bathroom in the hall where there was always a line. I soon learned to queue up way before I needed to, just in case the urge should overcome me.

The first time I ventured out into the crowded hall, I found Tanya sitting on the top step of the second floor. Moishe gave me his unfriendly gaze. One yellow eye, one brown.

"Why are you sitting out here?" I asked Tanya.

"My mother has company."

"When my father's violin students start coming, I'll be spending half my life on these stairs."

"It's only on Friday," Tanya said, stroking Moishe, who was more fur than flesh.

"Your mother teaches on Friday?"

Moishe jumped off Tanya's lap, and Tanya propped her elbows on her knees. "Teaches? I guess you could say that. One student, every Friday at two o'clock. But not the same one every week."

I heard muffled sounds coming from the apartment. "What's she teach? Voice? She's a singer?" Just then the door opened, and out came a man who was either Chinese or Japanese, I couldn't tell which, except that the uniform suggested that he was a Japanese soldier. Tanya and I both jumped to our feet as he rumbled down the steps two at a time, clearly in a hurry to get back on duty.

"Class is over," Tanya said with a sigh.

Soon our apartment swelled with music. Father lined his studio walls with quilts to muffle the sound, which poured out under the door anyway. Each day he said, "Don't worry, children. I'll play with an orchestra soon enough."

"Don't count your chickens," Mother said.

Every third refugee was a musician or a conductor or composer, and did they have work? Of course not. All the violin chairs were already filled in the Shanghai Municipal Orchestra and the music conservatory and the finest universities.

"Each one has another violinist or two greedily hovering in the shadows, rosin ready. Mostly Russians," Father said with a sneer. Obviously, Austrian musicians were the best in the world, or Mozart and Beethoven wouldn't have spent so much of their lives in Vienna. Viennese doctors, too, and bakers and cobblers. Just about everything from Austria was better than whatever came out of Hungary and Poland and Russia.

Discouragement was beginning to line Father's ruddy face and cloud his eyes. He took in a few students and made Erich and me continue our lessons on The Violin, the only instrument we'd been able to spirit out of Austria. Our parents liked to think of us as a musical family. Mother played the piano. Father, of course, was a virtuoso, famous all over Austria. But Erich and I—well, Father's consolation for having such tin-eared children was that he'd never have to compete with us if a seat opened up in a Shanghai symphony.

Within a few days of our arrival, we began to notice swarms of other foreigners, and that helped us feel more at home.

Mother said, "So many from eastern Europe. No class." She glared over the top of her glasses at the noisy Czech and Polish refugees on the streets. But I felt sorry for them because Germany had invaded their countries, and war was now raging in Europe.

Also there were French and Dutch and British and

Americans on the streets of Shanghai. A most curious sight were the yeshiva boys, pale as paste in their long black coats and fur-trimmed hats, with earlocks that fell to their shoulders in curlicues. They walked two by two, never looking at anyone else on the street, talking to one another and waving their hands as though they were always in an argument.

"Make a face; see if they notice you," Tanya said. "They're not allowed to look at girls, much less touch."

"What are they saying?"

"They're Torah learners. Arguing about Bible passages. They study all day and half the night." The pair passed, making a wide half-circle around us. "Did you notice the tall one with the ring of milk over his lip? He's cute."

"Oh, Tanya, be serious. They look like undertakers."

"But I have heard that their rebbe is looking for wives for those boys. Are you interested?"

"*Never!*"

Lots of other eastern Europeans clogged the streets of Shanghai. A bunch of White Russians who'd escaped the Communists years ago had set up their own neighborhood, Little Moscow, in the French Concession, but Mother wouldn't let us go there because the White Russians hated Jews. Everyone seemed to.

Oh, but good Jewish Russians lived in Shanghai, also, and some of them were refugees like us. Others had been in China for forty or fifty years and were now settled in Shanghai, the "City by the Sea." Well, it was hardly a sea, if you ask me. We had the smelly Soochow Creek that streamed off the

Whangpoo River, which itself was a fat, ugly sister of the Yangtze farther north. I never saw the Yangtze, but I knew it was huge. "Like an ocean," I said to Erich once, and he jabbed me with a spoon and said, "Crack open a geography book if you think that caramel-colored mess is like an ocean."

"Well, close," I insisted.

"Best you can say for the Yangtze is that it floods a lot," Erich grumbled. What a grouch, my brother!

Mother, who'd never worked a day in her whole thirty-seven years, found a job behind the counter of a Viennese bakery. Father was shamed, but what could we do? We had to eat *something*. We wouldn't get rich on Mother's pay, but at least she brought home fluffy loaves of bread, and every Sunday, a creamy napoleon or a thick wedge of linzer torte, which we divided and devoured even before dinner. Dinner, hah! We could finish it in two minutes or less, as there was nothing that involved actual chewing.

Across the Garden Bridge from where we lived sprawled Hongkew district, which smoldered under Japanese occupation. The Japanese were swarming all over China, but they couldn't get their hands on our International Settlement or the French Concession in Shanghai, so we were safe.

The first time Erich and Tanya and I crossed the bridge, I sucked in my breath at the sight of the Japanese sentry guarding the entrance to Hongkew. He stood at attention, as if he had a broomstick stuck in his trousers. His rifle had a bayonet fixed at the end of it, and I was sure he meant to run it through us.

We girls clutched Erich's arm. I said, "I thought we'd left such things behind with the Nazis."

"Shhh, just look straight ahead and walk briskly," Erich whispered as we crossed over into Hongkew.

"I've been in Shanghai months already," Tanya said, "but I never had the nerve to come over here."

No wonder. The streets were bursting with people— mostly Chinese and Japanese, and some poor German and Austrian refugees who couldn't afford even the hatbox we lived in. We stumbled over rubble in the streets, left from when the Japanese had bombed Hongkew two years earlier. Some of the bombed-out shells were already rebuilt, and how I loved reading their shop signs in German! There were shoemakers and sausage shops, a stationer, a hatmaker, a haberdasher, lots of cafés, a meat market, and even a kosher butcher, although we Shpanns didn't observe the Jewish dietary laws, and anyway, we couldn't afford meat.

In the dense Chinese section of Hongkew, beggars filled the streets. "Don't stare," Tanya whispered, staring at the men and children with oozing sores and empty eye sockets and stumps where hands and feet ought to be.

"How do you suppose they got that way?"

"Don't ask," Erich muttered, and I imagined the worst: Wretched birth defects or Japanese bombs, or worse yet, diseases like leprosy that made fingers and toes chip off like dry bark.

Smelly garbage lined the curbs. "I'm sure glad we don't live over here." I kept shaking my head as street peddlers slid tin pots, needles and thread, rubber shoes, and nubby blue fabric under my nose.

Tanya said, "Everyone's selling, but no one's buying."

Except at the letter writer's booth, since so many Chinese couldn't read or write their own language. Well, if you ask me, it looked impossible to read those squiggles going up and down instead of neatly across the page like proper language.

The folding street kitchens were doing a hearty business too. Men with foot-long chopsticks stirred mysterious foods in giant pans over glowing hot charcoal—green beans as long as sticks and fish heads with eyes popping.

"Know what that is?" Erich pointed to some see-through stuff shriveling in the pan. "Jellyfish. And those rings of striped meat? Snake."

"Oh!" I clutched my belly. Tanya was more daring. She bought a paper napkin full of snake bits. "I don't think snake's kosher, but here goes." She popped a chunk into her mouth and smacked her lips. "Um, not bad. Want to try a bite?"

Erich sampled it thoughtfully and spit it out.

I am quite certain that God never intended for us to eat things that slither on the ground.

Great clouds of smoke baked the walls of the buildings around us. A million flies swirled above all the snake and jellyfish, or whatever that stuff was hissing in boiling oil. Somehow the cooks made it all smell mouthwatering.

Tanya motioned toward some spotty black ovals and introduced us. "Meet hundred-year-old eggs."

"I'll bet they're not a day older than ten," I said.

Erich shrugged. "A rotten egg's a rotten egg."

Chickens and ducks and monkeys squawked and poked their noses out of bamboo cages hung all over the market.

"Careful," Tanya warned, sidestepping a pungent pile of steamy droppings. Mother would have a fit if she saw this. Fish, squid, frogs, and shrimp elbowed each other in tanks filled with murky river water. My stomach churned.

"Still hungry?" Erich asked.

Still. My stomach growled despite the horrible sights and smells. Until we watched a vendor scoop out a net full of jade-colored frogs the size of Pookie's paws. She dropped the net, squatted indelicately, the way no Viennese lady ever would, and clubbed those poor little frogs with the wooden end of her cleaver until they gave up.

A toothless old woman started some high-pitched haggling with the frog murderer, which seemed to be the way business was usually conducted. Finally, when it looked like they were about to punch each other, both women smiled, and the deal was done. Fresh frogs for dinner.

Erich got a nasty gleam in his eye. "You know what they say. The Chinese eat anything with four legs except a table. You don't notice any dogs or cats around, do you? Keep a close eye on Moishe."

"Oh, Erich, honestly!" Tanya cried, punching his arm.

She was a little sweet on my brother, who rubbed his arm and said, "Come on, let's get out of here."

We darted through the crowd, running back to the International Settlement. The Japanese guard's eyes burned into my back all the way across the bridge.

It didn't take us long to figure out that the language of business wasn't the one we spoke, or even Chinese. So Mother taught English to refugees and to us.

"Mother!" I wailed each time she plunked Erich and me down for an English lesson. Secretly I soaked up the foreign words. I longed to speak English—not the stuffy British English that some of the rich Jews in Shanghai spoke, but American English, full of delicious slang: *Toot, toot, tootsie, good-bye; razz; nifty;* rolled around on my tongue like a lemon drop.

This was not the American English that Mother had learned. We were never encouraged to ask Mother about those years in America, or about her special friend, the one Erich and I nicknamed Molly O'Toole after the mysterious M.O. that appeared on the return address. Mother had been a university student in the state of California, we knew that much, and also that she hadn't graduated. She'd returned to Vienna in 1923 to finish her studies, but then Father came along, and how could school possibly compete with true love?

True love. Oh, yes, now into my twelves, how I yearned to be in love with someone. Someone other than myself.

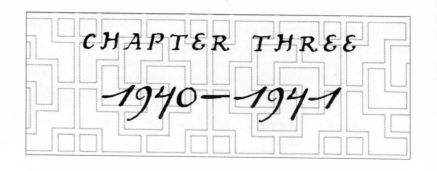

CHAPTER THREE
1940 — 1941

"Tanya, there's that little thief I told you about!" Tanya made a point of ignoring Liu and gazed in the window of Mrs. Kazimierz's house across the street, where a beautiful Tiffany lamp gleamed like a beacon in the shabby room.

"Why are you always following me?" I asked the boy, not that he understood a word of German.

His smile showed a bunch of chipped teeth as he said, "No ma, no pa, no whiskey, no soda."

Ma I got, Pa I got, but whiskey and soda? Liu stumbled around like a drunk.

"Ah, schnapps." And so we began a sort of pantomime ballet and managed to communicate a bit, at least I thought so. I motioned to my house and gestured. "Where do you live, sleep, eat?" And he jerked his grubby elbow toward a wide place in the gutter where he'd built a dwelling out of cardboard. It was smaller than Pookie's doghouse in Vienna.

"See? Close-by," he said. "Whistle, I come to you." He warbled some toneless tune I didn't recognize.

"You whistle for dogs, not people," I said indignantly. I pointed to the jagged scar on his leg, raising my eyebrows in question.

"Big fight," he said cheerfully, and pulled a knife out of his short trousers. Tanya spun around, eyes wide, as he faked a crisscross with the point of the knife over his scar. She pulled on my blouse, rushing me down the street. When I looked back, Liu was grinning at us, with the knife tucked back into his belt.

War news got to us slowly, and much of it was garbled. Holland and Belgium surrendered to Hitler, followed by Norway. The Germans entered Paris in June. And then Italy joined the war on Germany's side. Yugoslavia and Greece fell in spring 1941. But it was all so far away that we hardly felt the effects.

And we were all thankfully distracted by a wonderful parcel that came from America for Mother. The box weighed a good ten pounds, twenty maybe.

"Molly O'Toole must have spent a fortune on this, Mother. Open it, quick!"

She took the box over to her bed, loosening the brown paper carefully.

"I'd tear that box open and toss the paper wrapping out the window already."

"We can turn the paper over and use it," Mother said quietly. She raised her glasses hanging beside the key on a string around her neck and opened the envelope taped inside the box. I inched over to catch the first glimpse of the contents.

After an endless minute Mother handed me the note—the first time I'd read a word from her American friend. Mother had told us her friend was from an Irish family, which was how we came up with the name Molly O'Toole. So I'd imagined a loopy handwriting in blue ink, the kind that fades when you blot it. To my disappointment the note was barely a few words typed on onionskin:

January 29, 1941

Frieda,

I hear that many goods are hard to come by in the Far East. I am sending some things you and your family might need during these difficult times. Be well.

M. O.

Well, it certainly wasn't a warm note. There wasn't a hint of the Irish brogue I'd always imagined for Molly O'Toole. And the parcel had taken months to get here!

Mother dug deep and fished out one delectable after another—coffee candies, a tube of Ipana toothpaste, a tin of Hills Brothers coffee, two bars of Ivory Soap. Also in the package were some white shoelaces, a sack of kidney beans, red ribbons, and Doublemint chewing gum.

Mother blew the envelope open to put the letter back in and found a crisp American ten-dollar bill. We were rich!

Then she pulled out of the box four pairs of ugly gray wool socks and buried her face in them. When she looked up over the socks, I couldn't read the unfamiliar look in her eyes. Embarrassed, I reached into the box again and scooped out three packs of Lucky Strikes.

"We will sell them one by one. American cigarettes are worth a small fortune," mother said.

"I know."

Mother laid all eight socks out in a marching row on the bed. There was slick sweat dripping down my neck, so those itchy, nubby socks didn't look a bit appetizing.

"Remember winter, Ilse? Winter will come again," Mother said, "and we'll be grateful for these homely socks." She stuffed the ten-dollar bill under her bodice, into that handy pocket grown women have and I didn't have much of to brag about.

That night we had a whole roasted chicken for dinner, our first in seven months. Erich hid a wing under his pillow, or it could have been something else he hid. He was always full of secrets.

Me, I refused to wash off the chicken grease around my mouth or the delicious smell on my fingers, so I could taste them all night long.

Erich brought home the news that Germany was battling the USSR, and Soviet cities were being tossed back and forth between the two powers. Then right before my thirteenth birthday in October 1941, rumors reached us that the Nazis had murdered tens of thousands of Jews in the city of Kiev.

"Barbarians!" Mother said, listlessly stirring a pot of thin potato soup. "Ach, but tomorrow is Ilse's birthday. Life must go on."

We pretended cheer. Erich said, "You're anxious for us to learn English. You know what would really help? An American movie, that's what."

"A movie?" Mother repeated.

I quickly chimed in, "Cinema. At the Magestic Theatre. Imagine what two whole hours of hearing Americans talk to one another will do for our vocabulary."

"Sure, it's expensive," Erich said. "Maybe we can have half a dollar from your Molly O'Toole money?"

"A little, too, for popcorn?" I begged. "Americans always eat popcorn at the movies. Say yes."

"I will talk to your father," Mother answered dubiously.

By the time these movies crept across the ocean to China, they weren't exactly current Hollywood hits, but we didn't care. Everything American was wonderful. I couldn't think of a better birthday celebration than sitting in a nice, dark movie theater watching huge, beautiful Americans talk and kiss on the flickering screen.

"What is the movie they're playing?" Mother asked.

"It's called *Going Places*," I answered quickly.

"Going where?"

"Oh, Mother, I don't know! But it's starring Ronald Reagan. Very big Hollywood star."

"I never heard of him."

Erich hugged Mother. "You must have heard of a song from the movie. 'Jeepers Creepers'."

We bombarded Father at the door when he came home. "Please, please? For my birthday?" I begged.

"Jakob, there is a song in this movie called 'Jeepers Creepers'. Even in America I never heard this word."

"It's teenage slang," I proudly announced. "Erich and I will need to know such things when we get to the United States."

"If," Mother corrected me. "First we go home to Vienna."

Erich worked on Father, who was a softer touch than Mother. "It's a musical, Father." Erich hummed the opening bars of something by Mozart.

Father was hooked. "This film is an opera? What could it hurt, Frieda?" Father actually winked at her. Maybe they were glad to ship us out of the apartment so they could have a few hours alone.

Mother blushed and sighed, and it was settled. "Be careful of pickpockets," she cautioned.

All through my special birthday meal—two inches of brisket in with the vegetables, joy of joys!—Erich and I kept singing "Jeepers Creepers." By the time I blew out the match masquerading as a candle on a wedge of Mr. Schmaltzer's devil's food cake, Mother was humming the song, and just before Erich and I left for the movie, Father was plucking the melody on The Violin.

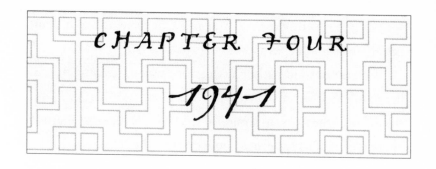

CHAPTER FOUR
1941

We'd weathered two miserable winters already. Our coats were worn limp as bedsheets, our shoe leather thinned to cardboard. Supper was no more than a few tired vegetables and a cup of rice, shared four ways. Mother was never hungry, or so she said, but her hollow eyes watched each bite Erich and I put in our mouths. If it hadn't been for the odd package that would come from Molly O'Toole, we'd have withered away. Every minute we were cold and damp, longing for spring. Then the rains came, and Tanya and I dumped bucketfuls of water out of our shoes at the door of the Kadoorie School, where we Jewish students tried to learn with steam rising from our soggy clothes.

Erich and I thought about staying warm and dry, and filling our bellies constantly. Tanya seemed to be thriving and shared treats with us every Friday night—sometimes half a melon, or baby bok choy that she handed to Mother upright, like a pale green bouquet.

Mother had three English students, who paid almost nothing. Mr. Shulweiss from downstairs was at least eighty years old and as dense as a rutabaga. Sputtering through the ABC's was his greatest accomplishment. He'd rub his elbows and pat his bald spot and treat us to three or four honking nose blows, then struggle to his feet for a trip down the hall to the water closet at around *m-n-o*. Though we'd miss the money, Mother politely released him from the torture, after which she said, "Ilse, I will give you an American expression you can add to your collection: 'You cannot teach an old dog new tricks.'"

Mrs. Mogelevsky, Tanya's mother, was her second student. She had dancing brown eyes and a small, heart-shaped face framed by a mass of brunette hair. Whereas Mother was lumpy here and there, Mrs. Mogelevsky had curves you couldn't help noticing. She made Erich very nervous. In the Ukraine she'd been a seamstress to rich ladies who'd sneered at anything less than the most elegant fabrics. Here in Shanghai, she had a knack for transforming any old cloth into stylish frocks that clung to her.

Mother loved teaching Mrs. Mogelevsky, who began each lesson with a sentence like a prayer: "I vant learn. I make English sewing business."

The third student was Dovid Ruzevich, who was a year or two older than Erich. The first time I opened the door to this boy, late in 1941, something odd happened to me—it was like touching the top of a radio and feeling the sounds hum through my hands. I backed away from the door as he asked in fractured English, "Meezis Shpann, de Anglish ticher?"

Behind me Mother said, "Ah, yes, Dovid, please come in." They sat down at the table, and Mother asked her usual first question: "Tell me, why do you want to learn English?"

He was from Poland, and in his own language, Yiddish, he explained, "I will not forever be in China. I must learn quickly so I can work in New York, America. Many jobs there for bookbinders. That is my trade."

Mother tested him to see just how much English he knew. "Meezis Shpann, de Anglish ticher" was his entire grasp of the language. Mother plunged right in, while Dovid's face struggled with the awkward sounds and his lean hands rolled around as if he were trying to wave the words right into his brain.

I tried to be home when Dovid appeared in our apartment each Wednesday at four. Sunday, Monday, Tuesday—these were just the days leading up to his lesson. Thursday, Friday, and Saturday were the disappointing days after. As I shivered in my useless blanket each night, Dovid's face—his chin with its small tuft of wiry dark hair, his blue-black eyes so intent on learning—was the last thing I saw before sleep wiped it from my mind like jottings from a blackboard.

Father barely noticed the cold because he was playing with a string quartet that practiced in a ramshackle warehouse and eked out one paying concert a month at a Shinto temple in

Hongkew. "Chamber music," Father told us, "balm to my frayed soul."

Well! All our souls were frayed as more and more war news reached us. Our beloved Austria hadn't been *ours* for three years already. I wondered what it was like for Grete and her family—if they were still alive. I don't know how Erich heard things, but one night he told us that ten thousand Polish Jews had fled for Lithuania before Hitler had gobbled it up. I wondered if they were still safe.

"Thank God we are alive, children," Father said over and over. Me, I wasn't at all convinced this was *life*.

"Tanya," I asked one especially cold, hungry night as we huddled together out on our porch, "is this the way life is meant to be?"

"Maybe. For Jews," she replied.

I'd been wanting to ask her a very personal question, but the time had never been right. Yet, tonight I took the risk, though I couldn't look at her as I asked, "I'm wondering what happened to your father."

She squirmed beside me, offering a mild wave of warmth under our thin quilt. "In Vinnytsia he stayed. Our town is about 250 kilometers from Kiev."

"And he let you and your mother go, just like that?" I couldn't imagine Father allowing such a thing to happen. "Oh, but maybe he couldn't get papers to leave. Is that it?"

Minutes passed before she said, "Papa isn't Jewish."

I didn't know anyone who was married to a gentile, but blood is blood. Mrs. Mogelevsky was so gorgeous, and

Tanya! How could he let them go? "Wouldn't he come with you anyway?"

"No."

I thought that was the end of the discussion, one sharp *no*, until she took a deep breath and said, "Promise you'll never tell a word to anyone, especially not to your brother. Promise?" I nodded. "Papa was a Communist. His comrades, they didn't know that my father had a Jewish wife and daughter. He doesn't like Jews, you know, Stalin."

I sighed: the usual story.

"Or Orthodox Christians, either. But mostly Stalin doesn't like anyone who could be a threat to his power. Even his own Communist leaders in my country. But, we had a roof over our heads and enough to eat. Until the massacre."

I braced myself for another tragic story; I was swimming in them in the sea all around me. But I listened.

"Papa was not just a Communist," Tanya said, twisting a handkerchief into a thin pretzel. "He was a member of the NKVD, a Blue-Cap."

"Which is what?"

"The Soviet secret police," she whispered. "It was 1938, a terrible time in Ukraine. Before the Germans came. Stalin ordered the police to round up everyone in Vinnytsia who was an enemy of the people. Some because they didn't go to work on a religious holiday, or they put up a fuss when the Soviets took their property to starve them, or they moved houses or jobs without permission of the NKVD. Others, no reason at all. They were shot in the back of the head. Some of the young women—don't ask. Truckloads dripping blood came every night and threw hundreds of bodies into a mass grave. The grave was left open in the daytime. You can imagine the smell. Three years later, it's still in my nose."

"And your papa?" I asked, with my hands pressed to my heart.

"He was a guard, to make sure families didn't take their loved ones out of the grave." Tanya told me this in a calm, no-nonsense way, but a quick sideways glance revealed the tears filling her eyes.

"I'm so sorry, Tanya."

She shrugged under our quilt; our shoulders bumped.

"One day Mama saw the bodies down in the deep grave. Some were still alive."

"Oh, God!"

"Mama started to yell and scream and tear at her hair and beat on my father's chest. Papa acted like he didn't recognize her."

"How could he *do* that?" I said, nearly gasping.

"Who knows, Ilse? Maybe that's why we're alive today. So, two men on his guard detail dragged her away from him and dropped her at our door."

"Then what happened?" I asked quietly.

"In the dark, Papa came home. My mother spit in his face and slammed the door on his boot. He threw stones at the window to make us open up again. The NKVD had its eye on Mama, he said. She was now an enemy of the people. They'd come for her. I'd be swept along with her."

"You must have been terrified!"

Tanya shrugged again. "Those things happened in my country. That night Papa gave us forged papers and put us on a truck into the countryside. We crossed over into Byelorussia, then to Lithuania, and to the other side of the world. Here we are. We left him behind, my father. No regrets."

"Oh, Tanya!" There was nothing else to say so I was glad that Moishe padded up the stairs just then, with a mouse dangling from his teeth.

Tanya said, "At least someone's eating meat these days."

That night, when Mother and Father were wrapped around each other for warmth and snoring in their bed, Erich and I bundled ourselves into every towel and blanket in the house and played chess by the moonlight from his little frosty window.

I tapped my bishop a square or two. Erich said, "What kind of a move was that?"

"My fingers are numb. I can barely pick up my pieces." Excuses. Truth is, Erich was a much better chess player. "I'm a block of ice. Feel." I thrust my hand at Erich's cheek. "And hungry enough to eat the whole chessboard." No comment from my brother. "I'm so miserable. I wish I were dead."

Erich suddenly backhanded the board, and all the pieces went flying. "Don't ever, ever say that—unless you're prepared to die for something beyond your own skin."

I was shocked by his outburst and the realization that my own brother saw me as a selfish, empty-headed girl. "Die for what, then?"

"Freedom."

Fancy word, but what did it mean in practical terms, such as food in our bowls? "What would *you* die for?"

"I'd be willing to die fighting the Nazi bastards or the Japs."

"Erich! You wouldn't know which end of the gun to use."

He scooped up the chess pieces. "There are many ways to fight, such as the Resistance."

"And what's that?" I asked hotly.

He started to say something, then changed his mind. "You're not old enough to understand."

"Oh, really? I'm still taller than you."

"As if brains were measured in millimeters." Erich pulled his blanket up to his ears. At nearly sixteen his whole face looked different—wider, longer. His reddish hair, once like mine, was browning up and dry. I wondered if I looked different now. I'd avoided mirrors for months.

Erich began sorting the pieces on the board. "Start over. Your move."

"Forget it!" I stormed off to my own dark icebox of a room. In the middle of the night, I shivered myself awake, and Erich's words flooded into my mind: "fighting . . . the Japs," "freedom," "the Resistance," and I was stabbed by a frightening thought: Erich was caught up in something dangerous. I could lose my brother. Lose him.

Was that what I should prepare to die for?

CHAPTER FIVE
1941

One Sunday afternoon, bored to death, I coaxed Erich into taking a walk in Hongkew. We trudged through the streets of the Chinese section, but as soon as we rounded the corner on Chusan Road, you'd have thought we were in Austria.

A sign in a window said, LITTLE VIENNA CAFÉ. We hovered around the doorway. Erich's eyes were drawn to three young men hunched in a tight circle. Though my brother had no ear for music, he could hear things only dogs could pick up. I only caught fragments of the whispered conversation, even though it was in German.

"Midnight . . ." "Moral obligation . . ."

"What's so interesting about those guys?"

Erich shushed me. One of them glanced up, and I could swear he recognized Erich. His eyes shifted away instantly, and Erich turned his back.

I was more intrigued by a smartly dressed couple at the next table. Their knees touched under the table, which thrilled me, but not half as much as the white starched tablecloth, the likes of which I hadn't seen since we were on the ship bound for Shanghai. I stood close enough to feel the cool cloth brush my knees.

Though the air crackled with cold, the woman looked cozy in her red suit and shimmery silk stockings, with just a wool shawl draped over her shoulders. Suddenly I wasn't thirteen, I was twenty-five, sophisticated, cool and composed, like she was. I took a closer look at the man across from her. He was dashingly handsome and worthy of this lady and me, both of us so genteel, with our ebony cigarette holder in the ashtray, smoke curling upward in a lazy spiral.

The man was eating ice cream. In winter. In occupied China! I held my breath as he spooned soft mounds into his mouth, and I stared at the coated spoon as it slid off his tongue. Never mind the woman; just then I was the man, mustache and all.

No doubt I was drooling on him, which was why he looked up at me and offered his cup of ice cream and a clean silver spoon. I grabbed them and let that beautiful, thick, frozen cream glide luxuriously down my dry throat.

Surely this was heaven. I'd have licked the cup clean if I'd thought Erich wouldn't blab the news to Mother.

"Thank you," I whispered, placing the empty cup and spoon on the table.

If only I had a job, then I could buy ice cream whenever I wanted it. But jobs were scarcer than blond hair in China, and even Mother had been cut back to ten hours a week at the bakery. Of course, no one would hire a girl my age, but Erich was promised four hours a week as a delivery boy—if he could only scrounge up a bicycle.

Somehow Erich came home with a rusty specimen of a bicycle that guzzled oil, but at least its wheels spun. "I'm calling the bike Peaches," he announced proudly.

"That's a ridiculous name," I muttered.

"Ridiculous? Why? Peaches are what I miss most from home. Now I'll have peaches every day."

How on earth could my brother get such a treasure? The suspicion in Mother's face mirrored my own, but we'd learned to simply be grateful for every windfall.

Indoors was nearly as cold as outside, and Mother could barely grasp the pages of her English grammar book when Dovid came for his lesson. I watched him lean across the table and turn each page for her.

In frustration she slammed the book shut and said, "Forget nouns and verbs. Today we will work on vocabulary, also comprehension. So, Dovid, please, you must tell us your story. Everyone in Shanghai has a story. Ilse, come to the table. We will have an English conversation."

I eagerly leaped off Mother's bed and slid onto a chair across from Dovid. My hands were warm inside the white furry muff Mother had traded for a loaf of Mr. Schmaltzer's bread too burned to sell. It was how he'd paid her that day.

Dovid cleared his throat. "Where to begin? Poland, we are Polish, my family."

Though I knew that, I felt the familiar pang of disappointment: better if he'd been Austrian. Mother would approve of a boyfriend from Austria. But, I reminded myself, Europeans are Europeans in this sea of Chinese. And besides, he isn't my boyfriend.

"Your parents?" Mother asked.

He shook his head, unsettling a nest of dark curls that he brushed away. "Who knows?" He searched for each word and haltingly told us, "Also my sisters . . . twins, Shayna and Beyla. German soldiers come. Take them away."

Mother asked gently, "How did you find out, Dovid?"

"A neighbor, not Jewish."

Mother supplied the word, "A gentile, yes, what did he do?"

"He put his own family in danger to tell me. Also to let me sleep in his . . ."

"House? Barn? Shop?"

"Where *chazers* live."

"Ah, pigsty," Mother said.

"Pigsty, yes. Two nights while I think what to do, where to go. In the end, I alone go out from Poland."

"Without your family?" I cried.

"Worse things there are," he said brusquely.

Mother nodded. "You expressed yourself very well. That is enough for today."

Dovid started to get up, then slid a paper out of the back of his book. "For you, Mrs. Shpann."

I studied the black-and-white charcoal drawing upside down—trees, a few houses with smoke swirling out of the chimneys, a gentle hill in the distance with smudges that could have been goats. No people.

"Lovely. And where did this come from?" Mother asked.

"I draw myself. My village in Poland, after they take my family."

Tears sprang to my eyes.

Mother propped the drawing up on the bookcase behind her. "Come next Wednesday," she said. "Ilse, show Dovid to the door."

My arm brushed his as I opened the door to a blast of hall air even colder than in our apartment. "Stay warm out there," I murmured.

He smiled. Crinkly half circles on his cheeks enchanted me, but I also saw that his lips were badly chapped. "I am used to Polish winters," he said, tipping his cap to Mother.

Once he was gone, the apartment felt even colder. Mother lay on her bed cradling her sore hands. Gently, I slid them into my white muff.

The next morning, December 8, I was jolted out of bed by the sound of explosions. We rushed into the hall.

"They bombed Pearl Harbor! They bombed Pearl Harbor!" everyone was shouting. "Thousands of Americans dead!"

Details were hard to pin down, but we learned that the Japanese had launched a surprise attack on Pearl Harbor, which was in the American territory of Hawaii. Now they'd bombed a British gunboat in our harbor.

Then we joined the rest of the house huddled around Mr. Shulweiss's shortwave. The static cleared every few seconds, so we heard the shaky voice of the announcer: "Ladies and gentlemen, I regret to inform you that the war in the Pacific has begun."

America was in the war.

Suddenly, it was not just Hongkew under Japanese occupation but all of Shanghai, including us in the once-safe foreign settlements. We poured back into the frosty streets. I saw Liu hiding behind a garbage bin. I didn't know if he was watching for pickpocket prey or whether he was just as scared as the rest of us hounding one another for information on how our lives were going to turn.

I cried bitter tears, lost in the horde of frightened people. Father was stunned, and Mother had to rush off to the bakery, so Erich tried to comfort me awkwardly. I shrugged him off. Why, I don't know. Maybe it was because of his smug look that said, *I warned you all; you didn't listen.*

Asian countries all around us were reeling under Japan's atrocities. If before Pearl Harbor we were hungry, *after* Pearl Harbor we would surely be starving. In weeks we would feel the effects of the war in the Pacific right where it hurt us Jewish refugees most. Once the United States had declared war on Japan, and days later the Germans had declared war on the United States, we'd get no more American movies, no more packages from Molly O'Toole. All American money for the refugee settlement, all Red Cross money, all Hebrew Immigrant Aid money, would be cut off cold.

That night after we found out about Pearl Harbor, Erich didn't come home. Mother and Father were frantic, and I was no help. I pictured him pierced through by a Japanese bayonet or drowned in the Whangpoo. Then something clicked for me. Those men at the Little Vienna Café who'd recognized Erich and turned away—maybe they were some of the Resistance fighters Erich had hinted about. And my brother was working with them.

They were the ones who'd given Erich the bicycle. I was sure of it now. What had only been talk—talk among Erich's friends in Vienna—was turning into dangerous action in Shanghai. Who they all were, where they headquartered, I didn't know, but that night I vowed to find out.

"Where were you the whole night?" Mother patted Erich's face, his arms, his chest, to make sure he was all in one piece. "We were worried sick, your father and I."

"With friends," Erich said, slipping out from under Mother's probing hands and eyes.

Father was practicing. The Violin was one string short, and he was making do. The music vibrated a filling in my back tooth.

"Who are these friends?" Mother asked, closing Father's studio door.

"You don't know them."

"You spend too much time with them," Mother said sternly.

"They use the time well," he retorted. He'd gotten very sassy with Mother in that new deep voice he so eagerly showcased for us.

Her back was to Erich as she stirred a pot of soup. "Where do you go every day with these people?"

"Here, there."

"Where?"

Ilse to the rescue: "He plays soccer, Mother."

Mother's spoon scraped lazily across the pot. "You play soccer all night? And the bicycle—"

"Why are you interrogating me?"

"So many hours, and I don't know where you are?" She turned around and offered Erich a spoonful of the potato-and-leek soup—a peace offering.

He shook his head. "I go to meetings."

"Meetings, Erich?"

"What do you think, everyone sits around like you do waiting for the Japanese to take over every corner of the city?" He paced the room, drumming his fingers on his thigh. "Some people act, Mother. Action."

Mother pulled her shoulders together in resolution. She handed me a Thermos and some bamboo chips, which we used as currency at the hot-water shop. "Go down and get us boiled water for tea."

She was getting rid of me so they could talk, as if I was a child and Erich wasn't. I looked at my brother closely. His shoulders were broader, his waist narrower. There were rusty shadows on his cheeks. A wave of fear scuttled through me as Erich tore out of the apartment, slamming the door behind him.

I snapped up the Thermos and bamboo chips, followed

him and sensed somebody following *me*. I looked over my shoulder, and there was Liu, a half block behind. What did he want from me? He knew I had no food to share with him, no money.

Three boys I'd never seen before waited for Erich at the corner of Kinchow Road and Baikal. He must have known they were waiting; that was why he'd picked the fight with Mother—so he could bolt from the house.

He fell right into step with the boys, all of them walking so fast that I needed three steps to each of theirs just to keep them in sight.

At the gate of the Baikal Cemetery, one of the boys gave a lit smoke to Erich. The tallest one snuffed his out with his bare fingers and tossed the stub of it over the fence into the cemetery. Then, as if on a signal, all four of them turned around and walked back down Baikal Road, laughing and punching each other and generally acting like obnoxious boys. I ducked into Ah Ching's Bird Shop, where it was dark and jammed with cages and fluttering wings.

"You don't buy a bird, you don't stay in my shop," Ah Ching growled, and his mynahs and canaries cackled in agreement.

Finally the boys passed the store, and I raced up the street to keep a respectable distance between us.

At Yangtzepoo Road the tall boy dangled a key around his neck and bent toward the lock of a godown, one of the decrepit warehouses along the docks of the Whangpoo. The four of them disappeared into the building. The door slammed shut; all the windows were boarded up. I listened at the door, but not a sound escaped the building. Was this one of the *meetings* Erich talked about? Just what were they discussing so quietly in there? I held my breath and listened more closely. Nothing.

Straddling a wide stone bench next to the godown, I waited. For what?

Liu darted in and out between the godowns, clearly hunting for something—dropped coins, maybe, or food. Each time he appeared, he studied me and once got close enough that I snapped, "Why are you always following me?"

"Whistle, I come to you, missy," he replied.

"I didn't whistle."

"I come anyway!"

I groaned, and he got the hint, disappearing into an alleyway just as the door of the godown opened. My first instinct: hide. In wartime Shanghai the impulse was always to sneak, to lie, to make yourself invisible. I jumped off the bench and crouched under it, hidden by the great lion's claw legs.

The men were in their twenties, blond hair cropped short, smooth-cheeked, and crisply turned out in pressed khaki shirts and trousers. Whispering in German and shifting from foot to foot with their trousers tucked into their high boots, they looked so much like Nazi soldiers that for a moment my heart stopped. I tightened myself into a smaller target and studied them.

They weren't Nazis at all! They were two of the men

we'd seen at the café. Before I could scuttle out from under the bench, the short, stocky one spotted me.

"Look here, there's a rat in the sewer," he said to the other man, who yanked me out from under the bench.

I struggled up from the dirt and landed on the stone seat.

"Why are you spying on us?" he growled

"I'm not spying, I'm . . ."

"Just hiding under a bench. And you speak the mother tongue? Who sent you?"

"Nobody. I was just following someone, no one you know, really, just a friend, just exploring," I stammered.

"What do you want me to do with her, Gerhardt?" the shorter man asked, his beefy hands pressing on my shoulders.

I looked up at the one he'd called Gerhardt, whose eyes narrowed into tight slits, but there was a hint of a smile around his lips. "Get rid of her. I don't care, Rolf. Throw her in the river, feed her to the pelicans. Just make sure she remembers not to come sniffing around here ever again." He disappeared inside the warehouse, slamming the door.

So, Rolf was left with me. *Get rid of her,* Gerhardt's words echoed in my head, but I sensed that this man had no idea what to do with me.

"On your feet, girl," he commanded, not too convincingly.

I jumped up, hoping I could dart around him, but he was a wall between me and fresh air. My feet couldn't get me anywhere. Would words? "I'm Ilse, Erich Shpann's sister."

"You're *what?*" He shoved me back down on the stone bench with a punishing thud. "The idiot brought you here?"

"No, not really. I followed him. That is, I sort of guessed where he was going." There was no way he'd buy this lie, but I forged on. "My mother sent me to find him. She's feverish, burning up, and she needs him to come home right away."

He seemed to consider this. Maybe he had a heart after all, or a mother.

"Our mother will be so upset if I don't bring him before she dies." I sounded whiney, even to my own ears, so I swallowed and boldly asked, "What does my brother do inside that warehouse? What's so top secret here?"

"None of your business," he growled, "and if you have half as much sense as your brother, you'll forget where *here* is."

Did I dare take a chance? I stared right into his cold, blue eyes and said, "I know you're all in the Underground resistance."

The color drained from his cheeks. He hoisted me up by my elbows; my feet swung off the ground in front of him. Now my heart thudded; what business did I have nosing around in this mess?

He shook me. "I can haul you over to the river in about three giant steps. You a good swimmer?" Suddenly he was pulling me across the road to the river bank, my legs flying behind me. I looked down at rushing water that was deep and clogged and stinking with garbage and the morning's chamber pots. I really didn't expect that he'd throw me in, but I kept thinking, *Mother will kill me if I drown in this filthy water.*

He still gripped me by my elbows. My shoulders ached;

every muscle in my middle stretched into tight ropes. If I relaxed my body I could maybe drop, shimmy down and roll away from him on the grassy bank—or maybe I'd plunge right into the brackish water. My bones jiggly with fear, I closed my eyes to the rushing water below. And whistled. Beethoven's Fifth.

Rolf seemed startled. Then out of nowhere Liu appeared and shouted at the man's back, "I have a knife, boss!"

Rolf dropped me right at the edge of the riverbank and put his hands up. I scrambled away. Liu waved the knife, motioning for Rolf to run.

"Don't ever come around here again," the coward shouted from a safe distance, as Liu slipped the knife back into his belt.

"I don't know what he would have done if you hadn't shown up," I said breathlessly. Liu grinned and put his hand out. "I have nothing to give you." I tapped his grubby palm.

"You owe me next time you whistle and I come."

He walked me as far as the Garden Bridge, guarded by a Japanese soldier, but he went no farther. Chinese people crossing the bridge usually felt the blow of a boot, or spittle on the back of their necks, or worse, if they didn't bow to the guards, and Liu didn't seem like the bowing sort.

We westerners were virtually invisible to the soldiers. Of course, running could attract the guard's attention, and as I sprinted across the bridge, waving to Liu on the other side, I thought, *I didn't survive nearly floating in a putrid river just to be shot in the back by a Japanese guard.*

49

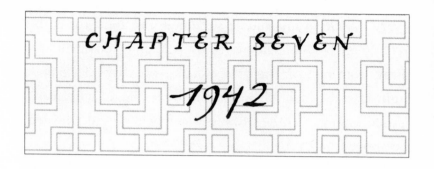

CHAPTER SEVEN
1942

I was terrified that something would happen to Erich hanging around with men like that. All through January and February I followed him to the warehouse, watching him tie Peaches to a post outside and tap a sort of Morse code on the metal door. Three knocks, pause, two knocks, pause, four quick taps. Usually the door opened a crack, and Erich slid in like a shadow.

Boldly creeping closer one day, I heard voices inside. They were arguing, shouting, but because of the street noise, I couldn't make out the words. I barreled an empty paint drum over to one of the boarded-up windows.

What if they caught me again? Had to take the risk. I glanced over at the rushing river across the road, took a deep, fortifying breath, and climbed onto the paint drum to peek between the window slats.

Gerhardt and Rolf were there. Erich sprawled on an overstuffed chair in the corner, surrounded by two of his cigarette-smoking friends.

Gerhardt seemed to be in charge. He passed a bowl of something around. Each of the others reached into the bowl and drew out a piece of paper, read it, and tore it into confetti, tossing the scraps into a blue-speckled tub. I watched the leader's eyes move from one person to the next; each one nodded as the leader tossed a lit match into the tub.

Suddenly something caught my eye outside the warehouse. Liu was cutting the rope that tied Peaches to the post! I tore over to him and leaped on his back. "Get away from that bike!" I shouted in German, in English, and I don't even know *what* I said in Chinese.

Surprised to find a girl nearly choking him, Liu dropped his knife. I let go of him and snatched it up. His eyes blazed. He seemed paralyzed, expecting me to slice him in two. But I just passed him the knife, handle first, the way Mother had taught me to hand scissors.

With the hilt of the knife firmly in his palm, he shook a head full of filthy hair and said, "Whiskey? Schnapps? Dollar for shoeshine, missy?"

"Go away, I'm just as poor as you are," I grumbled, slapping his hand with my palm rather than a coin.

He flashed me his grin again and flexed his muscles. *What* muscles? He was all bones, no meat. "I know tap-tap code," he said.

I shook my head. "Not a good idea."

"Okay, missy." Liu tugged at my sleeve again and led me around the building. The window I'd peeked in only moments before was now covered with Chinese newspapers. Had they heard me? Seen me?

Liu scaled the side of the building. Clinging to a rotted windowsill, he wedged his knife in a slot where the window didn't quite meet the sash. The window slid up, and Liu disappeared inside the warehouse.

I circled the building again. By the time I'd worked my way around to the front, Liu was standing at the open door grinning. A slight jerk of his head instructed me to follow silently.

Voices. I followed Liu up metal steps to a dark mezzanine overlooking the main open space of the warehouse. We hid in shadows, behind a couple of the beams. I had a clear view of Erich and the others below.

They had a huge map spread across several crates. The leader tapped a spot on the map. "The pharmaceutical plant, right here."

"Not impressed," the other man said.

"I say we go for a military plant—ammunition, explosives, blast 'em all to hell and gone," one of the boys said.

The second man said, "You crazy? Whatta we know about explosives? We'd be dead before we blew the hide off the first Jap."

The leader took a pen from his pocket and circled a spot on the map. "This is it, Red Poppy Pharmaceuticals up here in Chaipei. You think they're really making medicines out of those little red posies? Morphine? Before the occupation, maybe, but now it's all chemical warfare. We blow the plant sky-high!"

"And release poison gas into Shanghai?" Erich said. "That'll help Hitler along. It'll kill ten thousand Europeans and countless Chinese, too, along with the Japs. Smart."

The leader shrugged. "Chance we take. No war without risks. You in, mates?"

"That's way out of our range," the second man said, wiping his forehead with a red handkerchief. "Lunatics, the lot of you. Especially you, Gerhardt."

The leader, Gerhardt, lifted the map and held it like a shield in front of him, jabbing at the circle he'd drawn. "I say we wipe out the whole installation. We're men, and this is war. I'm right, Rolf, admit it."

"Right game, wrong playing field," Rolf said.

One of the boys thumped the map. "I still say hit the explosives. Light up the sky at midnight so the Japs can't miss the show."

Erich's voice was calm and measured, the way he got when his fuse was about to blow. "You said we'd be doing things like crossing wires, jamming radios, smuggling messages in and out, planting false intelligence. That's how we were going to help the Allied war effort. You never said anything about explosives and poisonous chemicals."

Gerhardt glared coldly at Erich. "This is war, Shpann, not a Boy Scout field trip. Last chance. In, or not?"

Just then a brown rat scurried across my feet, lashing

my leg with its rubbery tail. I released a tiny whimper of revulsion—just enough to cause Gerhardt to look up.

"Who's there?"

Silence. Could they hear us breathing?

"Shpann, go up and look."

Liu and I plastered ourselves to the back of the beams. I willed my heart rate to slow with shallow breaths. Erich clambered up the steps, the noise resounding off the metal walls. His flashlight painted the corrugated walls with a hard yellow light that darted into every dark corner. Rats raced to get out of the glare.

I was blinded by the light when it finally found my hiding place.

"Ilse? My God," Erich whispered, clicking off the flashlight.

Liu silently crept up behind Erich with his knife drawn. He recognized Erich, but his eyes asked, *Right now, enemy or friend?*

"Liu, no!" I whispered frantically, and he lowered the knife—a hair's width away from Erich's shirt.

My outburst brought Rolf tearing up the stairs. "You again?" he snarled.

"My sister," Erich said miserably.

"Yeah, we've had the pleasure. Is your shadow around here, that Chinese kid?"

I shook my head, watching Liu move in the dark behind Rolf.

Rolf said, "Give me some light, Shpann. I should have

drowned your sister when I had the chance. Okay, spill it. What'd you hear?"

You'd expect to panic, but instead, I took a deep breath and went absolutely calm. No sudden moves. "I heard everything." Erich spun on his heel, furious, but there was no stopping me now. "I heard enough to know that you're soldiers in the war against the Japanese."

"Yeah? What else?" He stepped on my foot to lock me in place, and I forced myself not to respond, no matter what. I kept my eye on Liu, hovering in the shadows, waiting for a signal from me.

Erich's flashlight darted around the dark space we occupied.

From below, someone called, "What's up there?"

"Under control." Rolf assured them.

Whose control?

A thousand emotions flooded Erich's face—horror, rage, regret. I feared he'd try to wrestle Rolf to the ground so I could run. Erich was outsized, and what good would it do anyway? I'd be caught in a flash. I signaled in the silent language of brothers and sisters: *I'm okay.* And I was, really. My fear had burned off.

Erich tried to coach me with his whole face. His eyes flamed. "Just let my sister go. She doesn't know what she's doing. She'll keep her mouth shut. I can handle her."

"Well! When have you been able to do *that?*"

"Shut up, Ilse."

I looked Rolf right in the face. "I guess you'll just have to drown me in the Whangpoo after all because I know too much, huh?"

"Are you insane, Ilse? Keep your stupid mouth shut," Erich warned.

I put my hand out to silence him. It glowed white under his flashlight. "I'm old enough to know what I'm doing." Erich's flashlight jumped around until it fell steadily on Rolf's hip. A gun! I didn't bargain for a gun!

Puddles pooled under my arms. Streaming through my mind at lightning speed were images of Vienna and the life we Jews left behind: our home and Pookie and Grete and her family, maybe dead by now. The scene changed violently to fierce Japanese guards booting and spitting on the Chinese whose country they'd taken, and stripping all of us of our metal, our cooking fuel, our gasoline, our bread, and our dignity.

In the split-second it took these pictures to cascade through my mind, my resolve hardened. "I want to help. I can. I'm quick and smart."

"You think we need *you*? A snively girl who hides under a bench?"

"You do," I said confidently. "I can't blow things up, or drive a truck, or carry four hundred pounds of explosives, but I can sneak around and bring you valuable bits of information."

Erich was shaking his head.

"Who'd suspect a girl?" Brave words. My voice wobbled.

I couldn't hold it together much longer, but in that one frantic moment, I *knew* I had to work for the underground.

Last chance. My eyes were fixed on that gun at his hip,
as I stuck my hand out to Rolf. It branched out there, small
and steady, totally alone.

He paused, considering the options. "Depends on what
Gerhardt says." Keeping his boot on my foot, he leaned over
the railing and shouted down, "Hey, Gerhardt, better come
up here."

I moved only my eyes to watch Gerhardt run up the
clanging steps. Spotting me frozen in Erich's spotlight, he
started laughing. "I knew you'd be back, Miss Shpann."

Rolf's shoulders went limp with relief. He stepped back,
and I wiggled my foot. Nothing broken. Rolf swaggered a
little, clearly trying to look much more important than he
was. "Just yesterday you were telling us we needed somebody skinny to slip through the cracks."

"Yeah," Gerhardt said, "she's a runt, all right." I was surprised to see that my hand was still sticking out when
he grabbed it in the big mitt of his own hand, shook it
vigorously, and said. "Welcome to the team, Shpann Number Two."

I was in! I glanced over at Erich and saw two messages in
his eyes: *You did a crazy, stupid thing, Ilse,* along with, *I'm proud of
you, little sister.*

Liu slid silently away.

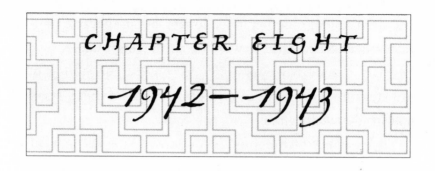

CHAPTER EIGHT
1942—1943

Mother and Father were sitting at the table when I burst into the apartment, gasping for breath. Also, Dovid was there, which caught me by surprise. It wasn't his time. I immediately smoothed my hair and bit my lips to give them some color. Odd that Father didn't let go of Mother's hand. Erich and I almost never saw them touch when they were awake, even though we knew they loved each other. But to be holding hands in front of a stranger? Unheard of. Something was terribly wrong.

Erich? I'd just left him with Gerhardt and the others. What could have happened in twenty minutes? "What is it?"

News far more urgent than our family troubles. Father said, "Hitler is gassing people in Poland. Dovid has heard."

I jerked my head toward Dovid. "Gassing?"

"At deportation camps in Chelmno, Belzek, Sobibor," Father said. "Hundreds of thousands already. Not only Jews. Gypsies, also."

"Dovid?" I asked. "Your people?"

He shook his head, and Mother said, "No one knows."

I sank into a chair. "Can't anyone else escape?" I asked in a whisper.

Father pulled his hand away from Mother's. "There's no way to get out now."

I looked from face to face. All three of them were stricken with grief. My head throbbed, but I didn't how to feel. And then Father said, "Last month many Jews were sent . . . to camps."

My breath was sucked out of me. "To Chelmno?" I gasped.

"We don't know where they are." Mother clasped Father's hand again.

He said, "The Nazis want to erase Jews from the face of the earth. My God, Frieda, what are our people going to do?"

Stalling for time, I said, "They'll do what we did, Father." I turned to Dovid. "We took an Italian liner here. Can't they do that?"

I watched anger, maybe disgust, cross Dovid's face. He saw me as a spoiled brat, jabbering on about our sea voyage.

Father shook his head. "No ships, not since Italy entered the war. Those Jews are trapped in Europe, Daughter. Dead."

"No!" I shouted. "Oh, I'll never see Grete again."

Mother's hand flew across my face in a sharp crack. "Selfish child. You, it's always you! Think about Grete and her family. Think about Dovid's family."

My cheek stung more from the embarrassment of being slapped in front of Dovid than from the slap itself. I ran into my closet, slammed the door, buried my face in my pillow. Father's words echoed in my head. *"Those Jews . . . trapped . . . dead."*

I heard the murmur of voices in the other room, then a chair scraping across the wood floor. In a minute a slice of light brightened my room and Mother knelt across my bed with her arms outstretched.

I followed her out and splashed water on my face. My eyes were probably bloodshot, my cheeks all stretched and raw from crying. Dovid was still rooted in his chair. I sat down in Erich's place at the table and asked, "What about your people, Dovid?" My voice echoed tinny in my own ears.

Dovid splayed his beautiful fingers on our table and began. His English had improved so much—a tribute to Mother and to his own hard work.

"I am alive today because of soccer. Soccer and Sugihara. The ball game you know. Sugihara I will have to tell, but later."

Father asked, in German, "Where is your home, Dovid?"

Dovid kept reaching for English vocabulary to tell us: "A small village sixty kilometers from Kraków. For five generations my mother's and father's families live in that village."

A hundred questions tumbled out. Some he'd already answered on other visits, but now it seemed important to get every single detail. "You left when? How old were you? How did you get out? How long did it take? Where did you go?"

He went on with his story. "Nearly two years ago I leave, summer, nineteen forty. I am sixteen then."

Perfect. A boy should be a few years older than his girlfriend.
Quick, I asked another question so he wouldn't see me blushing over that thought. "You went to school? That's where you learned to draw?"

"Drawing, before I can read a word. But school, different. It is nineteen thirty-nine. Already the Jewish school is closed, but the soccer team at Saint Ignatz Catholic School is happy to let me play. The coach says, 'You are a good goalie, for a Jew.'"

"The nerve!"

"Daughter, be quiet and listen," Father said.

"One day Germans come by. How do you say it, the way they walk?"

"Goose-stepping," Mother supplied.

"Yes. We are playing a game. We freeze, all of us statues on the field, watching."

My heart seized.

"Our coach blows his . . ." Dovid pursed his lips to demonstrate.

"Whistle," Mother said.

"Whistle. He shouts for us all to play again. I should go home right away." Dovid closed his eyes; his eyelids fluttered sadly.

"But you didn't know what they would do," Mother said gently.

"Yes, yes, and so we play soccer. Poorly, no spirit, you can imagine. I don't remember who wins. After, both teams go to drink beer. I never go with the boys. A Jew in a tavern with so many Catholics? Who hears such a thing? I start the long walk home. Everything feels—how do I say it?"

He reached for his teacup and gulped the last of the cooled water. He motioned for me to put my hand out, palm up, and then set the china cup on the flat of my hand and flicked the rim. Mother watched nervously, maybe afraid we'd break one of her two remaining cups.

"You hear?" Yes, I heard a faint ringing that lingered in the air. He flicked the cup again. "What is it you feel?"

"It's vibrating, like it could shatter."

"That is what the day feels like, like glass will shatter into many sharp pieces. When I am at my home, the glass is already broken. My father, my mother, my sisters, all gone, all the Jews in my village. Vanish like smoke."

"No doubt to a concentration camp," Mother said. "We must believe they are safe."

Dovid raised his dark eyes to Mother's face. "People say no one lives long in such a place. My mother, I don't know the English word, she has the sugar disease. She needs every-day the shots. My sisters, Shayna and Beyla, are little." He pulled his head back to have a good look at me. "Younger even than you."

He thinks of me as a child! My heart sank like a stone.

"Any age is too young, also too old, for such a place," Mother said.

Father was at a disadvantage with English, but he added, "Your father, Dovid?"

"He is strong. Maybe . . ." Dovid's voice cracked. He

didn't need to complete the thought for me to understand him clearly.

Suddenly Dovid stood up. "Enough for today. Who needs another sad story?"

"Yet, we all need to tell them," Mother said.

Dovid pushed his chair back and nodded toward Mother and Father. "Mrs. Shpann, understand, please. No more can I come for English. No money."

"Starting today, lessons are free," Mother said.

"You are kind, but I am shamed to take from you with nothing to give."

Mother motioned around us. "We stare at blank white walls. Bring me the pictures you draw. In exchange I will give you words."

"Not enough, Mrs. Shpann, a few drawings." He seemed to search for some English words to leave us with. "Good-bye, farewell," he said soberly, and quickly let himself out, leaving such a heavy cloud of sorrow in the room.

Never mind how Hitler had swooped up European nations as if they were no more than smudges on a map, or his plans for Jews. At that moment—petty, selfish girl that everyone accused me of being—the thing that stabbed at my heart was the fear that I'd never see my Dovid Ruzevich again.

CHAPTER NINE
1942—1943

Dovid played like a happy-sad movie in my mind while I waited for my first assignment from the underground. Erich wouldn't discuss any of it. Days passed without a word, while he was sneaking out at night. When would it be my turn?

Now that the war in the Pacific was raging, every American, French, and British flag had come down, and up the poles had shot the flag of the Empire of the Rising Sun with its ugly, big ball of blood on a huge white bandage. There were troops and tanks all over the city and Japanese sentries outside the British and American consulates and the cable offices and newspapers. Every scrap of news was censored, so it was pointless to greet friends with the usual, "Have you heard anything?" because none of us could get word from the outside. It was like living on an island surrounded by shark-infested waters; no one could reach us except the sharks.

While I was walking home from school with Tanya one day, my frustration twisted around to an unkind attack:

"How can you stand to have those soldiers visit your mother?"

"We eat; others don't." She thrust out one meaty hip; I was all skin and bones. "You don't mind when we bring you oranges on Fridays."

"I'll never again take anything you buy with their money!"

"Starve, if that makes you happy," Tanya said. "Anyway, I saw your father going into the bank."

"Yes, but when Father went to draw out what little money he'd saved, our account was frozen. We've got nothing but small dribs my mother stashed away for living expenses."

"So? My mama and I, we have no one to bring home pay. Nobody can buy the dresses she used to sew."

"But *Japanese soldiers?* Honestly, Tanya."

In hot silence we passed a beautiful hotel, its awning fluttering in the wind. The invaders had taken over all the finest hotels and foreign clubs, along with every thriving company in Shanghai. "Foreigners are tossed out like yesterday's rubbish," Father had said bitterly.

We'd reached our block, both of us mad, when Tanya pointed to the house across from us. "It's gone. The Tiffany lamp. Mrs. Kazimierz must have sold it." Suddenly Tanya burst into tears. "The only pretty thing in any of our windows, gone. Everything gone."

I put my arm around her and let her tears soak my

blouse. "Let's not fight anymore, okay?" I felt her nod her head, her nose pecking my bony shoulder.

We were just getting used to all the new indignities when the Japanese began rationing cooking gas. Since our hot plate was electric, we were able to slip in one cooked meal a day without going over our electricity allotment. *If* we could find food.

Gasoline disappeared—shipped to Japan—so hardly any buses or streetcars ran. We didn't have carfare, anyway. That meant hearty business for rickshaw pullers and pedicab drivers, whose fuel was their feet. Sometimes three or four coolies pulled gigantic wagonloads like a team of horses. Even the richest foreigners who used to have chauffeurs were now trundling bicycles, so we had to watch Erich's Peaches more closely. Of course, she still drank oil, and there wasn't much of that, so Peaches had a very dry, rusty winter. Her grinding sounds made my teeth ache.

Electricity rationing worsened. Mrs. Kazimierz wouldn't have been able to turn on her Tiffany lamp even if it were still sitting in her front window. We were only allowed to light one room at a time—no problem for us, since we *had* only one room—but even that room was limited to a ten-watt bulb. You could hardly see your hand in front of your face, much less read. The wraithlike shadows in our apartment haunted me, awake and asleep. I saw them as Japanese soldiers looming over me; tree branches outside the window were their drawn bayonets. When lights of the occasional passing car slid across our walls, I imagined them as the headlights of a Japanese tank headed straight for our building. For my own protection I forced the hot-liquid fear in my belly to congeal into jagged-edged anger. How I wished that I had Erich's courage to fight back, or that the underground would give me a chance.

Tanya came pounding on our door. "Did you hear? They're making all Americans and British and Dutch here register with the Japanese police. Not so, Ukrainians, I am happy to say."

"Or Austrians," I added haughtily.

Tanya held Moishe with his head over her shoulder like a human baby. I heard his cat-motor running. As usual, he refused to turn around and look at me. We were sworn enemies. Tanya and Moishe came in and sat on the bed. "They're called enemy nationals now. They've got red armbands with the initial of their country."

I sat beside Tanya, so Moishe jumped away and hid under the table. "Dovid says in Europe, Jews must wear yellow armbands."

"Yes, yes. Just like us Jews at home, now the enemy nationals aren't welcome in restaurants or theaters. Not even in parks. Now *their* stores are being shut down. I love it! Finally, thank you, Emperor Hirohito, we Jews have it better, can you believe this?"

How could things change so fast? The winter of 1942–1943 was as bitter as horseradish. The piercing cold wasn't helped a bit by the Japanese soldiers who burst into our apartment one day and yanked out our radiator pipes as scrap metal for their war effort. Without heat we froze, even with Molly O'Toole's ugly wool socks, which we darned and saved from year to year, knobby in our thin shoes. The few pipes left in our building froze and burst, sending water streaming through the ground floor.

For once I was glad we didn't have a kitchen or bathroom in our apartment. The people downstairs were squishing through icy water that oozed under their doors. The bathtub was useless, the toilets—well, I couldn't even describe that part. Imagine the worst.

One day Mother came home from the bakery pale and jittery. "They're going to round up the so-called enemy nationals and send them to internment camps. Brits and Americans."

Could they do that to Americans? To the rich Iraqi Jews, who were now British citizens? They'd practically ruled the foreign settlements before the Japanese came.

"At least we don't have to worry about that," Erich muttered. "One advantage to being a stateless refugee."

"Erich, I have told you a hundred times, we are not—"

"Face the truth, Mother."

I believe that day she finally did.

Tanya and I had patched up our argument, and I promised never to say another word about her mother's Japanese visitors. In the winter our long walks to school were miserable enough without fighting. I rubbed my hands and stomped my feet to keep the circulation going, scared of frostbite as much as I feared the Japanese bayonets.

I longed for the hot, steamy days of July, seven months away.

At last winter began to give way to spring, and with spring would come more daylight and a few fresh vegetables. It was easier not to despise the Japanese as the weather warmed. At first we'd thought that since they were allied with the Germans, they'd hate us Jews; but they didn't. They didn't love us, either. We were just foreigners to them, like any others.

"We can live out the war this way," I told Erich.

He spit out his response: "Like hell I will."

CHAPTER TEN
1943

News! Erich used the cover of his screechy violin practicing to tell me all about my role in the Underground, called REACT. "I'm the go-between. It would look too suspicious for a girl to hang around down at the docks. Ask me, and I'd say you shouldn't work with us at all, but Gerhardt says you're plucky. God, my sister, plucky. He also thinks you're useful for our purposes." The bow slid back and forth across the remaining strings, and the sound was terrible.

"And what exactly are our purposes, Erich?"

"Simple. Doing anything, great or small, to flummox the enemy. Jam communication, supply lines, toilets, whatever. Smuggle food and supplies and, most important, information to our comrades."

"Who are?"

He shook his head. "Not our business to know. All I've been told is that the head of our division is Madame Liang."

"A woman?"

"Keep your voice down." Erich arched his head toward

Father, who was reading across the room. "Maybe not a woman. Maybe an alias, just a code name. Don't ask so many questions."

So, I'd never know who they were, or whether they were all over China or only in Shanghai. I was just a tiny cog in the whole huge wheel of freedom fighters, of which Erich reminded me over and over. Maybe he was afraid I'd outshine him, as if I ever could.

"Not a word to that blabbermouth, Tanya," Erich warned.

"Of course not. I'm no idiot." I wiggled my eyebrows like that American comedian Groucho Marx. "Tanya likes you, you know."

"She likes anything in pants. It runs in her family."

"The Japanese soldiers, I know."

"I might have to accidentally trip one of them on his way down the stairs next Friday." Erich gave me a diabolical smile, something so rare on his face that I just melted and reached over to kiss his forehead as he sawed away at a strain vaguely Brahms.

Father sprinted across the room to snap the fiddle out of Erich's hands.

"You are a fine son, but a hopeless musician." He cradled The Violin as if it were an abused child. "I concede. I will not encourage you on this instrument any further."

"Me neither, Father?" I asked eagerly.

Father's deep sigh rolled over me like a wave.

"Neither of you displays a calling to music. I pray that you'll find your talents, your passions elsewhere."

Erich's burst of relief saddened Father, and to compensate, I tried to look heartbroken.

"Someday when we have a place to call home, we will have a piano again," Father said. "Perhaps that is your instrument, children. That would please your mother."

We both nodded in somber agreement while Erich flashed me a look that said, *not a chance on earth.* And in this way the music-loving world was spared any further assaults from the sausage-fingered Shpann children. I only hoped we'd make better spies than musicians.

"Now," Father said, "I'm off to the café to make a cup of coffee last all afternoon with the other useless men."

Once Father was gone, Erich handed me a street map and a letter he'd hidden under his mattress. It was handwritten on creamy vellum stationery thick enough to line our shoes with. I broke the chop seal on the envelope and read the note written in precise English:

February 1, 1943

Mr. Wushan Xi
Kwan Ho Employment Agency
Hongkew, Shanghai

Dear Sir,

I seek the assistance of a clever servant girl, as I anticipate considerable company. Due to the vicissitudes of wartime, I do not know when these guests will arrive. Thus I would require that the aforementioned housemaid be available immediately and on duty shortly. As you well know, I am an impatient and exacting employer. Needless to say, the girl must be eager to work like a beast of burden, yet willing to waive all benefits save modest recompense. Though I live well, my resources are not as they once were. The girl's reward will be the assurance that she is serving the aristocracy of Old China in a time-honoured capacity. I believe you have my telephone number in your file. Please contact my butler, Sheng, with details. Time, as always, is of the essence.

Cordially yours,
MADAME LIANG

"What a snotty woman. So, what does this mean?"

"It's the final go-ahead for your first assignment. See the words *shortly* and *waive*? Before the week's out, the Japanese will confiscate all shortwave radios."

"Who cares? They have everything else of ours."

"Think. Shortwaves are our only means of contact with the outside. They'll just barge into people's homes and steal the few radios left, you'll see."

"And I'm to stop them?" I asked hopefully, though I couldn't imagine how.

Erich laughed at how naïve I was and playfully pinched my arm until I yelped. Satisfied, he tapped the street map. "A REACTor, that's you, will go to all the families in this area and warn them to hide their shortwaves. Bury them, if necessary."

"That's all?"

"Ilse, don't you see? It's a test. Gerhardt wants to check how well you handle this mission. You think it's easy? There's an art to it. You have to convince each person that it's vital to maintain secret communication with the Allies, and you have to do all this without scaring anyone, and above all, you can't tell a soul who put you up to this job and how you know this piece of intelligence directly out of Japanese headquarters. Do you understand?"

Then it was starting to sound a little more complicated, but I nodded in agreement.

"Good, so I'm instructed to send you off, right away. Zigzag. Don't go house to house in a straight row. Only go into a house when the guard turns his back." He pulled me to him for an awkward hug. "Be careful." Pushing me away, he looked at his watch. "I will go to the telephone down the block and tell them when you start. You have two hours to finish. Beyond that it begins to look suspicious. When you're done, I telephone to Rolf with your report."

"Oh, so that's what Madame Liang means by 'contact my butler, Sheng, with details'?"

"Coded, of course." He handed me the map and rushed me out the door, and that's how I began my first assignment as a saboteur.

The two hours raced by, and I was totally frustrated by my neighbors who just didn't see the importance of my mission. I slunk home to report my pitiful progress.

"I covered thirty-three families in seven buildings, and

only six promised they'd hide their radios. Most didn't have radios, and the rest acted like I was a lunatic."

Erich digested my report soberly. I followed him to the telephone two blocks away and crowded into the booth with him, thrilled by the sound of real coins jangling down the throat of the phone. When had I last had more than one coin in my hand? Erich wouldn't let me see the number he dialed, and what I heard on his end told me nothing:

"Already thirty-three people have applied for jobs at the Peking Road Pencil Factory, but unfortunately, there are only six positions open. Um-hmn. Um-hmn. Yes. I will." And he hung up. "You passed the test. Tomorrow you hit Frenchtown, same story."

Not even a week passed before Japanese signs went up all over the place and messages blasted from megaphones up and down the streets:

ATTENTION! ATTENTION!
ALL RESIDENTS ARE COMMANDED TO TURN IN
SHORTWAVE RADIOS IMMEDIATELY.
VIOLATORS WILL BE IMPRISONED. NO EXCEPTIONS.

REACT was right on the money. I began to feel I was truly part of something important, that even a girl like me could make a difference.

I came home from the Kadoorie School one day and found Mother curled on her bed. A tentative tap at the door woke her before I could. "It's probably Mrs. Kazimierz from across the street. Back again," Mother said under her breath. She got up and tidied her hair.

But it wasn't Mrs. Kazimierz. It was a man as bald as a watermelon, wearing plaid suspenders that hitched up his trousers nearly to his armpits.

"Mrs. Span?" He was an American, judging by the way he pronounced our name—Span, like it was the span of a bridge, rather than *Shpohn.*

"Yes?" Mother was wary; strangers seldom came to our door, and Americans, never.

He showed Mother a blue air letter with USA on it. "May I come in?"

Mother went pale. "Yes, of course."

I edged forward to see that the letter was from M. O., but all sorts of postmarks and scribblings cluttered the envelope after months, and thousands of miles, of travel.

Mother offered the man the other chair at the table. I stood between them.

"Mrs. Span, I am Joseph Foley. I am in the employ of Laura Margolies. You know the name?"

"Yes, the social worker, God should bless her."

"Yes, the *American* social worker," Mr. Foley boasted. "We both work for the Joint."

Mother offered Mr. Foley a cup of coffee. I knew what a sacrifice that would be if he accepted; Father would have no coffee for dinner.

He politely declined. "Yes, the JDC, the American Jewish Joint Distribution Committee. We are here in Shanghai to help the refugees at this unfortuitous time."

"May I see my letter?" Mother asked, reaching out.

He handed it to her. "Mrs. Span, you know that Americans cannot send mail directly to Japanese-occupied China."

"I understand." Mother held the letter to her heart.

"Your letter has taken a circuitous route. It reached China months ago. A delegate from the Swiss consulate happened to be in the office of a certain Japanese officer when the decision was made as to what to do with a bagful of old mail. The Swiss, as you know, are neutral, and they often serve as go-betweens."

Like Erich does for the Underground.

"The Swiss man tried to convince the officer to entrust the mail to him, to no avail. But the officer must have felt playful that day." Mr. Foley rubbed his shiny head and held up three lean fingers. "He offered the Swiss the chance to randomly draw three letters from the mail pouch, and those he was authorized to distribute. The remainder would be burned." He folded his fingers down one by one and twisted the fist in the air. "Your letter, Mrs. Span, was one of the three. To make a long story short"—*it was too late for that*—"the Swiss consulate delivered the three letters to the Joint, and I am delivering yours to you. However, I must inform you that a certain enclosure has been, shall we say, *appropriated* by the Japanese. Not by the Joint, I want you to know."

"Thank you," Mother said, rising. "I shall keep that in mind."

Mr. Foley took the hint. "Good day," he said, showing us the top of his pink scalp.

As soon as he was gone, Mother carefully peeled the envelope open. I read over her shoulder.

Dear Frieda,

This is the last you will hear from me. With the war in the Pacific raging, I am a liability to you. I didn't dare send a package. As you must know, there is a blockade against parcels from any of the Allied countries. But I hope the twenty dollars in this envelope will help to ease your family through the days ahead.
M. O.

There were Japanese characters in the margins, and the M. O. was enclosed in a blood red box. My heart sank—the money was gone. The outside of the envelope was all marked up, too, and the same red ink encircled the Santa Rosa, California, return address, as if the tentacles of the Japanese Kempetai, the dreaded secret police, could extend as far as America.

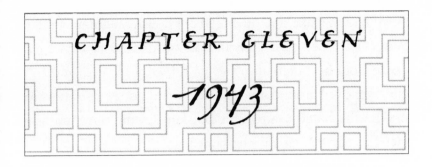

CHAPTER ELEVEN
1943

I had barely a second to think about this letter because REACT had another assignment for me.

"No letter from Madame Liang this time, so listen carefully," Erich instructed me. "You're to go to the Shanghai Club on the Bund."

"And do what?"

"You're to slip into the water closets on the main floor and bend the rods of the copper floats in each toilet."

"You're joking."

"I am perfectly serious," Erich said. "Disable the toilets and you create, well, let's say, a messy problem for our Japanese friends."

The European Shanghai Club had become the social gathering place for the Japanese navy. I couldn't just waltz into such a high-security building and ask to jam their plumbing. I was outfitted as a delivery boy—another way to be invisible—complete with a uniform and cap, into which I stuffed my pinned hair.

I had to make sure no one in our house caught me in this getup. I tiptoed past Tanya's door just as Moishe jumped down from his perch atop the trash boxes. He meowed and curled his tail around my leg and turned gooey eyes toward me. So, he hated the real me but fancied the telegram-boy me. Too bad he was still the same cat.

I did not fool Liu. As usual, he tagged along behind me all the way to the Bund. He was wearing a newish, red-and-white-striped shirt that hung below his knees. I wondered what dead body he'd stripped it from. Somebody a lot larger than he, that was clear. I waved him away, and he hung back a few paces.

If I'd fooled Moishe, maybe I'd fool the angry-looking navy guard who blocked the giant front door of the Shanghai Club. REACT had learned that Admiral Imura conducted a lot of navy business at the club, with a glass of vodka balanced on his rolling belly.

I fluttered a manila envelope under the guard's nose and struck a deep boy's voice: "The Swiss consulate sent this for Admiral Imura. Extremely important."

My heart skipped a few beats and wild doubts raced through my head, mostly on the theme of *just possibly I wasn't cut out for sabotage.* But I tapped my foot and rolled my eyes to suggest that the fate of the Japanese navy, even the whole war, maybe the world as we knew it, hung on whether this particular guard allowed the message to get through to the admiral promptly.

He studied the envelope with his face pulled together

like a drawstring pouch, and then it dawned on me that the man was faking. He couldn't read the German. He probably didn't even read Japanese. As Mother often said, "Such guards are selected for qualities other than their literary proficiency." Finally he waved me in.

"*Arigato*, thank you," I said, bowing low. He bowed, I bowed, he bowed, and I slipped past him into the Shanghai Club.

I couldn't pause to admire the beautiful blackstone foyer, because of those mean sentries, stiff as department store dummies, every few paces along the wall. I was dying to get a glimpse of that hundred-foot-long bar we'd heard about. I wanted to knock everything off and slide across the smooth, polished wood in my socks. But this was war; no time for trivialities. No, I had to hurry to the toilets.

A guard's eyes followed me, without his head moving, as I scampered into the men's room. I glanced at the urinals. How could men be so immodest? Well, as Erich said, men had outdoor plumbing, so no one cared.

Disappointing to count only six stalls—not enough toilets to stop the Japanese march through China, but I'd do my part. Rolling up my sleeves, I set to work in the first stall. The copper float was green and coated with some sort of scum. It was slippery and hard as steel. I couldn't bend it a millimeter. Dismal failure on my first attempt. The best I could do was unhook the float and move on to the next stall. That toilet was more accommodating because the float was corroded and easier to snap. The third ball cock cracked in my palm like a raw egg. By the last one I was the underground's expert on dismantling plumbing, and I was feeling quite smug, when someone came into the men's room.

I climbed onto the toilet, crouching so nothing of me would show under or above the divider. Shiny boots appeared two stalls away, then trousers draped over the boots, suspended above the floor by thick fingers. Assuming he was alone, the venerable officer of the Japanese navy began singing.

And then came the moment a saboteur lives for. The officer tried to flush the toilet. The handle jiggled feebly, followed by a string of Japanese curses. Success! I heard him open the door of his stall. Changing his mind, he threw the lock on the door and crawled out under it, so no one would stumble into that stall and discover his shame. An officer of the Japanese navy who didn't flush? Unthinkable!

Water furiously splashed in a basin, the linen towel loop was yanked, and the officer stomped out of the men's room. I finished my work and stuffed a huge wad of tissue into each basin for good measure, then slipped out the swinging door, confident that officers with their elbows on the long bar would have an interesting day or two thanks to REACT. Mission accomplished, I stuffed the manila envelope under my uniform coat and sauntered over to the building entrance. I bowed to the guard, he bowed, I bowed. The Japanese were always polite.

*　　*　　*

"What a lark!" I bragged to Erich. "I just wish I could keep that nice, warm uniform."

"Not a lark if you get caught."

I stopped my mugging around and stared at him. Until that moment I never considered getting caught or what would become of me if I did. I could be tossed into a Japanese prison. We'd all heard reports of the brutal treatment innocent captives got at the Bridge House. Or they rotted away with typhus in the Ward Road Jail.

I could die there. My stomach flip-flopped as the blood drained from my face. *Something worth dying for.* I remembered Erich saying that, but now? So young?

Erich tapped my head. "Just don't get caught, Ilse."

All winter there'd been rumors floating on the chill winds that we Jews would be herded into a ghetto. That all of us would be forced to wear armbands, just like in Europe. That Americans and Brits would be sent to dreadful internment camps. That fewer and fewer provisions would reach us, even through Swiss intermediaries, since America's law against trading with the enemy was being strictly enforced. That we'd slowly starve to death, as if we weren't already.

Father dismissed these dire rumors as Japanese propaganda.

"I believe there is some truth to them," Mother quietly responded.

"Ach, they are simply hallucinations of minds consumed by relentless shivering and empty bellies. You'll see, Frieda. In the spring they will dry up and vanish."

They didn't. With the last gasp of winter, February 17, 1943, the proclamation came down on our heads, confirming the rumors.

CHAPTER TWELVE
1943

Newspapers shouted the headline:

PROCLAMATION CONCERNING
RESTRICTION OF RESIDENCE AND BUSINESS
OF STATELESS REFUGEES

The same notice was nailed to every tree and telephone pole in our neighborhood.

"Maybe it doesn't mean us," Mother said. She and Father sat at our table while Erich and I stood with our bowls raised to our chins.

Erich fumed. "We're the stateless refugees; who else would they mean? Don't deny it, Mother."

Father said, "Have some respect for your mother, for God's sake. What else have we but respect?"

Mother put her spoon down and lowered her eyes to our splintery table, but Erich ranted on.

"We're the ones who don't have passports. We're the

people without a homeland. We're the ones going to the ghetto."

Ever the hopeless optimist, I made a feeble attempt: "The proclamation doesn't actually use the word *ghetto*."

"It doesn't have to," Father said. "The meaning is clear. Go, children, see what it looks like for us there. Your mother and I need some time to make plans."

We were glad to break away from the heavy grief in our apartment. "Let's take Tanya with us," I said, knocking on her door.

She wasn't surprised to see us. "I heard already. Too grim for words."

"We're walking over to look at the neighborhood more closely."

"Neighborhood?" said Tanya. "It's more like a rabbit warren. Mama, I'll be back in an hour," she called over her shoulder.

We hurried past the guards across the bridge into Hongkew and walked the perimeter of the designated area. It bordered the International Settlement to the north, down Chaufoong Road on the west, to East Seward Road on the south, and up along the eastern border of Yangtzepoo Creek. Less than a square mile—forty square blocks tangled deep in the belly of Hongkew and hidden far from the river and the brightly lit boulevards. There wasn't even a small green square of a park to relieve the dreariness. Here, thousands of us were going to be forced to relocate our homes and businesses.

"Imagine, all of us in less than a square mile that takes under twenty minutes to cover," I said.

Erich added, "Twenty minutes only because we have to elbow our way through the filthy streets."

The streets were clogged with rickshaws and pedicabs; with overflowing garbage bins; with men in old-fashioned black silk gowns, and still older men clicking mah-jongg tiles on makeshift tables in the lanes; with laundry dragging from lines strung between houses or from poles sticking out of windows; with carriers balancing bamboo poles on their shoulders, the pungent liquids sloshing out of buckets hanging from either end.

"God alone knows what's in those buckets," Tanya said. "Could be soup, could be warm pee."

We stepped over people sleeping on the street, their heads nesting on gunnysacks for pillows. Of course, none of this was brand-new to us. Mother worked in Hongkew, though in the prettier Viennese section, and we'd been in and out of the district during our years in Shanghai. "How colorful it is," I used to say. But there, deep in its core, *color* gave way to squalor. I eyed the drab surroundings, not as a visitor now, but as a future resident, and I simply couldn't imagine this place as a neighborhood for people like us.

Shaken, the best I could manage was, "Well, it's certainly full of life."

"And reeking of death," Erich added, tripping over the body of a rail-thin man in one of the lanes—maybe sleeping, maybe dead.

"There are a few exemptions," Tanya said. "The Mirrer Yeshiva boys, for one. I hear they'll be allowed to stay at the synagogue on the outside. There must be other exceptions." Her voice trailed off. "I think I'll have to leave Moishe behind," she said mournfully.

Well, so there was *some* good news!

Later, we dropped Tanya home, and we four Shpanns sat on Mother and Father's bed for a conference. Lately, I'd been having headaches. Stress, Father said. Probably malnutrition.

Everyone was despondent about the three months we'd been given to relocate—and to such awful surroundings. I didn't want to be like the rest of them; but rubbing my forehead to stave off the shadowy vision that sometimes came with my migraines, I wondered where the chipper girl was who'd first set foot in Shanghai, ready for adventure. Where the *good* girl was. In a futile effort to find her again, I said brightly, "At least we won't have to go far for groceries."

Erich rolled his eyes, but Mother listened to every detail. Setting her jaw squarely, she said, "I know some people in Hongkew, Mr. Schmaltzer from the bakery, others. I'll inquire about suitable quarters."

"There aren't suitable quarters," Erich grumbled.

"There must be," said Father. "Thousands of people manage to live there respectably."

Erich slammed his fist down on the table. "That's the problem. Too many thousands. Already about eight thousand refugees and Japanese, and a hundred thousand more

Chinese who're used to living without indoor plumbing. Without *plumbing*, Father."

Mother winced. "So thousands *with* plumbing will evacuate to make room for us. Surely we'll be able to trade our apartment for a larger one." Her statement was more like a question, and I wanted to answer, "Yes, of course," but our stroll around the district that day had filled me with doubts. Mother said, "Tomorrow after I leave the bakery, I'll begin looking."

Father patted her crooked hand. "Frieda, it is possible that we will do worse."

"No!" she shouted.

But the next day's news was more discouraging.

"Key money we're going to need," Mother said. "They say as much as four months' rent, on top of the rent. A bribe to get people out of their houses so we can move in. Where do we find money like that, I ask you, Jakob? Where?"

"We'll find a way."

I glanced over at The Violin, but Father took off his pinkie ring that had belonged to Grandfather Rudolf—his last memento of his parents. "You'll know where to sell it, Erich?"

I snatched it out of Erich's hands. "I know where." Liu had connections, and he'd only take a small fee.

Mother set her lips in a tight line, a sure sign that she was fighting back tears. "We might all four have to crowd into one room. Not even our three tiny closets. There's more." We waited. "Erich was right, most of the buildings don't have plumbing."

Squatting over *pots?* I would die of mortification.

Father spread a map of Hongkew on the table, with our small designated area shaded in gray.

"Looks like prison walls," Erich mumbled.

I kicked him under the table as Mother asked, "Jakob, when we're in Hongkew, you will still be able to play with the chamber quartet?"

"I cannot live without music . . ." Father began.

"Music, music, music! What about money, Jakob? We depend on the miserly money you get from your concerts and a bit from Erich's deliveries now that Mr. Schmaltzer's cut my job back to a pittance. I have one English student left, Ludmila Mogelevsky. A fen or two. And where will you teach your students if we all live in one small room? Think, Jakob, think beyond the treble clef for a change, yes?"

Father hung his head like a scolded child, and suddenly I realized something shocking about my father: He wasn't a strong man, and yet all my life I'd thought *he* was in charge. Now the truth was clear. Mother, a wall of granite, had always fortified Father and made him appear steady and able. How frightening! What was a family with a father who couldn't handle the unexpected, the terrifying dark that we were headed into?

Within a day or two we learned there would be a few more exceptions. The Russian and Polish Jews who'd arrived in

Shanghai by 1937 wouldn't be sent to the ghetto. Of course, we came in 1939, so we weren't exempt. However, some people who had documented or essential jobs outside the ghetto would temporarily be able to get passes to go to work, but no one knew how long *temporary* was. That meant Father might be able to continue with the chamber quartet for a while, and maybe share space with someone to teach the three or four students who could still afford violin lessons, at least for a while. Hope rose again. Erich laughed at me.

"You're a dreamer, my sister."

"Someone has to be, around here."

"I suppose. Come," he said gruffly, "we're going to enjoy the freedom of the city while we have it."

We walked for hours and hours along the Bund, all through the French Concession, out into the country, into the Badlands, where the gambling houses were, and the opium dens and nightclubs, even one named Hollywood. We climbed fences and prowled around the estates of the wealthiest Jews in Shanghai—the Kadoories, the Sassoons, the Hardoons—knowing that within months they'd be forced to abandon their fancy estates, carry what they could on their backs, and march with thousands of other enemy nationals into primitive Japanese internment camps. Mean, I suppose, but it gave me a delicious lift to know that they'd lose their elegant houses and kow-towing servants, and would have to look after themselves for the first time in their lives.

We tried to look like normal people meandering through Jessfield Park, through the countryside—not like saboteurs, not like Jews about to be shut into a choking ghetto.

Erich reminded me of the risks around the country estates. "Listen, there are guard towers and firing squads authorized to shoot intruders at the whim of the Japanese soldiers. But if a sentry spots the two of us strolling down a country road, laughing and singing, he'll just think we're ga-ga young lovers and wave us on."

"Any moron could see that we're brother and sister," I snapped.

"Ach, we all look alike to them, anyway."

It worked. We charmed one stern-looking guard, who stood so straight that you'd swear his shoulders were glued to the fence behind him. He apparently heard us singing a German drinking song before we poked our heads out of the woods. He barked something to us in Japanese.

My heart held its breath as Erich whispered, "Just skip, keep singing."

We clasped hands and swung our arms, bowing our heads in his direction. A smile spread across his face. He stabbed his bayonet into the hard ground and pulled out a wilted picture of his sweetheart and him, seated in some sort of Ferris wheel car. She had a stick-out ponytail pulled to one side of her head, and her eyes were wide in mock fear as the two of them were ready to take off into the cloudless sky.

He obviously loved the picture, loved the girl, jovially

explaining the scene to us in Japanese. We didn't understand a word, but we nodded and uttered oohs and ahs, which pleased him.

All the while we memorized his uniform, the number of stripes; his boots, to assess whether they were steel-toed; the buildings behind him, the number of chimneys puffing smoke out into the late-winter air—every detail we could see or smell or hear, to report to REACT. I knew that any second he could pull out of his lovesick wallowing and turn on us. I squashed my fear down inside. Wartime, I kept reminding myself. Individuals don't matter. I don't matter. Families don't matter.

But they did.

The guard reached toward Erich. His hands were thick, strong. For an instant I thought he might choke Erich, but then I saw that he was offering a cigarette. A peace offering, one lover to another? Erich took the gift in fingers trembling ever so slightly, as the Japanese guard reached into his pocket for a match, which he struck on his boot. The soldier jabbered and motioned something to me, the gist of it apparently being, *don't smoke; my girlfriend doesn't smoke.*

Erich and I reviewed the abrupt turn our lives were about to take. He picked at the skin around his thumbs, which was raw and bleeding. I slapped his hands every so often to stop him.

At Mr. Bauman's café, Erich said, "We'll have to lie and cheat to get passes to leave the ghetto."

"Oh, I'm good at that. Grete would be amazed to see how devious I've become." My words were jaunty, but deep down I grieved for the *good* girl, the before-the-war girl. I caught the last of Erich's sentence:

". . . a pass just to go to school."

I leaned toward him, covering my mouth, and whispered, "What about our REACT assignments? How will we manage?"

"I'll smuggle and lie and sneak and bribe my way out of the ghetto. You, my sister, will stop the work."

"I won't! I can do all those things just like you can."

Erich studied me closely for a few seconds and took a sip of the tea we shared. Secondhand tea leaves—free at Mr. Bauman's café. "For once in your life, listen to me, Ilse. I'm your big brother." Why couldn't he say, *I love you?* Instead, I heard, "I know what's best for you. They'll have guards planted at every entrance. They're saying that our own men will be drafted as Pao Chia guards. Tell me, Ilse, how is it different from a prison?"

"But our own men, won't they be more lenient?"

"Don't count on it. You've heard the rumors like I have, about the camps in Germany, in Poland, with our men as *kapos?* Who can blame them? They do what they must to survive."

Yes, I'd heard. Terrible stories trickled down to us. Just rumors, we reassured ourselves. Also, we got news through REACT, which had ears in the German consulate. We knew about the horrible gassings at Chelmno and Sobibor but the rest of those places in Germany and Poland were just *concentration* camps, where many people were crowded together. True, some families were split up and a few people died of hunger or exposure and disease and sheer exhaustion from hard labor. This *was* wartime, after all, but the strong survived. We believed that our concentration in the Hongkew ghetto would be very much like what was happening in the camps of Europe, and that all we had to do was stay healthy, and we'd make it to the end of the war. "At least here in China," we murmured to one another, "families can stay together for strength."

At least people still fell in love.

"Erich, do you ever think about being in love, maybe with Tanya?"

"Certainly not Tanya! She's as lovable as a ball of barbed wire. Even her cat has more sex appeal."

"Somebody else, then. Do you ever daydream about marrying the person you adore most?"

Erich laughed cynically. "Never. We're too young to be in love."

"We are not!"

"Anyway, love is a luxury we can't afford, like chocolates."

I lowered my eyes and kept still, but I *knew* that love in wartime wasn't a luxury like chocolates. It was a necessity, like bread, like breath.

And my work for REACT would continue, as long as I drew breath.

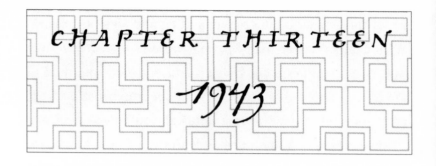

CHAPTER THIRTEEN
1943

Bored and restless after school, we needed something, *anything*, to do before the Hongkew gates were to slam in our faces. Mr. Bauman was kind enough to let us young people twiddle the hours away in his café without spending a fen.

Tanya and the other girls and I looked over the crop of boys who crowded around the table across the room. We had a capsule summary for each one: "Buck-toothed." "Looks like a rabbit." "Ugly yellow shirt." "Never stops talking." "Name's Hershel, bad name." "So dumb in school that Miss Klein acts like she doesn't see his hand waving in the air." "Midget." "He'll be bald in a couple years." We giggled with each pronouncement.

And then one day Dovid came into the café, and my heart leapfrogged. Despite the spring warmth he wore a mothy tweed sweater and patched, shiny trousers. An American-style baseball cap, too small for his head, perched atop a mass of dark curls. One curl endearingly fell over his forehead. He needed a haircut; well, didn't we all? Although he sat at the table packed with other boys three-deep, he seemed to be alone, drawing something on little scraps of paper.

All us girls perked up at the scent of fresh blood across the room. We bunched up to compare notes. "Nice hair." "Funny clothes." "A melancholy artist." "Very intense." "Looks like he hasn't eaten since a week ago Tuesday."

"But he's a little bit cute," Tanya said. "Ilse, you're falling out of your chair. You know this boy?"

"He used to be my mother's student," I whispered.

"Well, he keeps looking over here. Go on, pretend you want to admire his artwork." The other girls agreed, and Tanya shoved my chair away from the table with her sturdy legs.

He sat at the corner of the table, outside the ring of boys. I passed him with my cup for Mr. Bauman to refill with boiled water. Those eyes, brown as polished wood, recaptured my heart after months of seeing them only in my memory. Slowly inching past him on the way back to my table, I noticed the little tuft of beard had given way to clean-shaven cheeks that were pinkish balls above hollows inflating and deflating like a balloon while he sketched on tiny stubs from Mr. Bauman's cash register.

My teacup clattered as I lowered it to the girls' table with shaky hands.

"Well? Well?" Tanya demanded. The girls all leaned into my circle for the report.

"His eyelashes curl back like with mascara," which, of

course, we couldn't get even if we'd had the money. "I can't tell what he's drawing."

"Go see," Tanya said.

"I can't go back. It would look too obvious."

"You want to end up an old maid? Go."

The girls all poked and urged me on, but I shook my head.

"Tomorrow, then," Tanya conceded, in a bargain I was only too willing to accept.

The next morning early, before the rowdy boys' table filled up, I gathered my courage and scraped my chair across the café. Talk about obvious! But I was determined. "Hello, Dovid, remember me, from Mrs. Shpann's?" He nodded and kept on sketching. "We still have your charcoal on our book-case." Another nod, no words. "I'd love to see what you're drawing."

His smile carved a dimple in those sweet, smooth cheeks. He slid one of his drawings across the table and spun it around.

"Amazing!" It was a tiny rendering of the café, down to the curlicues on the ornate coffee urn and the label on a small tin of sugar. "Every detail, just right."

Dovid slid a square of paper out of the little pile of his work and advanced it toward me, studying my face as I reached for it.

I recognized myself, but the face looked like the *me* I remembered, before the sallow skin, the sunken cheeks, the thinning hair, headaches, a nose too beaked. Before starva-tion. "I don't look like that anymore, Dovid."

He snapped it away from me and buried it in his pile. I'd wounded him. "No, no, I love it!"

"It is the artist's job to see what is not there," he said.

Then *I* was insulted. So, it was confirmed: I was just as ugly as I suspected.

Dovid Ruzevich played in my mind all that day and half the night. Every scrap of warmth or food or news had to be shared with my friends, of course, but Dovid was an indulgence that was mine alone, better than ice cream. The next morning, even before Erich was awake, I quickly dressed, stole past Tanya's door, and returned to the café.

"So early?" Mr. Bauman teased. "Sit. You're my first customer, so for you I have fresh tea leaves. Someone else can enjoy the leftovers." He poured steamy water over dry, fragrant jasmine leaves. I watched them swell and drift lazily through the yellowing water. Ah, luxury! I pulled the cup to my face, inhaling the heady aroma.

The door opened, and there was Dovid, in the same clothes despite the gathering heat and with just a hint of stubble on his cheeks, as if he'd been in such a hurry to get to me that he hadn't bothered to shave. My face flushed, and I quickly lowered the teacup. He sat down across from me. Mr. Bauman gave me an encouraging nod as he brought us a second cup of hot water. I spooned tea leaves into Dovid's cup, already mourning the loss.

And so during our last week of freedom, I began coaxing his story out of him. It's what refugees did; it's how we stayed sane. I spoke no Yiddish, or even Polish, but his English had improved enormously, as if he'd been practicing. With an English girl?

"The last time we were together, you told me you're alive because of soccer and some other word I don't know."

"Yes, Sugihara, a Japanese diplomat."

"What?! Tell me everything."

"Be patient," he teased. "So . . ." Dovid started slowly, then began racing through the worst of the story, waving his sketching pencil like a baton. "We are millions of Jews in Poland in nineteen thirty-nine. One minute we are under Russian occupation; the next, under German control. Suddenly in our own homeland we are not welcome."

"Yes, I know."

"Do you?" He looked at me crossly. "But you are here with your family."

"That should make me feel guilty?" I immediately regretted the words.

"Not guilty. Lucky," he said with a sigh, then jumped up and began pacing the empty café. Mr. Bauman discreetly stepped into his back room and pulled the threadbare curtain. "Nearly every Polish Jew is gone, or crowded into ghettos. The lucky ones, they escape to Russian Lithuania, with Germany pounding at their door." From the windows: "In Lithuania we cannot live, either, but what choice do we have?"

My tangle of hair was escaping the red ribbon I'd worn for Dovid.

"There we are, trapped in Lithuania," Dovid said, "maybe ten thousand of us. The Russians do not understand why we want to leave, and the Germans, they do not yet have Lithuania, thank God."

"Why *did* you want to leave, Dovid?"

"Why? Because survival is better than death." His words were slow, careful. "Who knows what is the right thing to do? The Russians say we are crazy to want to leave, and since we are crazy, what will they do to us? They will send us to Siberia for the cure."

"The cure meaning what? Exile?"

"If we live long enough. Death in the frozen land otherwise."

"And I thought we were miserable here in the damp winters? Human beings can't survive in temperatures like that, can they?"

"Outside, not for more than a few minutes at a time. So night and day we Polish Jews argue—is it better to try to leave? The Russians call this treason. For treason also they will send us to Siberia. Or is it more dangerous to stay in Lithuania and take a chance Hitler will not find us?"

I felt my chest tighten, and to cover up, I scooped some of the tea leaves back into my own cup and got up to pour hot water onto the soggy leaves. I returned to the table, and Dovid went on with his tale as if I'd not even moved.

"If we can scratch together the money, and I can sneak it into the Soviet Intourist office, and if the Russian official does not steal the money and send me anyway to Siberia—"

Just then Erich burst into the café. He always arrived like a freight train rumbling into the station. "Thought I would find you here." He jumped back, startled to see Dovid and me with our heads leaning toward one another across the table, nearly touching, and my finger hooked through the handle of Dovid's teacup. Such an intimate picture we must have painted, like the sophisticated man and woman who'd captivated me in that café so long ago—but younger, hungrier.

Erich glared at Dovid. "Come, Ilse, we have work to do."

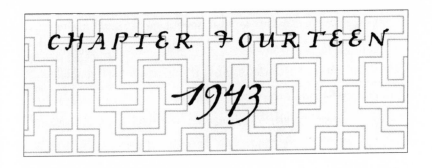

CHAPTER FOURTEEN
1943

Erich and I ducked into the doorway of Ping Low's Apothecary, and he pulled out another letter on the familiar creamy stationery.

May 12, 1943

Mr. Wang Choi Sing
International Agriculture Cooperative
Shanghai, China

Dear Sir,
I trust my name is known to you, as my late husband maintained vast farmlands in our home province of Hunan. He has recently joined the ancestors, and I am left a widow in my declining years.
*   An associate of my husband's has assured me that we might jointly prosper in the enterprise of producing sunflower honey. I, myself, shall not soil my hands with such labors, but*

those in my employ are loyal trustees. Thus, I should like to order a Shanghai Beehive sent to me immediately at my Foochow Road address for careful perusal. If we are satisfied, we shall increase the order to our mutual advantage.

As my resources are diminishing, I remind you that time, as always, is of the essence. I shall expect the package by Saturday, latest.

Cordially yours,
MADAME LIANG

"Translate?" I said to Erich.

"I have your instructions." He stuffed the envelope under his shirt. "This letter is the go-ahead that says now's the time to REACT. You're to tail a woman called Beehive."

"But, why?" I asked Erich as we walked back to our apartment.

"For once, can't you just do as you're told without a bunch of questions?"

"Okay, but I won't even know what to look for unless I know why they want me to follow her."

"No more questions until we get home. The streets have ears." So like Erich, suspicious of everyone and everything.

It was a week before we'd have to move, and Mother was in Hongkew still scouting out a place for us to live. At home, Father practiced in his studio-closet. Erich leaned close to me in case Father should stop playing. "She's a

REACTor, but they suspect she's also an informer. I don't know any more, so don't ask."

"Double-crossing us?"

"Don't look so shocked. You can't trust anyone."

"Not even you?"

"You can trust me." He handed me a scrap of paper. "Her address. She has a REACT assignment on Saturday, eleven o'clock. Follow her. Get as close as you can, until you're her second skin, but don't let her know you're on to her. Understand?"

"But I—"

"*Understand?*"

"Yeah, yeah," I said, but I didn't really get it.

Saturday morning. I needed courage for the REACT mission ahead, or so I told myself as I slid into the chair at the table I'd shared with Dovid. I hoped he wasn't religious, that he wasn't at the synagogue this Sabbath morning.

Saturday or not, maybe he was as eager to see me as I was him because a minute later he arrived, as if he'd been watching for me from the corner.

"Good morning, Dovid!" I got up to bring him a cup of hot water, transferred my tea leaves to his cup, and we continued right where we'd left off. That's how anxious we refugees in China were to tell our stories of home.

"So, it is nineteen forty. As I said, I take the money to buy an exit visa and a ticket for the train to Vladivostok. But this I can do only *if* I have an end visa. Somewhere to go."

"Our problem, too. I wanted to go to America." I clunked my elbow on the table. "But here we are."

He was impatient with the interruption. I promised myself that I'd be quiet and let him pour his whole story out.

"Yes, yes, everybody's problem. So we cannot get an exit visa unless we have an end visa. This is where Chiune Sugihara comes into the story. He is with the Japanese consulate in Lithuania." A smile spread across Dovid's lovely face. I wanted to jump up and touch the half-moons of his cheeks and his chin, which quivered ever so slightly.

"This man Sugihara," Dovid continued, "he sees what is ahead for the Jews of Europe, and he begins issuing Japanese exit visas. I am already on the train, doomed. I cannot stay, but I have nowhere to go. Ilse, I tell you, a miracle. The angel stamps my visa through the window just as the train is pulling out of the station."

"Oh, Dovid." I felt everything—the despair, the hope, the train clacking along the tracks. Then the little bell on Mr. Bauman's door jingled, and there stood Erich—again.

"Have a seat," I said with a sigh. Erich took my cup to slurp the last of my tea. I heard Mother's scolding voice ringing in my head: *You were raised without manners?*

"Dovid is telling me how he came to be in Shanghai. We were just getting to the good part."

A hint of a smile softened Dovid's face, and then it clouded again. I suppose he was thinking of being the big brother to his own sisters—dead, no doubt.

Erich asked brusquely, "So, how'd you escape Hitler?" That was our Erich—right to the point.

"Chiune Sugihara," I said importantly.

"Who?"

Dovid explained and set the scene all over again for Erich.

The excitement in Dovid's voice made my heart swim in a pool of warmth. "It is chaos that day, my friends. Picture it. People swarming the train to get on. Arms waving visas out the window to catch Sugihara's eye. The whistle howls. Then the train slowly builds into a *chug-a-chug-a-chug*, and there is Sugihara, running and stamping visas waving out the window until he can no longer keep up with the train."

"But visas to where?" Erich asked.

Dovid's smile fell behind his eyes like a setting sun. "Well, that is the problem."

"Ach, everybody's problem," Erich muttered.

"We are luckier than some. We grasp in our hands exit visas to Curaçao."

Even Erich, who knew everything, didn't know where Curaçao was.

"An island in the Caribbean Sea, south," Dovid explained. "Near the tip of Venezuela. Sea breezes all year around."

Here, it was May, and summer was already roaring toward us. It had rained all night, all morning, and the rain had turned the air to sludge. Dovid and I had sweat beading on our faces. Waving palms and sea breezes sounded glorious.

"I never get to Curaçao. It is only a trick to get us out of Lithuania."

Erich caught on. "So, that diplomat—"

"Sugihara," I supplied.

"Yes, so that guy could issue your exit visas. Clever scheme," Erich said, admiration clear in his voice. "How many got out this way, twenty? Thirty?"

"Two thousand," Dovid boasted.

"Impressive. Where did you go if not to Curaçao?"

Dovid was enjoying this parceling out of information a tiny bite at a time. "We had Japanese visas, you see. We went to Kobe, Japan. Where else?"

"You took a boat from Lithuania to Kobe?" I asked.

Dovid and Erich both laughed, at my expense. Erich said, "My sister has no head for geography. She thinks America's around the corner from Brazil."

"Do not!" I pouted. "Don't stop telling the story just because my brother's so rude."

Now Erich was deeply engrossed. He straddled his chair, facing Dovid. He looked so comfortable with his arms hugging the chairback. A girl would *never* be allowed to sit that way, and then I became aware of my elbows on the table—which Mother never allowed—and I pulled my arms down to my lap. "Go on, Dovid, please, we're dying to hear the rest."

By then even Mr. Bauman and three free-loading patrons were hanging on every word as well.

"All of us pile into the Trans-Siberian train. Through the Ural Mountains and across Russia. Until you spend eleven days on a train, you do not understand how big Russia is." He stretched his arms as wide as they'd go. "The first long stop is Manchuria. Happy surprise to find Yiddish-speaking Russian Jews there."

"So far north? In Manchuria?" Erich asked.

"Twenty-five years already. So, finally we reach Vladivostok, and we are loaded onto open cargo barges. Forty hours we travel this way. Don't tell anybody, but I am seasick all the way down the coast of Korea, into the port of Kobe."

"Japan," Erich said with contempt. "I wouldn't have gotten off the boat."

"No? In Kobe we are treated very well, but we are a—curious—to the gentle Japanese people."

"Gentle?" I asked. *Gentle* certainly didn't fit the Japanese who occupied Shanghai. We'd heard shocking rumors of the tortures in the Bridge House Prison, where the Kempetai, the Japanese secret police, ruled supreme, and of the massacre of thousands of Chinese in Nanking. "Gentle?" I asked again.

Dovid said, "No matter what you see, remember, the Japanese people—not the soldiers, not the secret police, but the people—they are kind, gentle souls."

"I've seen no evidence of that," Erich said, tapping a spoon furiously on the table.

"Then I hope you will soon, my friends. Our days in Kobe stretch into peaceful months. Gladly we would stay there. I draw a hundred sketches of the beautiful Japanese countryside. Very . . . mystery. On large pieces of paper, not on these foolish scraps."

Dovid's look was dreamy, far-off, but he snapped back to the present. "We cannot stay in Japan. Nowhere to go. Summer ends, nineteen forty-one, we come here. Thank God for Shanghai." At that, he looked right into my face. Thanking God for *me?* I'm quite sure I turned purple.

A stranger came into the café. We stopped talking to eye the well-dressed man. By *well-dressed,* I mean no holes or mismatched socks or plaids with stripes, and shoes that still faintly remembered a shine. Wordlessly, he bumped Erich, who shot out of his seat and left the café. The man followed. I watched them talking outside, the stranger waving his hands in anger, and Erich pulling at the skin around his thumb. Obviously, this wasn't a warm, friendly meeting. The man darted across the street between rickshaws and bicycles, even leaping over the front fender of a car. Erich, visibly shaken, came back into the café and said, "My sister and I have a job to do. Come, Ilse, we have a date with a cranky old dowager."

Outside, he hurriedly told me, "Beehive. It's all moved up, ten o'clock instead of eleven. Be careful, Ilse." Erich jerked his shoulder in the direction the stranger had gone. "He thinks Beehive might be on to us, and her friends are not known for mercy."

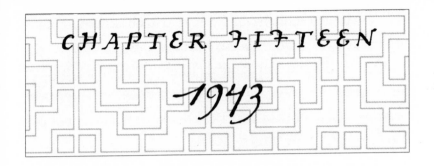

CHAPTER FIFTEEN
1943

This was a job for an expert, which I wasn't yet, so once on the street I looked for Liu. Wouldn't you know it—just when I needed him most, he wasn't in sight. I did something I swore I'd never do. I whistled Liu's toneless tune, and he appeared out of nowhere with something green and wiggly hanging from wooden chopsticks. I couldn't tell whether it was animal or vegetable, edible or fish bait. He popped the foul thing in his mouth and gulped it down.

I said, "We have to go to Foochow Road to find a lady called Beehive, okay?" He nodded eagerly and pulled out his knife to show me he was ready for serious business. The sun glinted off the knife as our busybody downstairs-neighbor passed by.

"He's a fishmonger," I quickly told Mr. Shulweiss. "Guts fish for his father." I motioned for him to hide the knife, which went into his belt along with the blackened chopsticks. As soon as Mr. Shulweiss was out of earshot, Liu said, "No father. No mother."

"Well, you must have had one of each at some point." He cocked his head, processing my words. For a second I thought he didn't understand my English, but then I realized he'd caught the words, all right. He just couldn't capture any memory of a mother or father. "Who do you belong to, Liu?" No recognition. "Who are your people?"

He mimicked a common American expression: "Me, myself, and I. We all three." He hurried along on feet of tanned hide, and I could barely keep up with him. I tapped him on the shoulder, and he spun around with enough force to knock me off balance. His eyes blazed until he realized it was only me.

"I didn't mean to scare you. Just curious about you, that's all."

He grinned—his customary expression when he was satisfied with himself. He poked two fingers at his eyes. "Open in sunshine one day long time ago." He turned a stained hand up, with a ropy scar healed across the palm. One finger looked like someone had bitten the tip off years earlier. Thumping each finger on his chest, he said, "Five."

"Five o'clock? Five days, what? Oh, you mean you have no memory before you were five years old?"

He didn't quite understand, but he nodded and pointed to the dark hole of the sewer on the street corner. "Water whoosh past me down there. I climb up to the street by the Bund." He spread his hands and shrugged his shoulders in a *that's all* gesture. "No ma, no pa, no whiskey, no soda." Yes, the standard cry of Shanghai street boys. "Okay, missy, now we do business."

He quickened his pace, with me nearly trotting behind him, and somehow led me right to the Foochow Road address. We waited and watched, though his feet were tapping and dancing every second. For a rest, he waved his toes, with their yellow nails curled over the tips.

Eventually, Beehive backed out of her door. I pointed to the prey, since I'd seen her photo, and Liu, the pro, caught on right away.

Beehive was tall, even for a westerner, with legs about twice as long as Liu's. She took giant steps up Foochow to the Bund, at the corner of the Hong Kong and Shanghai Bank. The wretched Japanese had taken away the elegant lions I loved that used to guard the bank, and I wished I could once again rub their smooth brass feet for good luck because I had no idea what I was doing tailing this woman. And what if she got on a tram? There was no money in my pocket, and only holes in Liu's.

She kept walking, leading us on a forced march north toward Nanking Road, where weekend browsers were already three-deep in front of shopwindows loaded with Japanese goods no one had any money to buy.

Beehive stepped into Fah Choi's House of Ebony. I pointed for Liu to follow her into the store, which I didn't dare enter, since the shop was deserted and she'd certainly notice me and identify me if we ever met again. I thought of Erich's words: *"Her friends are not known for mercy."*

Not to worry. Liu had the situation under control. He rolled his eyes up into his head as though he had no pupils, and suddenly he was blind. Patting his way to Fah Choi's door, he made the bell over the door jingle, then put on a big show of stumbling around inside the shop with his grubby palm out like a beggar.

He'd left the door wide open so I could hear what was going on inside, including his own heartrending beggar's chant. Fah Choi nearly leapfrogged over the counter to shoo the poor blind urchin out of his shop as Beehive disappeared behind a curtain separating the showroom from the back. Shoving Liu out into the street, Fah Choi slammed the door so hard that the windows shimmered. One of Beehive's merciless friends?

Liu grinned at me, flashed me a pair of ebony chopsticks he'd filched, brought his eyes back to normal, and said, "Lady-called-Beehive is gone." He pulled me around to the back alley, where we hid behind a trash bin swarming with jumbo flies. A few feral cats hissed and growled at us. In a minute Beehive slipped out the back door, clutching a flat bundle wrapped in brown butcher paper and tied with jute.

Was Fah Choi part of the Chinese Underground connected to Free China? Or a counteragent? Had he passed her something for REACT or for the enemy? Where was she taking it? What was inside?

She hurried down Nanking Road. We trailed her as far as the race course, where the street took a little jog to become Bubbling Well Road. Lots of people were enjoying a Saturday morning outing in the park, the only luxury left to us.

The Race Course was also a handy place for the Underground to exchange information, since sometimes the safest place to hide is in plain view. I hoped.

Beehive fell in with the moving crowd and didn't seem to have any purpose for about ten minutes. My eyes wandered to a man in a well-cut gray suit, wearing a hat pitched on his head at a jaunty angle. What westerner could dress so well this long into the occupation? I was almost on the man's heels when he turned and deliberately collided with Beehive. Liu yanked me back a few inches. Beehive handed over the package, which the man nimbly slipped into his suit coat.

He whispered in English, probably thinking no one could understand, "Eleven. Southbound tram on the Bund. Get on at the Cathay. Under the seat. Last row." Then louder, for the benefit of others in the park: "Are you hurt, madame? Forgive me, I must have been in another world."

He joined the flow of the crowd, and Beehive walked on briskly, bought a newspaper at the corner, and perched on a limestone bench, waiting for the right time to go back to the Bund and catch the tram.

Liu's sharp elbow dug into my waist to draw my attention to a half Asian, half western man the size of a brown bear. His slitted eyes followed Beehive's every step.

Liu darted into the path so suddenly that the bear toppled like a giant tree. "So sorry, so sorry," Liu said, bustling around the man and helping him to his feet. Meanwhile, Beehive disappeared in the crowd, and the man went lumbering up the path in pursuit. Suddenly Japanese soldiers began chasing the man, guns drawn.

"Run, missy!"

Liu and I took off in the opposite direction and hid behind a wide tree trunk until the soldiers were out of sight. Gasping for breath, I asked, "What was *that* all about?"

"I smell trouble, missy."

The clock tower said ten forty-five. Somehow I needed to find enough money to get on that streetcar before Beehive did. I gave Liu the universal sign for money—rubbing my thumb across my fingers—and he returned my message with his own universal sign, inside-out pockets.

"Why couldn't you have stolen somebody's wallet *now*, when I need the money?" I hissed.

"Ah, not mix business with pleasure!"

But the little conniver did have a plan. We dashed up to the Bund, where he checked out every rickshaw boy until his eyes landed on one carrying a featherweight passenger. Liu trotted alongside the rickshaw, pressing his case, until the older boy lowered the shafts almost to the ground, and Liu took them up in a handoff so smooth that the passenger barely noticed. The relieved boy sank to the ground along the seawall next to another napping rickshaw puller.

Liu was remarkably strong. He trotted along bearing the passenger, a small, elaborately dressed Chinese woman, to the Jardine Matheson building, where I imagined she'd be meeting a Japanese businessman for fun and profit. I was breathless by the time I reached the office building, just as the woman pointed an elegant boot out of the rickshaw and scornfully rained four coins into Liu's cupped palm. She straightened her peacock blue Chinese dress slit to the knee, patted her stiff hair, and vanished into the lobby of the building.

Liu proudly dropped two coins in my hand, pocketed one, and saved the other as the rickshaw boy's commission on the rental of the vehicle, which he, of course, was renting from someone else.

I got on the southbound tram at the British Consulate, two stops before the Cathay Hotel, and headed for the back row. Only because I knew to look for it did I see the brown tip of the package under the seat. A Chinese amah auntie stretched out, resting her legs on the length of the seat. I smiled and squatted down in front of her, and she didn't seem at all interested in why this redheaded foreigner was rummaging around under the seat of a streetcar.

The flat package slid out easily. Its crisscrossed string tie was gone, but it was taped up so neatly that you'd never guess it had been opened and something had been removed, or replaced. *What?* And for which side? Who was enemy? Who was friend? Curiosity gnawed away at me.

The tram stopped. People got off and on, and Beehive came up behind me.

"Give it. That's mine." She tugged at the package.

"No, mine. It's a gift from my sweetheart." I locked the package to my chest with both arms. She'd need a crowbar to separate me from it. She started pummeling me and swearing in German, in English, until the amah saw profit in the fight and got in on my side, since I apparently had the goods. She swung her powerful legs around and used them to shove Beehive back a few feet, causing her to fall in the lap of an ancient Chinese grandfather. The tram came to a stop; its doors creaked open. I quickly dropped my last coin into the amah's hand and ran out to the street to wait for Liu. Victory!

In a few minutes Liu caught up with me. Now all I had to do was get the package home to Erich, and my mission would be complete. Liu and I loped down the street like a couple of horses after the race is run. Oh, how I'd miss the pumping excitement, laced with a hint of fear, once we were sealed in the tomb of Hongkew. And Liu. I'd miss him, too.

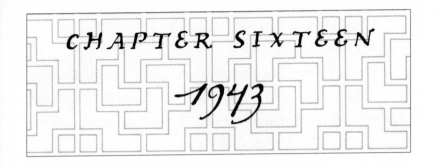

"So, Erich? Beehive *was* a double agent?"

"So, Ilse? Dovid *is* your boyfriend?"

"None of your business," I huffed. "I want to know what happened with Beehive."

"They keep me in the dark," Erich admitted. "Gerhardt and Rolf don't completely trust me. Or anyone. This much I know. There was a man watching you *and* Beehive."

"Yeah, we saw him. Liu tripped him in the park to get him off Beehive's trail."

"He what?" Erich pounded the table; forks jumped. "Not smart. Do you realize what could have happened to you?"

"Like what?" But I didn't want to hear.

"The Japanese Kempetai picked the man up and dragged him through the park. This morning his broken body was tossed out of Bridge House Prison."

"Alive?" I asked tremulously.

"Dead."

"Oh! Which side was he on?"

"Ours, the good guys."

"My God, Erich."

"Right, if there is such a thing as God in this hellhole."

"Shhh, here comes Mother." My hands shook as Mother's weary footsteps echoed in the hall. I opened the door, and she brushed past me, looking as worn down as a rickshaw puller and entirely defeated. She collapsed on her bed with her wrist over her forehead. "We have a place to move to on Houshan Road."

Erich and I bombarded her with questions. How many rooms? Plumbing? How many flights up? Windows? Neighbors?

Mother's voice was thin and wobbly. "One room, half the size of this one. No closets. Third floor walk-up. Plumbing."

"What kind of plumbing?" I asked. "Western toilets? Because I will not squat on the floor of a Chinese toilet."

"It has a western water closet on each floor," Mother said almost in a whisper, which made me wonder what she wasn't telling us.

The dead man's shattered body—I knew that's what Erich was thinking about, me too, but we couldn't let on to Mother, so we jabbered about the apartment in Hongkew.

Erich, the practical one, asked, "How much?"

"Too much. We can't afford it. All the way home I've thought about what we can sell. My winter coat, also your father's. Summer's coming. And my mother's silver kiddush cup should fetch some good money."

"Oh, Mother, no!"

Her voice gathered strength and turned hard. "We will sell everything we can except your bicycle, Erich, which you need for work, and The Violin."

I sighed. "The apartment, has it got a stove?" Mother shook her head. "Heating?" No, again. "Is it sunny?"

Mother exploded. "Sunshine? You want *sunshine*? And maybe also sour cream for your potatoes?"

We hadn't tasted sour cream since Vienna.

"Forget the sour cream. Even a plain boiled potato would be a miracle," Erich grumbled. "I hate the Japanese. Hate them with all my mortal being."

Mother snorted, a most unladylike sound for her. "Such a waste of energy. Use it to find boxes. We move on Friday morning."

"So soon, Mother?" I cried. "We have a whole week left on the outside."

"You think we make our own decisions these days? The Chinese family living there now on Houshan Road, they're moving in here on Friday afternoon. A mother, a father, six children, and a grandfather. Hah!" Mother suddenly burst into brittle-edged laughter mixed with tears. "Look at this place. To them it will be a palace."

It didn't take long to learn that there were worse places than our new apartment in Hongkew. Our school started a community service project to cheer us as we faced life in the ghetto. We adopted one of the "homes," the barracks that were room and board for the poorest souls among us westerners. Each pair of girls got a mop, a bucket of soapy water, a scrub brush, and a supply of rags to clean the walls and floors and windows on the inside. At the same time, the boys would wash the outside windows and whitewash the exterior walls of the rundown shell of a building.

The men who lived in the home were gone for the morning, working, or more likely scrounging for work, so the dormitory and dining room were empty for our whirl-wind spic-and-span operation. Six pairs of us marched into the building like soldiers, with our mops over our shoulders as rifles and our buckets as drums. Tanya and I were a team. Our bucket clattered to the linoleum floor and echoed through the cavernous dormitory, where sixty beds were lined up along the walls with about a foot between them. There wasn't so much as a shelf over each bed to hold a person's treasures or a nail to hang a change of clothes on. The sheets were nubby canvas, the blankets scratchy gray wool, and we counted only three pillows in the whole room.

As hard as I scrubbed, my mind kept drifting to the bearlike man in the park. I imagined his massive heap of broken bones, his battered face, in the street outside Bridge House. And then, God forgive me, I wondered who'd gotten the man's coat and hat, his leather shoes . . .

Tanya and I must have changed the wash water a hundred times. We were on our hands and knees on either side of the twelfth bed, scrubbing the floor under it. Tanya whispered to me in the dark shadows under the bed, "Pray we never come to this, Ilse."

"Never!" I vowed. My back ached, and I rose up on my

knees for a mighty stretch. That's when I noticed some charcoal sketches tacked to the wall over the next bed. The corners of the drawings were curled, and when I flattened the first one, the work was unmistakable.

"Tanya, come here!"

"What?" She slid across the floor on her knees, retying the kerchief that held her curls back. "What's so important?"

"This is where Dovid lives." I pointed to the sketches. "I've seen drawings like these. This one on top? His village in Poland. And this one is Kobe, Japan."

Tanya sank to her knees again. "Your Dovid lives in this hovel?"

"We have to get out of here before he comes back. He'll be so embarrassed." I spread my palm to the dismal room the color of oatmeal, the depressing rows of gray beds, the walls blank and dingy except for the relief of these sketches.

Tanya nodded. "Anyway, I can't scrub one more millimeter of floor. Already my skin's peeling."

We wrung out our rags, grabbed our pail and mop, and headed for the door, but not fast enough. Men were beginning to stream into the building for lunch, and suddenly, there was Dovid.

"Hide!" I whispered to Tanya, and we ducked behind a reception desk, hoping Dovid wouldn't notice our mop and bucket sticking out of the cave. I crawled out just far enough to watch him march down the row and flop on his own bed. Rusty springs creaked in protest. He kicked off each shoe and caught it, stuffing both under his head for a pillow. The whole picture was so desolate, so lonely, that I wanted to run right over and comfort him, take him home with me. But that would have hurt him worse. I reached behind me for Tanya to follow, and we silently crawled to the exit, to the surprise of the boys whitewashing outside.

The following afternoon I met Dovid at Mr. Bauman's café to tell him where we'd be living in Hongkew.

"Very close to me," he said with some glee in his eyes. "I live in the Kinchow Road Home." To my surprise he asked, "Want to see my castle?"

"I haven't much time. We're packing to move tomorrow." Excuses. But he looked so disappointed. "Okay, if we hurry."

We ran through the streets and stopped in front of the ramshackle building, improved only slightly by the white-washing.

"Do not fall over in shock," Dovid said. "It was never rebuilt since the bombing in 1937."

"Ah, but that's only the outside," I assured him, faking optimism.

"Inside it is worse. You will see." He led me into the dormitory I'd scrubbed only yesterday. Since it was late in the day, men and boys of all ages sprawled on their cots, staring at the ceiling. Such odor from so many bodies in one room! I tried not to breathe through my nose. The snores of some of the men bounced off the bare walls. I thought of Mother's rule: Unless you're feverish and half delirious, you are not to fritter away precious time sleeping during the day. Yet what else had these men to do?

"You must guess which place is mine," Dovid said playfully.

I lied. "They're all alike. How could I pick yours out?" I pretended to scan the empty cots with their grim gray blankets until I came to the charcoal sketches tacked to the wall above his bed, the bottom corners curled up as if struggling for release. The work was so obviously Dovid's, with bold lines defining space on the page, and the spidery lines and black smudges, and then the startlingly precise detail captured in intricate pencil strokes.

"They're breathtaking, Dovid." We sat on his bed; where else was there to sit?

The blanket was woolly, itchy on the back of my legs. Some of the men stared at us. An awkward silence fell between us, and it passed through my mind that Mother wouldn't approve of my sitting on a gentleman's bed, even with at least twelve chaperones watching our every move. I slid to my feet. "I really have to get home. There's so much to do before we move tomorrow."

"Yes, I understand," Dovid murmured. Our footsteps resounded in the dormitory, and one of the men flipped over on his cot and shouted, "Have a heart. Can't you see I'm trying to get some sleep?"

Outside, Dovid took my hand as we crossed an intersection. My hand was sweaty, and his felt dry as ash, but we fit together neatly, as though I'd been born with my hand in his.

CHAPTER SEVENTEEN
1943

Tanya and her mother weren't able to find an apartment in our building, though they would be living two houses away. Every little disappointment like this seemed major as the unknown stretched out ahead of us. As a farewell-to-freedom gift the morning of our move, Tanya came by with a huge bundle of fresh spinach her mother had gotten from a Japanese soldier, and you would think it was a bouquet of orchids the way Mother lovingly brushed and blew the sand off each leaf.

Tanya also brought over a blouse her mother had sewn. "It's called patchwork," she explained about the odd splotches cut from an old nightgown, a chintz apron, and the remains of a brocade curtain. "Very stylish in America," she added. While we were taking turns trying the blouse on, we heard an odd scratching at our door, like someone was raking fingernails down the wood. I threw the door open, and in strutted Moishe, who took a shortcut over our table.

"Get that cat off my kitchen table!" Mother cried. "I'm sorry, Tanya, how rude of me when you've brought us this marvelous gift of fresh spinach." The huge bouquet hung over the sides of Mother's one pan, now steaming with boiling water.

Tanya snatched Moishe off the table and cradled him, palming his face and giving it a good shake, which he loved.

We watched the spinach shrink into the pan and boil down to a limp black saucerful of seaweed.

"At home," Mother said forlornly, "I would make a fresh spinach salad with sweet onions and hard-cooked eggs. We would chew and crunch for twenty minutes."

"I'm sorry, Mrs. Shpann. I wish I could have brought string beans. They don't cook down so much."

"No, no, Tanya. Please don't think me ungrateful." Mother made an apology, offering a quick pat on the cat's back. "I'm just . . . nostalgic. This morning we move to Hongkew—who knows?"

Moishe nodded in agreement.

Father had hired two pedicabs to carry all our goods except our thin mattresses and our table and chairs, which needed a costly truck. The bed frames we had to leave behind for the Chinese family who'd be moving in. Mother, Father, and I walked the two miles to our new home, while Erich bicycled beside the pedicabs to keep an eye on our things.

Tanya and her mother traveled in style, compliments of the Japanese soldier of the week. He'd borrowed a flatbed truck to move their belongings, and Tanya and her mother rode into Hongkew in the back of the truck, cushioned by their mattresses.

The pedicab drivers dumped all our things on Houshan Road, in front of an entire audience of neighbors. Erich and I hurried it all up narrow stairs to our apartment. Apartment? *Room.* It was beyond my worst expectations. Its one window, barely a foot square, was painted shut and darkened with about a hundred years' worth of grit. "At least it won't be drafty in the winter," I said, and ducked the pillow Erich flung at me.

Our so-called apartment was about fourteen feet square.

"Moth-*er!*" I wailed. How on earth would we get three mattresses in there and still have space to plant our feet on the floor? Mother paced off the room and told Father where to pound nails into the bumpy ceiling so she could hang sheets to make *rooms* out of the one room. The bathroom was down the hall, on our floor. That was a plus. And yes, there was a western toilet that mercifully flushed. But my heart dropped when I realized there was no bathtub—only a deep, rough cement basin suitable for doing laundry, although I couldn't guess how we'd manage that, since the one spigot dribbled only cold water.

It's not as bad as Dovid's dormitory, I kept reminding myself. *Not as bad.*

And far better than Tanya's place. Erich and I helped them move into a dark square of a room with peeling plaster walls and warped floorboards crusted with filth. You could even see the imprint of Chinese vegetables in the wood, as though they'd fossilized there. Moishe took one look at this horror and ran off for good.

Back in our own apartment that was palatial by comparison, Erich said, "Moishe's someone's steak dinner tonight. Medium rare, very tender, purr-fect."

"You heartless creature!" I scolded.

"Come on, you hate that cat as much as I do."

We heard voices on the other side of the wall, which was only a thin sheet of plywood that separated us from our neighbors. They were whispering to one another in Japanese.

Suddenly Erich's good humor evaporated, and he turned hard. "Japs live there?"

"Shoosh," I warned.

The neighbors turned out to be a sweet older couple, Mr. and Mrs. Kawashima. They'd been in Shanghai since way before the occupation because Mr. K had worked for the Shanghai Municipal Council as a Japanese translator until his retirement. Mrs. K knew a little German and a lot more English. That first night she told us what it used to be like in Hongkew before the Japanese bombing in 1937.

"Oh, such a nice market," she said. "Countrymen come with their finest. We have cabbage, artichoke, mango, pomegranate, lemon. Chicken, pheasant, squab. Fresh fish— tuna, shad, mackerel. Big tank slosh with water from the sea, squid and shrimp swimming in. You pick the best. Cheap, too. Not like now," she said with a deep sigh.

* * *

The good thing about having wafer-thin mattresses and no bed frames was that we could roll our beds up and stand them in a corner like smoke stacks during the day so we'd have room to move around. Mother learned to cook on an old-fashioned Chinese stove that burned coal briquettes by watching the Chinese cooks in their portable kitchens all over Hongkew. The smoke from their briquettes hung in the air like low clouds. They sold their hot dishes to people on the street, who clicked their chopsticks in appreciation, but Mother didn't quite have the knack yet, and our food had an odd undertaste.

"We're being slowly poisoned by our own mother," Erich said with a wink. It was meant as a joke, but Mother was in no laughing mood. She gave Erich one of her famous fingernail-flickings to the cheek. It didn't amount to much with her swollen joints. Her chipped, split nails made little of a thumping impact. He just laughed, which riled her even more.

All morning we watched the barbed wire go up. The gates of the ghetto were still open for another week. At night I lay awake for hours, so close to Mother and Father and Erich that I could pick out their separate breathing patterns. When I finally fell asleep, I dreamed of doors slamming shut, echoing for miles around. And of Dovid.

On May 18, 1943, signs went up at all the Hongkew exits: STATELESS REFUGEES PROHIBITED WITHOUT PERMISSION, and then the Japanese closed the gates. There was no resounding echo, as in my dream. In the din of activity on the Hongkew streets, we barely heard a clatter. I expected my heart to leap into my throat as I watched the bar slide across the gate nearest our apartment. I expected a resonating clang, but there was only a faint click of the lock, and I simply felt numb.

We needed passes to leave Hongkew. Erich was beyond school age, but I had one more year at the Kadoorie School, which entitled me to a day pass beginning a half hour before school started and ending an hour after school let out. That left no time for any REACT assignments, although I knew Erich was sneaking out of Hongkew and slipping home at odd hours. Mother stopped asking questions in exchange for the meager money Erich earned for the family kitty.

I had to learn the pass system, which meant cozying up to a man named Kanoh Ghoya, who called himself King of the Jews.

Tanya had already enjoyed the pleasure of a chat with the horrid little toad. "He comes up to my shoulder. My mother says he's like a lawn ornament, but ugly. My word, as ugly as a fat *tuchas*, this man is! Wait until you meet him."

I could wait. And I hoped he wouldn't become Mrs. Mogelevsky's new Friday visitor.

There in the ghetto, we Jewish girls and boys had all sorts of discussions about how to handle Ghoya. People who'd had dealings with him, to get clearance to go to a funeral or a job interview or a doctor's appointment, reported that sometimes he issued three-month passes when you'd only asked for a day, and other times he slammed his hands on the desk and refused even an hour's pass. The "king," they said, was known to jump up on his desk to slap the face of anyone who irritated him.

I gathered what ammunition I could before daring to face Ghoya because I knew someday I was going to feel desperate to get beyond the gates to roam through Shanghai like a free person. Besides, REACT needed me. At least I hoped it did.

Mrs. Kawashima told me that the Chinese had a saying in Shanghai, *maskee!* It meant, "never mind, don't worry, things will get better." Winter will melt into spring, summer will ease into fall. As Mrs. K said, "When summer heat make you itch like you have flea, you say '*maskee!*' Don't worry. Soon be cold again and flea will die." She was so full of good cheer; but as Erich reminded us, the Chinese and Japanese in Hongkew didn't have to show passes, just the Jews.

In June the rainy season hit us again, but at least our apartment was watertight. The streets, though, were ankle-deep in filthy water. Underground sewers were an unknown luxury in the Hongkew section of the city. The streets doubled as sewers. Chinese children splashed in the water as if all of the neighborhood were one big swimming pool. Slogging through it to get to school was a nightmare. My galoshes filled up with slimy scum water, and each step was like lifting weights. Steam rose from the water as the hot weather began to set in. Imagine the smell.

So, there was good news and bad news. The good news

was, school would be out soon and I could look for a job. The bad news was, the day that school let out for the summer, I'd lose my pass.

Maskee! I kept telling myself. It would get better. When? How long before we all gave in to the gloom, even me, even Mrs. Kawashima?

CHAPTER EIGHTEEN
1943

Once we were pent up in the ghetto, changes came rapidly, and they weren't all for the worse, either. We all had jobs to do, not that we got paid for any of them. Hour by hour, our job was to survive to the next meal. Day by day, our job was to keep from dying of heat prostration—until winter, when the challenge would be to keep our fingers and toes from snapping off like twigs. Week by week, our job was to lift up our sagging spirits with culture and activity, and to rebuild our rickety, dreary surroundings into a place fit for living and working and dreaming. Well, dreaming, that was tougher. We were planted in practicality.

Tanya and I sauntered around our neighborhood to check daily progress, and there was a lot. Put a bunch of enterprising people together, with too much time on their hands, and it's amazing what pops up.

"It's almost as good as a Hollywood movie," Tanya gushed as we watched a bombed-out building slowly being transformed into something humans could actually live in. "What do you think, they put flush toilets in there?"

"Oh, of course," I answered indignantly, remembering how in Vienna, Erich and I used to share a bathroom with a deep marble tub and gold faucets. "I just hope no one tries to jam their plumbing."

"Now, why would anyone do such an idiotic thing?" Tanya asked.

Bigmouth, me.

But she didn't expect an answer. She looked into every alley, up every fire escape, to find Moishe. "My poor, lonesome kitty-cat."

I tried to comfort her. "Maybe he's found a home on the outside and is eating well." There were enough rats in Hongkew for Moishe to have a six-course banquet every day.

Tanya stopped and turned around to face me. "You never liked my cat, did you?"

"I did, I thought he was beautiful, fluffy . . . No, not really."

"He didn't like you, either. He only loved me."

"I'm sorry, Tanya. I know you miss Moishe." I took her hand, and we walked some more, our thoughts punctuated by the constant hammering all around us.

"They're gone," Tanya said. "My mother's Japanese soldiers. Now we're even poorer than you are."

I squeezed her hand; there was nothing to say.

Some of our ghetto streets were looking more and more

like European neighborhoods, especially Little Vienna, with its shops and open-air cafés. Herr Bauman struggled to stay open, but he could no longer keep pouring free tea water. Doctors and dentists and lawyers opened offices upstairs from Little Vienna's shops, sharing space with one another by the hour so each could do a little business, make a bit of money, eat now and then. The watch repairman downstairs rented the space two hours a week so his customers could pick up his handiwork.

Newspapers on the outside called us "efficient" and "resourceful." We called ourselves hungry—for food and for culture.

So, we had newspapers and radio programs in a variety of languages. We could go to a restaurant or club such as the Roofgarden, and the heart-thumping American-style jazz would overflow the walls so we could listen outside. We couldn't afford to go *inside* these clubs, of course. Only the few wealthy among us, or people from beyond the ghetto, or the black marketeers could do that. One rare night, Erich joined the crowd with us outside the Roofgarden Café. Tanya and I danced on the sidewalk—our own version of the jitterbug—until we were soaked with sweat. Then we three sat on the curb and talked about what we missed most.

"Me, I crave things to crunch, like fried potatoes," I mused.

Erich said, "Meat. The kind that needs lots of chewing down to the bone. I'd suck the marrow out of the bone."

Tanya's eyes swam: "A bowl of custard and berries, so sweet that for a week I've got a toothache."

We yammered endlessly about fresh peaches and plums. Leafy salads, tart and oily with vinaigrette. Waxy, cold white asparagus on a bed of red-tipped lettuce—while at our apartment we peeled off mildewed leaves and chopped moldy stubs off vegetables to salvage the inner cores that the rot hadn't reached yet.

In a short time our ghetto boasted Yiddish theater. At first, Father and The Violin stayed busy, but without pay. Also, we had lots and lots of sports. The Chaufoong Road Home had a huge soccer field, and we watched the matches for free. People with a little money bet on them.

Dovid and I were walking along Yangztepoo Road, hand in hand, when I asked, "Why don't you go to Chaufoong Road and play soccer? You said you were the best goalie Saint Ignatz School ever had."

Dovid stopped to glare at me. "I told you about that day, Ilse, remember? My last soccer game, my parents, my sisters. Do you think—"

"Do *you* think that kicking the ball around a field will make your family disappear all over again? Stop punishing yourself, Dovid. Have some fun."

"I sketch," he said by way of defense.

"What fun!"

"So? What do *you* do for fun?" he asked.

That required some thought. Finally I came up with a

paltry something. "Tanya and I hang out on the curb outside the jazz clubs lots of evenings. We jitterbug and imagine that we're gobbling huge platefuls of food like the rich people inside."

"This is fun?" Dovid asked.

"Better than drinking lukewarm tea made with three-day-old tea leaves at Mr. Bauman's," I retorted. He reached for my hand; I pulled it away. "Erich's right: There's no place for chocolates or love in wartime."

He flinched at the word *love*. How stupid of me.

"I can't stay here any longer," he began.

Now I'd scared him off. "You have a pass?"

"I refuse to curry Ghoya's favor. No pass. I'm . . . disappearing."

Tears clouded my eyes. "What do you mean?"

"I will find a way to go into the interior. China's a vast country. I can get lost. Tibet, I may go there. The landscape is mystical, good for sketching."

"But why, Dovid?"

"Why? Why? Because! Nothing keeps me here."

"Me?"

"There's no future here for us."

"But the war will end someday. Soon, I believe."

"And then what?"

No one knew. America was a faint hope, or maybe we could go to Argentina, where Mother's brother lived. Argentina—it seemed worlds away.

"You see? You have no answer," Dovid said, tauntingly. "You will grow up."

"Dovid! I'm nearly fifteen. That's old, for wartime."

We stopped at a flinty bench. An old couple made way for us, maybe seeing in us the young lovers they'd once been. Young lovers, hah! We were in the middle of an ugly fight. We whispered, and it wasn't easy to argue in a whisper.

I made a brave effort, anyway. "How selfish can you be, leaving this way?"

"And I thought selfishness was your gift alone."

"That's cruel, Dovid, and you know it."

"You say anything on your mind. No thought for other people's feelings."

"As if you have any!"

The old couple struggled to their feet and left us to our battle.

Dovid's voice rose to a whiny level I'd never heard before. "Do you think I *like* living in a bombed-out tenement like I do, without so much as a hook to hang my coat on? Where is my self-respect? Gone. But I suppose it's what I deserve."

"Yes, because you let the Nazis take your family. It's all your fault for playing soccer when they came to your village, right? Stop feeling so sorry for yourself. It's not attractive."

"What do you know, Ilse? You have led a charmed life, in the shelter of a mother and father and brother."

"Charmed? Look at me, Dovid, look. I'm in tatters, my

hair is leeched straw, my nose runs constantly, I'm hollowed out. Charmed? I should say so." Also, I wouldn't give him the satisfaction of knowing that he'd caused a throbbing in my temples that would gather into a fierce headache before the night was over.

"Here, I'm useless. Maybe I can do something for our people somewhere else."

"Just what do you think *you* could do? You're no Sugi-hara!" I shot back—a mean, low blow that I regretted the minute it was out of my mouth.

Dovid jumped to his feet and stood in front of me. "Let's stop this. We're saying things that hurt. It is our last time together. Tomorrow I go."

I nodded, swallowing hot anger. "Will I ever hear from you again?"

He held my face, brushing tears off each cheek with his rough thumbs. "I will find you," he promised, "if we are both alive at the end of the war." We walked back to Houshan Road in silence, close, but not touching. He left me at the shadowy door of our building. "Be selfish, it is okay," he advised. "You will need to watch out for yourself, to survive." And he was gone.

CHAPTER NINETEEN
1943—1944

I cried myself to sleep for several nights, but I had to do it silently. There was no such thing as privacy in our apartment, and I didn't want Mother and Father to know about Dovid. He was the only possession I refused to share, even if he was gone. Those memories were mine alone to hoard.

We heard more and more horror stories about Ghoya, who had absolute control over our comings and goings. In July, Mr. Shaum, an old man in our building, pleaded with Ghoya for a pass to visit his wife's grave on the *yahrzeit*, the anniversary of her death. He caught Ghoya at a bad time— and was sentenced to a week of house arrest in his airless room on the fifth floor. When a foul odor seeped from under his door, Erich and another boy in the building broke the door down and carried Mr. Shaum's decaying body to the local cemetery. A week later, Ghoya forced a pregnant woman to kneel in his office for an hour while he stared at her and shouted, "No more Jews! Too crowded!"

But with school out and no chance of a job, I longed to see things outside the ghetto walls, so I began thinking of schemes to charm Ghoya. Erich had tried it the week before, and that turned out to be a disaster. He told me the sorry story as we were killing time. So much time on our hands.

Chang, the beggar whose territory was our lane, waited for us to pass, palm outstretched. Erich gave him the usual two grains of rice. To me he said, "Ghoya was in a rat-foul mood."

"When *isn't* he?"

"Worse than usual. Maybe he'd just eaten some spoiled sushi, or his wife had spent all his yen at the Race Course."

"The toad is married? So, what lie did you feed him?"

"I told him, 'I have to see Song Lingyu at the docks. He promised me a job,' which isn't true, but if I could get there and convince Song Lingyu to write a letter, that's all I'd need."

"Would a letter from Madame Liang help?"

"Are you crazy? Anyway, Song Lingyu wouldn't have to hire me or pay me, just write the letter confirming that he had a job for me, and that would get me a work pass out of Hongkew."

"Ghoya wasn't buying it, right?"

We passed the table where Mr. Hsu ran his letter-writing business. He wore the long black gown and black skull cap typical of old China. An impatient line formed by his table, some people fanning themselves with blue envelopes to read, and others chomping to get their letters written.

"Man, Ilse, you should have seen the Little King." That

was our nickname for Ghoya. "He shouted, 'Song Lingyu! Ghoya don't like Song Lingyu!' He started jumping up and down and calling me names in half a dozen languages. I tried to keep a straight face, but it was hilarious watching him dance around like Rumpelstiltskin. I couldn't help it, I started laughing and couldn't stop, couldn't even catch my breath."

"Oh, Erich! What happened?"

"Well, you do *not* laugh at this asinine little gnome." My brother did his best to hold in howls of laughter; they exploded, anyway. Mr. Hsu looked up from his calligraphy, and all his customers stared at us loud westerners.

"No, you don't laugh at the Little King," I said, biting my lip. "Okay, so he didn't give you the pass?"

"Worse. He put me on probation. I think he knows I'm the one who found Mr. Shaum. It's a warning to me. I can't apply for another pass for twelve weeks. But I have ways of getting out, and incidentally, I will personally strangle you if you try sneaking out yourself. Don't be stupid like I am."

"Dovid got out," I said.

Erich registered only mild surprise. Maybe he already knew. "Lucky man."

"I'll never see him again. What about me? I'm the one that's grieving." I put my hands on my hips, elbows jutting out in indignation. "Erich Shpann, don't you *dare* think about leaving me alone with Mother and Father. We'd never see you again. God only knows where Dovid's gotten to, or if he's still alive."

"Lucky man," Erich repeated, and I wondered if he

meant lucky because he'd escaped or lucky because he was dead—which I refused to believe.

Father had very little paying work. The chamber quartet had disbanded. He still had two or three willing students but nowhere to teach them. Days passed and The Violin stayed in its case, propped on top of our rolled-up mattresses. Maybe Father would take it out and rub a little oil onto its belly, maybe tighten its strings, but he stopped playing, even at the free concerts. Instead, he sat by the hour in cafés grousing with other fathers who had no work. From Tanya I'd learned the Yiddish word *mensch*, man, but it meant more than that. It meant a real, full, functioning, righteous human being. I could hardly stand Father's swimming in self-pity, and I'm ashamed to say, there were days when I just wanted to shout at my father: Be a mensch!

Not that Reb Chaim, the head of the Mirrer Yeshiva, was the perfect example of Jewish manhood, I quickly learned. He came to our house one afternoon while Mother was at Mr. Schmaltzer's bakery. Although it was hot enough to burn your feet on the sidewalk, the rebbe wore a long black coat and a fur-trimmed black hat that covered his ears and floated on the edges of his bushy sideburns. He must have been sweltering, especially inside our airless little apartment. We'd scrubbed the window and pried it open, but you'd think it was an insult to its reputation to let a breeze waft in.

Father asked me to leave while he talked to the rebbe. I

listened at the door, of course. After all, I was practically a trained spy, thanks to REACT—which hadn't used me at all since I'd been in the ghetto.

Reb Chaim's mission was almost too horrible to contemplate. He led a whole tribe of pimply, pious student scholars—future rabbis, no less! And they were all, as he said to Father, "in need of virtuous wives." One had his eye on me. "His name is Shlomo Leibovitz. From very good stock," Reb Chaim told him, as though Father were shopping for cattle. "But your lovely daughter—what is her name?"

"Ilse." It sounded musical on Father's lips.

"This is a Jewish name?"

"In Austria, yes," Father replied.

"Austria, ah," Reb Chaim said dismissively. "Reb Shpann, you've studied the holy books?" Fortunately, he didn't wait for an answer, because Father was far from a scholar. "Ah, then you know that when the Holy One, *baruch hashem*, blessed be His Name, when He made the world, at the same time He matched all future brides and grooms. So your daughter, Ilse, maybe she meets Shlomo Liebovitz, and she doesn't feel a spark. Not a problem. She can take her pick of a dozen of my boys, every one brilliant, I say with humility."

Take my pick? I'd sooner jump in Soochow Creek. Father must have heard me groan outside the thin wall. He opened the door then and silently shook his finger at me, motioning me to go away so he could talk to the rebbe.

I waited in the lane until Reb Chaim left, then dashed upstairs to beg my father to be reasonable.

"Father, if you said yes, I'll never forgive you. Never!" I shouted. I heard things go silent in the Kawashima apartment. It was their way of pretending they weren't home when we had a family squabble. Calming down, I whispered, "Please don't make me marry one of those rabbis. All they do is study, study, study. Please, anything. I'll take up The Violin again. I'll practice twelve hours a day. What did you tell him?"

Father wrinkled his forehead and gazed up at the ceiling. Oh, God, he'd promised me to one of those horrid boys; I was sure of it!

Then Father smiled mischievously. "'Reb Chaim,' I said—"

"Yes? Yes?"

"I told him 'Thank you, my family is honored, but my Ilse makes up her own mind who she's going to marry.'"

I leaped to my feet and hugged Father. It had been a long time between hugs.

"Violin lessons again, daughter? We can begin at once," he teased.

The really odd thing was, Mother believed I should consider marrying one of those deathly students. "The yeshiva boys eat well, they have a nice roof over their heads— outside the ghetto, I might mention. They have winter coats, fur hats. They're good boys, smart. Don't thumb your nose at such things."

"But they're going to be rabbis!" I protested. "Besides, I'm only fifteen. Look at me, Mother. Do I look like a rabbi's wife, really?" I made a face that brought laughter to Mother's eyes, as she said, "Still, it's not a bad prospect for a Jewish girl in China. We *are* Jews, I remind you."

We were Jews, all right—especially to Hitler—but religion was a different matter. In Vienna we weren't at all religious, and during our four years in Shanghai we'd only been to the synagogue once, on Pearl Harbor Day. Since we'd been penned in Hongkew, though, Mother had begun blessing Sabbath candles in halting Hebrew and talking about how we, too, should learn the Hebrew prayers of our ancestors. This religious awakening seemed to be happening all over the ghetto, and maybe it was comforting to some people in our dire circumstances, but marry a rabbi? That was going too far!

Tanya and I window-shopped along Chusan Avenue. We'd heard that the milliner had an exotic, new red hat in the window, perched on a blank-faced wooden head that someone forgot to give eyes and a nose and a mouth.

"Oy, the hat. So gorgeous," Tanya said dreamily.

That's how dull our lives in the ghetto were. A clutch of red felt, a tight ribbon bow, a couple of inches of netting, and a feather—that's all it took to hold us enthralled at the window like spectators at a soccer match as the dummy head slowly rotated for our entertainment.

"Guess what, Tanya?"

"Hmm?" She had her nose pressed to the window to catch the hat at every angle.

"The rebbe from the Mirrer Yeshiva came to talk to my father about marriage."

Tanya jumped back from the window as if I'd poked her with a stick. "You're going to marry the rebbe? He's at least fifty years old!"

"No, no, one of his ghostly boys."

"But what about Dovid?"

"Who says we'll ever see each other again? And anyway, I'm not going to marry the yeshiva boy."

"He's handsome?"

"How would I know? I never saw him, but he's seen me on the street, and to hear the rebbe tell it, the boy's totally love struck." Okay, I was bragging, and pleased that Tanya fell for it.

"Oh, Ilse, that's soooo romantic."

"Romantic? Tanya Mogelevsky, look at me." I slid between her and the window, blocking the hat. "Do I look like a girl who'd marry a rabbi? I'm not a bit religious, and we'd never, ever go to movies, because my brilliant husband would be studying a hundred hours a day, and anyway, movies aren't allowed in the yeshiva world."

"No movies? Well, I don't know. I'll have to think about it." Tanya shouldered me away from the window and turned back to the hat. The peacock feather shimmered its rainbow colors as the dummy head turned. "I've given it a lot of thought."

"Two seconds' worth."

"Enough to know what I'd do. I'd give up movies to marry a handsome, brooding rabbi."

"Tanya, you can't be serious!"

"Oh, yes, Ilse, very serious. I'll make a wonderful rabbi's wife. I'll take care of everything so he can study as much as he likes. I'll clean our cottage and cook delicious kosher meals and sew all his clothes after the babies are asleep. Lots of babies."

"Sounds perfect . . . ly wretched," I said, but she didn't hear, because she was floating in her own dream.

"And I'm going to wear that gorgeous red confection under the *chuppah* on our wedding day, you'll see. He'll lift the veil and see my eyes, so full of love."

I pictured the magnificent hat on Tanya's profusion of black curls, its feather tickling the underside of the wedding canopy, and tried to dredge up some feeling of joy for my friend. Curiously, what I felt was . . . betrayed.

I told Erich about Reb Chaim and the yeshiva boy who had his eye on me. "Marriage to a scholar, it wouldn't be so bad. At least you wouldn't starve."

"Erich!" I found myself drumming his chest with my fists, tears spilling down my hot face. So much to cry about. Losses piled on top of losses, and not a single gain. Erich let me carry on this way for a few minutes, then grabbed both my wrists and pulled me toward him.

"You're a wreck since Dovid left. You'd be no good to REACT this way." He paused, considering his next words. "I can't stand seeing you so unhappy. A little brotherly advice? You need to get out of here. The King of the Jews, he has the key. Go get it."

CHAPTER TWENTY

1944

I waited so long in the sun outside Ghoya's office that I about melted into a puddle of hot jelly. But finally, a peek at the devil.

The loathsome man sat on the front of his desk, swinging his little feet. He looked cool, and why not? A powerful fan blew at him from each side, as if he were the meeting place of the east and west winds. Such extravagant cool air, and with electricity rationed for the rest of us! But the cool wind revived me, and I got to work trying to enchant the man, the way yogis charm snakes.

I smiled, waiting for him to speak. "Ilse Shpann, sir," I answered when he asked my name.

"Ilse Shpann, it is supreme pleasure," he said in his peculiar English where *r*'s were *l*'s, and vice versa.

He never asked me to sit down. "Kind sir, I need to visit a certain doctor outside, on Avenue Joffre."

"You have many fine Jewish doctors in Hongkew." He

swung one ankle over the other knee. His eyes sparkled. The little reptile was flirting with me!

"Yes, sir, but I have a particularly delicate problem." I let him draw his own conclusions.

"Ah, Ghoya understands. And not married?"

"No, sir." I tried to look ashamed.

"This is a pity, such a pretty redheaded girl not married."

"So, you can see why I must consult with this doctor at once, sir?"

"Doctor's name?"

I handed him a slip of paper with the name and address of a German doctor, one of the refugees allowed to live outside the ghetto, since he'd come to Shanghai before 1939. Ghoya read it and read it, as though it were an indecipherable poem. Now his feet were together, swinging like a pendulum, with his heels thunking the desk.

He looked up at me with a zigzag grin. "Many pretty girls like you in Hongkew." He smoothed back his greasy hair and pointed to my head. "Ghoya loves pretty girls with pretty curls. Ha-ha!" He laughed at his clever rhyme, eyeing me luridly.

I lowered my eyes as if his so-called compliment had enchanted me instead of turning me nauseous.

His eyes still fixed on me, he slapped the desk behind him, knocking over a fishbowl full of red and white wrapped candies. My mouth watered for just one of those peppermints and the feel of sticky candy lodged in my teeth. He left the peppermints spread across the desk, never offering me one, of course, while he located a pad, scribbled something in Japanese, and pounded it with a red stamp. Handing me a slip of paper, he said merrily, "Come back to see me. Ghoya likes redheaded girls!"

I'd charmed the snake into a one-month pass. As I backed toward the door—we weren't allowed to turn our backs on Ghoya—he said, "You know the name REACT?"

My heart skipped about forty beats. "REACT, sir?"

He leaped to the floor, like a child jumping out of a swing. "Pretty girl like you don't talk to REACT men. Bad men, stupid men." He stared up into my face, his eyes cold and mean, then shouted, "Next!"

Mr. Schmaltzer generously gave Mother an hour a day to work at the bakery, but it was only a matter of weeks until he'd have to close. How could you run a bakery without flour or butter or sugar? And no one had money for his pastries, anyway. Even humble black bread was out of the reach of most of us. Instead of customers, Mr. Schmaltzer had flies and cockroaches and rats. Mother's hour at the bakery was mostly spent sweeping up the droppings.

So, it was Mother's hour at Mr. Schmaltzer's, and as soon as Father went to join his fellow grumps at the café, I planned to flee Hongkew for a glorious day in the city. But before Father left, there came a knock at the door.

"Ilse, go and see who."

It was Reb Chaim with a boy so thin, the rebbe could

slide him under our door. As soon as the boy saw me, he cast his eyes to the back wall and pulled at his patchy beard with sinewy hands.

Reb Chaim blustered in. "You should excuse me, miss, your father is at home?" Well, it wasn't like we had a gracious front hallway, with thick carpeting and flickering sconces. Reb Chaim could hardly overlook the fact that Father stood two feet away.

"Come in, come in." Father jerked his head to remind me to vanish—this was man-to-man talk. I ducked into my corner of the room and dropped to the floor, with the sheet-curtain yanked around me. We called this privacy in the ghetto.

"Reb Shpann, let me not hit around the shrub," the rebbe said in a conspiratorial whisper. "This is Shlomo. I told you about him. You remember?"

"Yes, Reb Chaim, but I also told you my daughter has a mind of her own."

"Of course, of course. What woman doesn't? Our curse, ever since from Adam's rib was formed Eve." I heard him slap his knee, chuckling.

Father forced up a weak chortle. I peeked around the curtain. There was Shlomo standing in the center of the room, his hat brushing the fly trap that hung from the ceiling. Towering over Father and Reb Chaim seated at the table, Shlomo rocked to and fro, as if his feet were screwed to the floor.

"Reb Shpann, Shlomo is a very enlightened boy. A great

scholar he'll be someday. Already he's memorized six trac-
tates, and he studies fourteen, sixteen hours a day."

Shlomo bent his chalk-white goose neck toward Father.
His back was rounded from poring over the books so many
hours. *By the time he reaches sixty,* I thought, *he'll be kissing his belly
button.*

He wasn't at all like Dovid, who was so handsome with
his back straight, his eyes dazzling, his cheeks smooth and
rosy.

"Reb Shpann, here is the heart of the matter. Shlomo
believes it is *beshert* that he should marry your daughter. You
know *beshert?*"

"No, Reb Chaim, I do not," Father said impatiently.

"Fate. Their marriage is ordained." Reb Chaim looked
up at the ceiling, then brushed his palms back and forth, as if
to say, *"See, Lord? We've taken care of that little earthly task for You."*

Father beckoned Shlomo to come closer, and the ghost
shuffled over toward Father, who asked, "He speaks German,
Reb Chaim?"

"Enough like Yiddish, he'll understand."

Father stood up and put his arm around Shlomo. I
thought the ghost might flicker away with human touch.
Father said, "I'm sure you're a fine boy, a brilliant learner, and
you'll make a kind husband, but not for my daughter, you
understand? With my daughter it is definitely not *beshert.*"

"So you say," Reb Chaim singsonged like a warning.
"Come, Shlomo." At the door Reb Chaim said, "You'll call me

if you change your mind? You can find me at the Beth Aharon shul."

Once they were gone, Father fished me out of my corner. "You heard?"

"Every word. Thank you, thank you, Father."

"Ilse, my daughter," he said, pulling me to my feet. "Believe me, I have higher hopes for my grandchildren than Shlomo. The boy does not look at all musical."

"My thoughts exactly, Father." Well, not *exactly*.

Then Father said, "When the day comes, Daughter, you will choose your own husband, and I trust you will choose wisely. Look how well your mother did." His weathered face crinkled in a smile that made my heart flood with love.

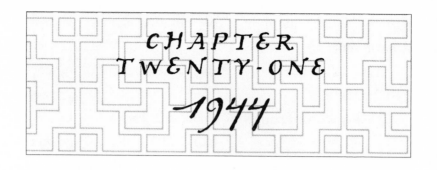

CHAPTER TWENTY-ONE
1944

I walked around the International Settlement, absorbing the sights and sounds and smells. I caught glimpses of Liu here and there, negotiating a variety of schemes, and once nabbed him by the back of his shirt.

"Have work to do, missy," he said, squirming away from me. "Important job for big lady on Bubbling Well Road."

"Wait. Have you eaten today?" The customary, polite Chinese greeting.

He tapped the ground with his crusty boot toe and thrust out his skinny belly with the knife tucked into his waist. "Liu don't eat much," he said jovially, as though starvation were a badge of honor.

Survival, war was all about survival. I thought about Dovid. Somehow his giving me permission to be selfish for my own survival freed me to be curiously generous.

I reached into my pocket for a thin coin. So what if I went without lunch? I was used to hunger gnawing at my belly. I offered the coin to Liu.

"No no no no no no no!" he said. "Beggar! Not Liu! I work job. You got job for me, missy?"

"Not today."

He shrugged his sharp-boned shoulders. "Okay," and he scampered away in search of a paying customer.

In the Old City, I watched a group of artisans carve ivory and jade into incredibly intricate tiny figures. A few steps away, professional letter writers enticed customers with chants that I could only guess at: "Your mother in the provinces wants to hear from you one last time before she closes her eyes to join the ancestors." "If your sweetheart doesn't get a letter, she'll marry Wang from the glassworks." "There is an inheritance waiting, you only have to write and ask for it."

I walked through the street market and marveled at the wild fowl in bamboo cages, their feathers snowing all around me. A woman who looked like she'd been alive for centuries tucked a skinny live chicken under her arms, trapping its wings. She hailed a rickshaw boy, who already had a customer, but he lowered the shaft to the ground anyway so the woman could tie the chicken to the bar of the rickshaw. The barefooted boy lifted the rickshaw and trotted with the chicken flapping up and down and protesting noisily. The passenger plugged his ears as the chicken screeched, "Quawk! Quawk!"

The woman tried to hold the chicken in place, plodding as best she could alongside the rickshaw. But the poor old thing hobbled on bound feet in threadbare silk slippers no bigger than a baby's shoes. I wanted to help, but how?

Help the chicken? Help the rickshaw runner? Help the old woman with the broken feet? I inched closer until the woman took notice of me. She shouted something to the boy, who dropped the rickshaw bars with a resounding clatter and stared at me. The woman, her face as creased as a walnut, gawked at my crowd-stopping nest of red hair. She smiled, not a tooth in her head. Even the chicken stopped flailing and peered at me as if he'd never seen a redhead, either.

Four years in China, and I was *still* every inch a foreigner.

Back in Hongkew that evening, I couldn't wait to get Erich alone to tell him about my day. We'd set up a chessboard on the curb, and while he studied his moves, I described the junks and sampans in Soochow Creek as though he'd never seen them before.

"The houseboats are jammed together, square and brown, with planks from one boat to another, so people can cross over. Each boat has a different gigantic eye painted on either side of the bow. Without those eyes, the boat couldn't see where it was going. That's what they say."

"Superstitious," Erich muttered.

"But there's such life on those houseboats, Erich, whole families. Some of those people never leave the boats their whole lives, can you imagine?"

"I imagine I'll be in this ghetto my whole life."

"I refuse to let you think that way, Erich."

He made a move on the chessboard. I could already see

I was doomed in this game. He picked at the raw skin on his thumb, his particular nervous habit. We all had them. Mine was twirling dry strands of my hair. I'd once had more hair than I could corral into a tam, but now it stuck out like a scarecrow's thin straw.

"Any more from the jolly world of houseboats?" Erich prompted.

"There was a sort of funeral." He looked up. Funerals, his cup of tea. "Lots of chanting and wailing, and the children on the boat stood quietly by. Then they slid it into the water."

"Slid what?" he asked, his eyes back on the board.

"The body, wrapped half in bamboo, half in tattered sails. He'll float toward the Yangtze, I suppose."

"Like we will someday, wrapped in our holey bedsheets."

"No, Erich," I told him firmly. "When the war's over, we'll go home to Vienna." Lying, even to myself.

Erich had no room in his heart for delusion. "Not possible."

"To America, then."

"Bah."

"To *America*. Do you hear me?"

Tanya and I lay on my thin mattress with our legs straight up the wall to absorb a bit of its coolness when we heard something teasing the apartment door as if it were a snare drum.

"Too hot. I can't move," I moaned to Tanya. "You go."

I rolled over to see who was at the door. Kneeling at Tanya's feet was the yeshiva boy, Shlomo Liebovitz. He jumped up just as Tanya squatted down to see who he was, but then she got up and *he* squatted. Up and down a few more times, as if they were on a calliope.

Tanya and I burst out laughing as Shlomo pressed himself against the far wall, lowering his eyes, of course. He wasn't supposed to be in the company of single young women without a chaperone, and the poor boy looked like we'd hexed him.

"Why are you here, Shlomo?" I asked.

His eyes were on the wall, as he pointed to a jar of something reddish purple at Tanya's feet.

"Borscht!" Tanya cried, snatching it up.

I came closer, watching that ugly liquid slosh in the jar. "What is that?"

"Soup, cold beet soup," Shlomo stammered while searching for the battered English words to state his mission at my door: "I bring betrothal gift for my *beshert*." He daringly shot a glance my way, blushed the color of the soup, then lowered his woeful eyes.

Tanya said in Yiddish, "I could love a man who brings borscht."

He brightened at the sound of his own language and subtly shifted his head from me to Tanya.

"I'm pleased to meet you, Reb Liebovitz. I am Tanya Mogelevsky, from Vinnytsia." She turned shy, hugging the borscht jar.

Shlomo backed toward the stairs, then ran. We watched him clutch the banister as he rounded each landing, his black coat flaring behind him like a cape.

From the bottom his Yiddish words echoed throughout the house, and Tanya translated: "I shall have Reb Chaim call on your father tomorrow, Miss Mogelevsky!"

It was no longer a rumor. Fact: All enemy nationals would be sent to internment camps, even members of our Shanghai Volunteer Corps, even its Jewish members. British, Americans, Dutch, and other people who'd lived in comfort in Shanghai would soon have to give up their homes and their businesses and their work and freedom, and live behind barbed wire. We Jews in the ghetto, at least we could get passes to come and go occasionally. *They* would be locked in for the duration of the war, however long that took. There'd be guard towers. Escapees would be shot.

"This is horrible, Mother. Can they do that?"

"The monsters can do anything they please," Mother said.

The Japanese had prodded us into our rat-infested square-mile ghetto like cattle into a barn. We had to lick their boots for the slightest privilege. They'd all but starved us. Word trickled down to us that the Kempetai brutalized political prisoners, and the luckier ones got sentenced to the Ward Road Jail, where they would most likely die of typhus. And there was the despicable Ghoya.

Even through all that, I hadn't hated our captors as

bitterly as Erich did, or the others in the Underground. Sure, the Japanese infuriated me, and I blamed them for the hunger that plagued me every minute of the day. Still, safely tucked in with my family, I thought of all those cloak-and-dagger REACT assignments—outsmarting our Japanese captors and brazenly flirting with danger—as adventures to enliven the wartime doldrums. As long as I didn't get caught.

But this—locking up American citizens—this was more than I could forgive. I loved all things American. Clear and simple, Japan was an enemy of America. Reason enough to hate them. Despite the gentle Kawashimas next door, and Dovid's reminder that the people were good, that only the soldiers were evil brutes, a new revulsion for the Japanese rose in me like bitter bile. Suddenly I longed for another REACT assignment, a vital one that I could carry out with a righteous vengeance.

It came during my month's pass out of Hongkew. Erich walked me briskly to the Baikal Cemetery, where we could talk without being heard.

"The dead have no ears," he said. We sat on a granite bench, surrounded by crumbling headstones. "REACT knows you have a narrow window of freedom for two more weeks. They want to send you by train to Hangchow."

A year before, I'd have protested. Send a western girl not yet sixteen alone on a train to a strange Chinese city? Maybe some *other* girl, not me. But with my new searing hatred for the Japanese brutes, I'd risk anything to get back at them.

"You're to pose as a tutor for a rich Chinese family.

Madame Liang has hired you to teach German and English to her twelve-year-old granddaughter. Spring Jade would like to study in England someday. Of course, you'll fail miserably as a tutor and will come right back to Shanghai."

"You don't have much confidence in me. What if Spring Jade adores me?"

"She doesn't know you like I do," Erich teased. "Anyway, this isn't a joke. You'll be carrying vital information for Free China, and you'll have to get back to Shanghai as quickly as possible, before anyone wises up. I don't know any more. Don't say a word about this, especially not to your blabbermouth friend, Tanya."

"She's so head over heels for that yeshiva boy that she hasn't got time for me. She's even stopped searching for that horrible cat of hers. But what will I tell Mother and Father?"

"Think of something."

"I'll say I'm staying at Tanya's house for a few days, a little holiday while her mother's away."

"Away where? Off with her Japanese lover?"

"No more soldiers, Tanya told me. Anyway, Mother doesn't ask questions these days."

"Just be prepared to leave at a moment's notice. I'll give you the details when I get them." He glanced left and right, to be sure a gravedigger wasn't listening. In the distance we heard hired Chinese mourners keening and tearing at their clothes, their hair. It was a way to make a living.

"This assignment could be dangerous, Ilse. Are you sure you want to do it?"

I nodded. What a great motivator hatred is! Walking toward the ghetto gates partway with me, Erich suddenly peeled away and vanished, leaving me alone to seethe about the inhumane way the Japanese were treating members of the Allied nations. We refugees were stateless, we had no political power, and no other country wanted us, so of course the Japanese could push us around. As well as the English and the Dutch. But who would guess that American citizens could be locked away so easily? I was sure Americans could *never* be so barbaric as their enemy. *Why?* I kept asking myself. *Why can't the Japanese behave more like Americans?*

Well, I'd soon enough do my small part to get even. I whispered, "Spring Jade, here I come!"

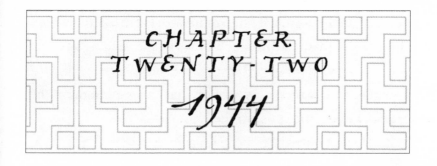
Why was it taking so long for my REACT assignment to come through? Each day I asked Erich, "Where's my letter from Madame Liang?" I waited, twirling strands of my hair until it was so snarled that I couldn't get a brush through it. I didn't care how I looked now that Dovid was gone.

One day in early June, word spread through the house: A Japanese soldier was on his way up the stairs! We were terrified. Mother and I scurried around like mice, stuffing into the rolled-up mattresses anything that might look the least bit suspicious or anything of value that might catch the eye of the marauding soldier. One by one, doors opened as his boot steps passed each apartment. Relieved, those lucky neighbors watched to see where he was heading; who was his victim?

He went directly to the Kawashimas' apartment. We heard the whole exchange through the plywood wall, although we didn't understand more than a couple of words. The tone was clear, though: It was a friendly visit, and also a hurried one. I watched the soldier back out of the Kawashimas' apartment, with much bowing and smiling on both sides of the doorway; but he looked nervous, and he bounded down the stairs so fast that our neighbors didn't even have a chance to slam their doors.

A few minutes later, Mrs. K came over with a letter from America. Since American mail couldn't get through to occupied China, her cousin had sent the letter to a friend in Switzerland with instructions to forward it to a Kawashima cousin in Tokyo, whose neighbor was that soldier who'd put such a scare in us. He'd been home on leave because his wife had just had a baby. Now back in Shanghai, the soldier violated all military regulations, and at huge risk to himself as well as his wife and new son, he personally hand-delivered the letter to Mrs. K.

Her husband wasn't home, and she was nervous about opening the envelope alone. We always expected terrible news. Mother and I huddled around her while she read the letter. Suddenly her face drained of color as she mumbled in Japanese.

Mother put her hand on our neighbor's arm. "What is it, Mrs. Kawashima?"

The woman slapped the blue letter against her chest. "My cousin Tamiko and her family, they are all remove to a camp, a few year ago already. Home, strawberry farm, all gone. All Japanese in America, this has happen. I do not understand. All their life they live in California, United

States. Never live in the old country. And now, barbed wire all around."

"Like us," Mother said gently, as though she expected this catastrophe.

But I was shocked. In America such things happened? My America? It was just a mistake in the translation. Had to be, I told myself. But the horrible truth seeped in through the cracks in my armor.

Still awaiting my assignment to Hangchow, I wandered through the teeming streets full of vendors and cooks. One ancient, black-robed man tapped his cloth shoe on a treadle and waved a drill at passersby. It looked like it was left over from the Inquisition. His sign, in both Chinese and English, read: DENTAL WORK, VERY CHEAP. Even Chang, the beggar, steered clear of the dentist!

Hsu Chen was the professional letter writer in our neighborhood. I'd passed his bamboo stool a million times, and it was always occupied. But that day when I felt so despondent over America's betrayal of my trust, the stool happened to be vacant, and Mr. Hsu beckoned to me.

"What is your heart's song?" he asked in perfect English. "My calling, you see, is to write letters for people who cannot write themselves. With reverent words I help them sing their heart's song. Times past, I wrote these letters on beautiful, handmade rice paper. Times past."

"Business is always booming at your table, Mr. Hsu. No

matter how poor people are, they always have a fen for a letter."

"Ah, but now my stool is waiting. Please, sit down. I will teach you."

The first character he taught me was *jên*, patience. "I have watched you pass here many times. Perhaps patience is difficult for you?"

How did he know?

He showed me what each stroke of the character means. "You see, young lady? *Jên* has a knife over its heart, symbolizing that it is unwise to provoke a person's patience. It is also unwise to lose one's patience."

He guided my unsure hand through the air and a dozen times dry across his table before he allowed me to dip the brush in the black ink he'd just ground and moistened on the inkstone. I was impatient to see my bold and beautiful handiwork on paper, even if the paper were only smudged Chinese newsprint, and not the lovely rice paper Mr. Hsu remembered so fondly.

Out of the corner of my eye, I spotted Erich rushing toward our building with a new suitcase. That could mean only one thing. I jumped to my feet. "I'll come back another day, Mr. Hsu. I'll be *patient* till then."

Erich had the orders and supplies for my REACT assignment. Mother and Father were out of the apartment— a lucky break—and I dressed behind my curtain while Erich quickly filled in the details. Pulling back the curtain, I tapped a wide-brimmed white straw hat onto the crown of my head.

My ever-sensitive brother blurted, "It wouldn't hurt you to comb your hair."

When I finally got the comb through my snarls, I twirled around for his approval.

Erich's catcall-whistle made me feel pretty for the first time in ages, and with a pang I remembered Dovid's drawing in which I'd looked healthy and beautiful. Where *was* Dovid?

My fancy clothes, plus the ones in my satchel, and the books and toys that were supposed to be for Spring Jade, were all compliments of American Underground resistance money. The fake passport in the patent leather bag was pure Jewish artistry, and it looked like the real thing if you didn't inspect it with a magnifying glass. I was Margaret Loeffler, citizen of Danzig, Germany. A letter from Madame Liang of Hangchow nestled in the bag, also. It was written in India ink on her familiar, thick, creamy paper:

May 12, 1944

Dear Miss Loeffler,

This is to inform you that you have been selected from among twenty-six lesser qualified young western ladies as a tutor for my granddaughter, Spring Jade.

You will kindly report to my family compound at 2 Fuming Road, Hangchow, at six o'clock Saturday of this week. My houseboy will meet your train. We are in the region of West Lake. You will find Hangchow to be a beautiful city.

I must warn you, however, that I am an exacting taskmaster. If you do not perform to my standards, you can expect to be back on a train within twenty-four hours. Others have failed before you.

Cordially yours,
MADAME LIANG

"Madame Liang is such an arrogant old witch!"

Erich signaled that we should be whispering; *thin walls,* he reminded me. "Don't worry, she'll send you right back. You won't even get a glimpse of Spring Jade. This is all just a front for Chiang Kai-shek's Free China Movement. Madame Liang will get the information to occupied Nanking, and from there to the Nationalist soldiers hiding out in the mountains. They have lots of American support, and in exchange, they supply information REACT can use against the Japs."

"Well, I'm not just mad at the Japanese; I'm mad at the Americans, too," I grumbled.

"That's beside the point. You'll give the suitcase to Madame Liang, then get on the next train back to Shanghai. She'll hand you a letter firing you."

"I'm insulted already." I rummaged through the satchel, feeling and sniffing the beautiful clothing and shiny toys. I hadn't seen anything so elegant and crisp-new since we'd arrived in China. Spinning the top on our rough wood floor, I watched the blue and red colors swirl dizzily. A new baby doll with stiff blond hair lay curled in a silk blanket. "Spring Jade's too old for this doll."

"Americans. What do they know?" Erich said.

There was some embarrassing lacy underwear that I tucked beneath the baby doll. Also a small makeup case with a wonderful fire-engine red lipstick that I smeared on my dry lips without even looking in the mirror. "Where's the message I'm supposed to be carrying?"

"Figure it out."

I inspected each item, including the underwear, turning each piece of clothing inside out, examining labels, looking for a secret compartment in the suitcase, in the doll. I opened every jar in the makeup case and flipped through each book. "I don't see a thing."

"Your vision is clouded by the headaches you get. You think I'm as blind as Mother and don't see you wincing and squinting and covering your eyes from the light? Headaches like that, you'd never travel anywhere without a trusted remedy, would you, Ilse?"

I puzzled over his words that seemed to come out of nowhere. A clue, but what did it mean? I pawed through the suitcase again and the makeup case, and it was making me so cranky that I actually felt a headache starting to tighten around my crown. I wondered if Mother had saved me an aspirin in that vial she hid behind the alarm clock. But here in the makeup case was a small brown bottle filled with cotton batting and—aspirin!

Erich nodded.

"Why, you clever boys, you!" With all the pills emptied out on the table, I held the bottle up to the light to read the back of the label. Through the prism of brown glass, nothing was visible but solid black lines. "This can't be it."

"Practically microscopic," Erich said. "Also encrypted. However, Madame Liang will be able to read and decipher a vast amount of information which you and I can't read, and shouldn't know anyway, about the locations of supply depots, munitions warehouses, radio transmitters, storage areas for synthetic fuel—that kind of stuff."

"All that on the back of an aspirin label?"

Erich plinked the pills back into the vial and kissed the glass with a theatrical flourish. "This you protect with your life. The most important information, at least hitting us directly, is about the location of political prisoners. If the Americans know how many political prisoners are here in Hongkew and how densely populated our area is, maybe they won't bomb us."

Bomb us? That had never occurred to me.

"So you see the importance of your assignment?"

I carefully packed everything back in the suitcase—except half the aspirin tablets, which I shook out of the brown bottle again and dropped into Mother's hidden stash. I snapped the suitcase shut. "Yes. REACT can count on me," I promised with a sickly excitement rising in my chest.

CHAPTER TWENTY-THREE
1944

Erich carried my suitcase as far as the Hongkew gate. For the sake of anyone who might be observing us, he said (lots louder than he needed to), "I doubt if you'll make much of a tutor, but at least Hangchow's a nice city to visit. Have a good trip." He stepped closer and gave me a brotherly kiss on the forehead, colliding with my hat. Under its wide shade he whispered, "Be careful. Don't trust anybody. Come back safely."

I wanted a simple declaration such as, "I love you, my sister." His eyes said what I wanted to hear, at least that's what I read in his worried expression as he gently pushed me toward the Hongkew gate.

I showed my yellow-striped Ilse Shpann pass to the Pao Chia guard, careful to keep my Margaret Loeffler passport tucked into my purse. I hailed a rickshaw boy, who tossed my suitcase in at my feet. As he was lifting the shafts of the rickshaw, I looked back at my brother behind the bars and barbed wire, and prayed that I'd do everything just right on this mission and be home with my family by dark.

Not easy buying the ticket at the train station. Slipping my money under the window, I shouted, "Hangchow." The Chinese man in the ticket cage clicked his abacus anxiously while a Japanese guard grunted orders. The guard asked to see my passport and moved his dark-dot eyes back and forth half a dozen times from my face to the picture. He was suspicious, probably because it just wasn't common for western girls to travel, much less alone.

"Purpose of trip?" he demanded.

I explained, but he couldn't understand either my German or my English. My hands shook as I smoothed Madame Liang's letter under the window. *"Don't trust anybody."* What if he kept it? He and the timid ticket seller discussed the English letter, half in Chinese, half in Japanese. Then the guard demanded to see what was in my suitcase, but there was nowhere to set it down. Standing on one foot like a flamingo, I hoisted my other leg up as a shelf, but human beings aren't meant to totter on one leg. The suitcase wobbled as I offered up various items for the guard's inspection. We never got to the underwear. I'd have been mortified if we had. And he never asked me to open the flowered makeup case.

A long line formed behind me, with people looking over my shoulder to see what the delay was, or to see what foreign treasures I harbored in my suitcase. Eventually the guard appeared to be satisfied and passed Madame Liang's letter back to me, so the ticket man was free to snap up my money. His fingers flew on the abacus, and he slid my change and my ticket back under the window. Completely frazzled, I ran to the tracks.

The conductor folded his arms across his chest and shook his head, refusing to let me on the train. We argued in our two languages. I had no idea what was happening, since I'd never ridden a Chinese train before. Maybe he was telling me that foreigners were supposed to ride in a different compartment. I started to run to the next entrance, my suitcase banging against my thigh; but he followed me, blowing his whistle and shouting something in high-pitched Chinese. He barred the next entrance. The train whistle was already blowing, and then I realized what the situation was—he expected a bribe! I dug two coins out of my purse, and like magic, a step stool came down and the entrance was no longer blocked.

I climbed aboard as the train began chugging out of the station, and I sank into the last seat in the last row, with my suitcase on my lap. My new shoes stuck to the floor, glued with God knows what. There were as many birds on that train as people, some caged, some not. Some of the people *should* have been. My informal survey during the first few minutes of the trip was that 50 percent of all Chinese train travelers smoked, and the other 50 percent batted away the dense cloud of smoke so they could see the cans to spit their tobacco into. Some just spit on the floor. Shuddering, I slid the suitcase under my seat anyway.

I assured myself that the smoke and flying tobacco wouldn't reach me there in the back row. The window slid down only three inches, just enough to let a black tornado of coal exhaust billow into the car until I had to shut my window or else swallow mouthfuls of the stuff, which was like liquid tar. A Chinese train in May is very hot, especially with the window closed, and I had 252 kilometers to cover and stupidly hadn't remembered to bring a Thermos of water.

I felt very *white* and foreign and schoolmarmish in my pert suit and straw hat. The other passengers and birds ogled me with curiosity. One woman offered to sell me a cigarette stub; another wanted me to make an offer on a half-dead goose. Two men asked to use my suitcase as a makeshift mah-jongg table. I was pretty good at deciphering Chinese by then, but I pretended not to understand the request. What if these men were spies, or thieves, or just careless travelers? What if they got off at any of the dozens of stops and took the suitcase with them? I pictured running after them, holding my hat on my head, yelling, "Hey, that's mine!" What if I never got it back before the train took off again? I'd have no idea where I was. I could be lost for days, plus I'd have to suffer Erich's disappointment and the wrath of Gerhardt and Rolf and Madame Liang.

So I kicked the suitcase farther under my seat and opened a book that the Underground had supplied me with for Spring Jade's enlightenment. It was *The Magic Mountain*, by Thomas Mann, who was an exile like me. Thick and satisfying, bound in fragrant leather, the book took me out of the chaos of a Chinese hard-seat train into a serene sanatorium in Germany, before the war.

The train rumbled along, and I was swimming in the beautiful German words of Thomas Mann when suddenly a line from Madame Liang's letter flashed through my mind: *"Others have failed before you."* I'd thought that meant other tutors for the imagined Spring Jade, but now I saw a darker meaning. The warning sent shivers through me despite the stifling train and the press of steamy bodies all around me. And the birds with unflinching stares.

Others *carrying information* had failed before me. Where were they now? Dead or alive? I thought of the huge man in the park on Beehive day—and his heap of broken bones outside Bridge House. I glanced around at the riders parading up and down the aisle, trading seats for no apparent reason, spitting seeds on the floor, squatting at the back of the car the way Chinese do for hours at a time.

Terror began seeping into my toes and slowly crept up my legs, up my chest, until my neck was hot and a steel band tightened around my head. Pounding, pounding, in counter-rhythm to the clacking of steel wheels on the track. My heart ticked like an overwound clock.

Relief. Get the aspirin before my head, before my heart explodes. Everyone on the train's watching me. My head's throbbing enough that all of them can see it expand and contract like a balloon. Just waiting for me to pop! Then they'll come and take everything. I will shatter, a hundred kilometers away from my family, and nothing of me will be left to identify.

Aspirin. I had to get to the aspirin before I burst. But the bottle was buried in my suitcase, far back under my seat, stuck to the floor, miles away, out of reach. I'd have to get down on the floor, tacky with spittle and stringy wet tobacco, to slide the valise out.

They'll all see me, even the blind man across the aisle. They'll watch me hunt for the aspirin bottle, fumble with the cap. They'll know what I'm hiding. They'll snatch the bottle out of my hand. They'll read the back of the label. The band's tightening around my head . . . I'm choking . . . can't move . . . can't breathe . . .

A Chinese amah came over to me and pressed a cool, wet rag to my forehead. She spoke soothing words in a dialect I'd never heard, then switched to Mandarin and said, "Foreigners, they breathe shallow; watch me." She pressed my hand to her stomach to show me the Chinese way to breathe. "Now you." My chest rose, and cool air flowed all the way down to my toes.

In a few minutes the amah saw that my panic had subsided. She patted my arm, took back her dirty rag, rejoined the noisy travelers at the front of the car, and left me alone. My heart slowly shrank and nested back in my chest, and an odd calm flooded me.

Two hours passed, and the train slowed down for the Hangchow station. Getting off, I waved to the amah through the window, but she'd apparently forgotten about me and didn't wave back.

No one was there at the station to meet me.

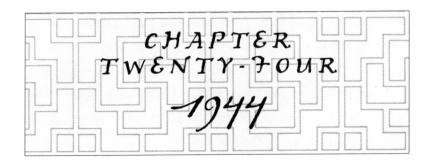

CHAPTER TWENTY-FOUR
1944

As the rush of people off the train cleared, I plunked myself down on a hard, bone-smooth bench. Tears filled my eyes.

Well, that'll get you nowhere.

I propped my feet up on the suitcase to wait for Madame Liang's houseboy. Lots of people bustled in, bought tickets, left, and while everyone gazed at me as though I'd sprouted a second head, nobody seemed to be looking for a lone western schoolmarm.

I kicked my suitcase across the floor to the ticket window. "Fuming Road?" I said. No sign of recognition. Knowing it was futile, I still had to ask, "Madame Liang?" The ticket man rattled something off in the local dialect. I scrolled through my limited Chinese vocabulary and retrieved the words that I thought meant, "Where is West Lake?" *"Xihu zai nar?"* I repeated.

"Ah, ah!" He came out of the ticket cage and shuffled to a map on the wall, encased in glass smudged with fingerprints. He pointed to this blue thing in the center of the map.

West Lake. I could walk there from the train station, but the lake was huge, like a small sea. I might wander around it for hours, lugging my suitcase, with no idea where I was going.

"*Xie xie,* thank you," I said. Defeated, I went back to the bench with my suitcase footstool. The clock dragged slowly.

A welcome cross-breeze rippled through the station, and so I sat and waited, not even sure what I was waiting for, reviewing and polishing every detail of this trip. Sometime in the future, when the war is long past, I promised myself, my children will be begging me to tell this story again and again. We'll be sitting in the kitchen of our bungalow in Santa Rosa, California, America, right down the road from Mother's friend, Molly O'Toole. Over bowls of chocolate ice cream—or peach, in honor of Uncle Erich and Aunt Whoever—I'll tell them about my adventure in Hangchow. If I survive it.

When had I turned the corner from *when* to *if?*

After an hour of this daydreaming, a man rattled a wobbly-wheeled cart into the station with a few snacks to sell, mostly fresh fruit, which was out of the question, of course, since they were no doubt fertilized with human night soil. I bought a cup of water, asking him over and over if the water had been boiled and therefore fit to drink. He didn't understand me, but he kept nodding yes, and in the end I took the chance. Malaria, dysentery, elephantiasis—who cared? I could die of thirst before one of those diseases set in.

I was nearly two hundred pages into *The Magic Mountain*, dozing off and on, when I heard a resounding crash. I dropped the book on the bench, grabbed the suitcase, and plodded outside to explore.

A slender Chinese girl brushed off her motorcycle, which had apparently just collided with a wheelbarrow loaded with rice sacks. Both she and the wheelbarrow man were hopping mad. His fists were flying, and she shouted curses at him and kicked the rice sacks with her rubber sandals until one burst and a grayish stream of rice poured onto the ground.

Wasted rice when so many of us were hungry! I ducked under the flying fists and kicking legs and stuck my finger in the hole to stanch the bleeding. The girl and the man must have thought me very clever. They stopped fighting to admire western ingenuity. The man smiled as though I'd just performed a miracle that inspired him to shift the bag so that the weight resettled and the hole was just an eye staring up at the sky. With deft hands the two of them scooped up every grain of rice and tied them in the man's oily kerchief. Grinning and bowing, he lifted the handles of the wheelbarrow and rattled down the road, with the girl shading her eyes to watch his progress.

As soon as he was out of earshot, she turned to me and said, "Looking for someone? I believe you've brought western clothing and makeup and books for Spring Jade, my granddaughter?"

My mouth gaped open; I was stunned by her perfect British English and her age, just two or three years older than me. She *couldn't* have a granddaughter!

She motioned for me to hand the suitcase over. I lifted it, but then I had an impulse to run as fast as my legs would carry me, along with the suitcase. This girl could be a counterintelligence spy. Maybe she'd captured the real Madame Liang and tortured her to find out about me.

Ridiculous! Yet, she wasn't at all what I had expected, which was a rich, manicured lady five times my age, dressed according to the latest French fashion. Not that I had any idea what the latest French fashion *was*. But it definitely wasn't this girl, with her hair chopped blunt across her jawline, wearing western trousers and a man's plaid cotton shirt tied at the waist.

She waggled her hand in a give-it-over-now gesture, one foot on the kickstand of her motorcycle.

"How do I know you're the right person?" I stammered.

"Come now. Who else would meet you here, Margaret Loeffler?" She flashed an envelope before my eyes and tucked it into the ribbon band of my hat. I recognized the same creamy stationery and thick black ink. Still, she could have stolen it from the real Madame Liang, who was probably tied up and struggling to keep her head above ditch water. Which could be my fate if I weren't careful. I remembered Erich's warning, *"never trust anybody,"* and I didn't know what to do, and anyway, if the girl had a mind to, she could just race off on her motorcycle, dragging me behind her, still stupidly clutching the suitcase in both arms.

I looked her in the eye, hoping it was a window to the truth. She didn't blink; she stared right back. Yes? No? Taking a deep breath, I let the suitcase slide down my body to the dusty ground.

She grabbed it and slung her leg over the seat of the motorcycle. Its motor began cranking.

"Wait!" I yelled. "When's the next train back to Shanghai?"

Her foot stamped the stubborn cycle's accelerator pedal until the engine finally roared into action. "Four A.M. tomorrow," she shouted, zoomed in front of me, took a sharp corner, and disappeared in a cyclone of dust.

Back in the station I read the letter:

To Whom It May Concern:

I appreciate Miss Margaret Loeffler's making the journey to Hangchow. While I found her to be bright and conscientious, I have determined that she is wholly unqualified as a tutor for my granddaughter, Spring Jade. I wish Miss Loeffler good fortune in her next assignment, which I trust will not include tutoring an impressionable girl. Should Miss Loeffler apply for gainful employment elsewhere, I shall be forthright in providing what information I can.

Cordially,
MADAME LIANG

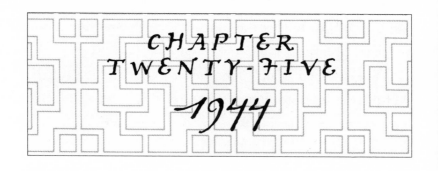

Mother gasped when I walked into our apartment. "Where did you get those clothes?"

How stupid of me. I was so exhausted and so relieved to be home from Hangchow that I didn't even think about the clothes. Then I became aware of those lovely silk hose latticed with runs and the dented hat. A heel had broken off one shoe, and the suit looked like I'd slept in it, which I had. But even with all that damage, the clothes were more glamorous than anything we'd worn in ages.

"Tanya's mother. She's a dressmaker, you know."

"Hats and shoes and patent leather purses also?"

"Can't a girl dress up now and then without an interrogation?"

Mother tamped out the dented fender of my hat. "How grown-up you are. Go in your room and take off the skirt. We'll press it with a little steam, and it'll look brand-new."

I pulled the curtain of my room and blew out a breath of

relief. Erich was right; Mother had stopped asking questions whose answers she was afraid to hear.

One day just as the spring term was ending, Tanya and I hurried home as usual before our passes expired. She was full of news about her *beshert*, Shlomo.

"Of course, I don't actually get to speak to him, but the rebbe says my Shlomo is his prize student. He has a memory like a steel trap; nothing escapes. We'll have babies reading Torah before they're three years old!"

"Wonderful," I mumbled, picturing midget Shlomos with thick eyeglasses and skin as white as rice paper.

As we sprinted by Kloski's Polish Restaurant, out flew Liu, with the aproned proprietor right behind him. "The scoundrel's stealing ice from me," Mr. Kloski shouted, raising a cast-iron frying pan obviously meant for Liu's head.

Tanya said something in Yiddish that I think was, "Go ahead, it's about time someone cracked his thick skull," at the same moment I shouted, "Don't hit him!"

The startled man froze, with the pan in midair, and then as though the movie reel began spinning again, he waved the pan and shouted Polish curses at Liu.

"Why can't the pest leave you alone?" Tanya asked.

"He's in trouble, Tanya. Have a heart."

I wondered why Liu didn't scamper away while he had the chance. Instead, he hunkered just enough out of Mr. Kloski's reach to avoid the collision with the pan.

A Japanese sentry came to investigate the hubbub, and Tanya dashed off. It must have been hilarious to passersby—all of us yelling at once, in Polish, Chinese, German, and Japanese. Mr. Kloski quickly retreated to his restaurant now that the soldier was involved, and if I'd had any sense, I'd have taken off in the opposite direction like Tanya did.

The soldier clutched Liu by the scruff of his neck, the way you'd pick up a kitten, and then I saw Liu's face. His cheek was swollen to twice its normal size, and his eyes swam in his head. Had someone beaten him?

Tangle with a Japanese soldier? Insane. Plus, I'd miss my pass deadline. I looked the soldier in the eye and bowed in mock respect. Layering on thick flattery, I said—half in English, half in German, with two or three Japanese words thrown in for good measure—"Officer, could you kindly put this boy down?"

Liu's focus sharpened enough to send me a silent signal, which I read as, *Run, idiot! I'm not worth it.*

"Officer," I began again, "this is a worthless mongrel, nothing but a footstool for the emperor, and beneath the dignity of a worthy officer in the venerable Japanese Army. He's a beggar in my lane. Please, let me drag him home."

The soldier, who certainly wasn't an officer, turned Liu toward him for a quick inspection; found him wanting, I suppose; then dropped him to the ground. I expected to hear brittle bones crack, but Liu was as indestructible as bamboo, and as soon as the soldier lost interest, Liu scrambled to his feet.

I dusted him off, gently fingering his swollen cheek. "What happened to you?"

He hooked a filthy thumb into his cheek and showed me a raw, inflamed place at the back of his mouth. "Bad tooth, missy."

I was no dentist, but any reasonable person could see that it was infected, abscessed, and had to come out. "We have to hurry, Liu. Wait here a second." I went back into Mr. Kloski's restaurant, and begged two ice cubes from him, which we tied into the ragged hem ripped from Liu's shirt. "Here, Liu, hold this against your cheek. We're going to the dentist near my house." We raced through the Hongkew gates two minutes past my deadline, but the guard wasn't in the mood for a battle.

My own teeth chattered, despite the heat, as the street dentist foot-treadled his rusty equipment. With no anti-septic, no anesthetic, not even a mouthful of cold water to deaden the pain, he ripped the tooth from Liu's mouth and tossed it behind him into the gutter. Then he gave Liu a small packet of herbs guaranteed to cure the infection. Liu already looked lots better.

Satisfied, the dentist put his hand out for payment. Liu and I hadn't a fen between us. But a workman must be paid, as Father always said, even though he rarely was. What could I use for currency? I had one barrette left, a yellow dachs-hund like Pookie. I unclipped it from my hair, which tumbled into my eyes, and I gave the barrette to the dentist with a shaky hand. He inspected the offering curiously and pock-eted it with a nod of approval.

When I got home, Mother said, "Get your hair out of your eyes, Ilse."

"I lost my barrette," I said, afraid to tell her how I'd spent it on Liu.

Mother sighed. "What else can we lose? You'll invent something for you and Erich to eat? I'm going to the concert hall. Your father is playing."

I glanced over at the roll of mattresses. The Violin was gone for the first time in weeks. "Wait a second, Mother." I reached for my Hangchow hat. "There. How's it feel?" The hat looked lovely on her graying auburn hair, turning her eyes wide and girlish and giving me a hint of what she must have looked like on her way to America.

Mother had given up all pretense of setting a proper table, since there wasn't much to put on our plates, anyway, and by suppertime the afternoon heat rose and settled into our third-floor apartment as thick as molten lead. Just walking around our tiny room seemed like too much effort. We took our kitchen chairs out to the lane for our supper, snatching every breeze that came by. The street cook in our lane sold the best sweet potatoes, steamed on his wok until the insides ran hot and juicy and sugary as caramel. We scooped them out with spoons, burning our mouths carelessly, but fried taste buds weren't much of a price to pay for the pleasure of this delicacy once a week or so. A small sweet potato—our whole meal.

Father was in a particularly jolly mood that evening. He'd had two concert dates with a little pay for each, and now he was smacking his lips over the last of his potato.

Erich said, "I'm saving half for a midnight snack."

"Very admirable, son," said Father.

"Very Austrian. I hate when he does that, Father. That half potato's going to haunt me all evening," I growled.

"I know," Erich replied with a grin. "That's what gives me the courage to stash half my supper away."

Our neighbors were all sitting or leaning against the wall. Our official lane beggar, Chang, crouched at his station in the gutter, waiting, and the atmosphere was relaxed because we knew that the spring nights would be pleasant and cool for a few more weeks.

And then the atmosphere in the lane suddenly tensed, as though an electric storm had jaggedly passed through it, and our neighbors' voices softened. Some shoved their little ones into the buildings, or darted inside themselves. Even Chang sidled into a competitor's territory because two Japanese soldiers came goose-stepping down the lane, chins haughtily in the air and bayoneted rifles shelved on their shoulders as if they were the color guard in a military dress parade.

I jammed my spoon into the potato as the soldiers stopped right in front of Mother.

"Shpann? Frieda Shpann?"

"Yes," Mother responded breathlessly.

"Why you do not wear armband?"

"I was not issued an armband. I have a resident certificate inside. Shall I get it?"

"You must wear armband!" the taller soldier barked.

Father stepped forward. "Excuse me, sir, but I believe you have my wife confused with someone else. We are Austrians. We came here in nineteen thirty-nine. We are stateless refugees designated for this area. We are not enemy nationals."

Mother's face drained of all color. Erich moved closer to Mother, not that he could protect her from these men.

The uglier of the two soldiers reached into his pocket and produced an official-looking document. Father took his reading glasses out of his shirt pocket and examined the document. Mother was a statue, with her spoon in midair, her eyes fixed as though she might never blink again.

"Frieda," Father said, his voice shaking, "this is you?"

The soldier snapped the document out of Father's hand and read the top line. Even in his awkward English, the message came through clearly:

"'In the matter of Frieda Shpann, citizen of the United States of America, who failed to register at the Enemy Aliens Office in Hamilton House by the December thirteenth, nineteen forty-two deadline.'" The Japanese soldier spit out the rest of his message: "You are a number one enemy alien. You are in violation. You will report tomorrow to receive your red armband."

"Mother? What's he talking about?" I whispered.

"Go inside, children," she said. "Inside at once."

Sick at heart, Erich and I obeyed, but we saw and heard the whole thing.

"Frieda Shpann, you will be relocated with other Americans to a civil assembly center in two weeks' time. Prepare yourself." The document was tossed onto Mother's lap. The two soldiers clicked their heels and did an about-face, marching out of our lane.

Erich bolted toward our parents, me right behind. Mother was stricken, Father perplexed, and we three were spilling over with questions. Father motioned for us to pick up the two chairs, and he hastily led us upstairs.

That night we found out the secret Mother had kept for twenty years: Her American friend, Molly O'Toole? *She* was a *he*, and *his* name was Michael O'Halloran.

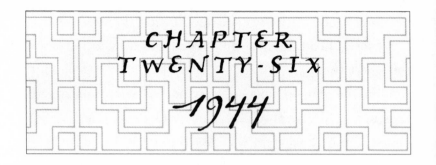

"How could you do this to us?" I demanded. "Lying to us all this time? Letting Erich and me believe those packages came from a girlfriend. Molly O'Toole, we even gave her a name, and you never said a word. You let us carry on like utter fools."

Mother sank into her chair, chin to her chest, and still I pummeled her with jagged, cutting words until even Erich said, "Hush, Sister. Give her a chance to talk."

We four circled around the table in our hot apartment, Mother at one end, Father at the other end, Erich and I standing on either side of Mother.

Erich was the one who kept us all from spinning out of orbit in our separate swirling pools of anger. "All right, Mother, what can you tell us?"

She twisted her handkerchief and spoke in a low, flat voice. The walls were thin, and this wasn't a matter for the Kawashimas.

Mother began, "I was young, impetuous. Like you, Ilse."

"Not like me. I would never make fools of my family!"

Mother looked off into the distance. "It was nineteen nineteen, the Great War had just ended. People were dying all around from the influenza that was sweeping the world, especially in Europe. A pandemic, they called it, which means it was everywhere, but not so bad in America, away from the big cities. My father sent me to America to study. My mother didn't want me to go. She cried and cried. From the ship hundreds of people everywhere saying good-bye, and all I saw was my mother soaking my father's handkerchief."

"Get to the point, Mother," I snapped.

"I must tell this in my own way, Ilse. Be patient."

"It's not my style to be patient!"

Mother ignored my latest outburst. "So I went to Berkeley, California. A wonderful university there, students from all over the world. It was a libertine place, everyone free to come and go. A glorious, colorful circus it was."

Jealousy bolted through my body like lightning: Why could *she* have a life of freedom and plenty in America, whereas *I* was stuck here in a decaying ghetto in China?

"Maybe you can see how appealing this was to the stiffly proper girl from Austria. My father had always been strict—you remember Grandfather—but then, why had he sent me to a place like Berkeley unless he wanted me to taste the fruits?"

Everything she told us felt like a knife to my heart. I wanted to know all of it at once, and at the same time, I didn't want to hear any of it. I needed all my questions answered, and I hated every question.

I hated her for deceiving us.

Mother twisted a dishrag into a tight rope. "There was a boy."

"What?" I shouted.

Father leaned forward, his face twisted in agony.

"I'm sorry, Jakob. May we talk about this privately?"

Father shook his head. "Tell us, all of us."

Mother took a deep breath. "Michael O'Halloran, a graduate student. He taught my American literature section. I barely knew any English, and American literature seemed so loose and unwieldy compared to the classical German literature I'd studied. So I went to the teacher for tutoring."

Not so bad, I thought, calming down. Of course Mother had boyfriends before Father. I had Dovid, didn't I? And someday I'd marry and tell my husband about my first love, about Dovid. *Not so bad.*

Mother's eyes darted toward Father and away. "I fell in love . . . with everything American. I went around the dormitory quoting Walt Whitman. In my thick German accent. How foolish I must have sounded. He was a kind man, Jakob. I was very fond of him. Not the same way I've loved you, not so wholly and deeply."

Erich and I glanced at each other. We'd never heard our parents talk of love. They'd been devoted to one another, respectful, even playful occasionally, but *love* had always been a private matter between them. I was embarrassed to hear it made public. Parents had no business laying bare their hearts in front of their children.

Mother whispered, "Michael and I, we decided to marry."

My head snapped up, and Erich's eyes flashed in disbelief.

"You *married* the man?" Father said.

I reached over to clasp his hand.

"Yes." She searched each of our faces with sad, defeated eyes. "A civil ceremony. I never told my parents. Michael is not Jewish. I suppose this is not so shocking in view of the whole disturbing truth that's tumbling out.

"Back in those days, I thought nothing of giving up my life in Austria to be his wife. How else could I be as American as every other girl in Berkeley? Now, of course, I understand what it means to give up one's homeland; we all do."

"So, what happened?" I asked coldly.

"We had nearly two years together, this Michael and I. They were . . . awkward years. I was a little prudish, a little rigid. We were opposites. Each passing day I was more and more homesick for my mother and father, my city, my language. Especially my language. We had a terrible fight. I threw a lamp at him."

"You, Mother?"

"What sort of lamp?" I asked.

"Just a *lamp*. Yes. I was a rebellious girl, remember? We lived in a . . . how do I describe . . . what we called a co-op? Nothing more than a room in a sprawling house." She glanced around our cluttered hatbox. "Bigger than this, but not by much. One kitchen downstairs, everything shared, even painting the house, all of us on ladders." Her voice drifted away, then circled back. "That night he left and didn't come home all night."

"Well, what did you expect, Mother?" I cried.

Father pulled his hand out of mine.

"I was furious at Michael. How could he make me worry so? Especially since he knew I was frightened and homesick, every night crying myself to sleep. I stuffed everything I owned into one suitcase, plus a carton of English books, and I walked to the bus depot. The next day I was on a ship home. I never said a word about Michael to my parents, only that I'd missed them and needed to come home to Austria. After all, I was still an Austrian at heart, only a U.S. citizen because I was married to an American."

Father drummed his fingers on the table without a sound. "And the divorce?"

"This is very hard."

"Good. Why should we make it easy for you? Your whole life's a lie, Mother, your whole life." My words sounded cruel to my own ears, yet they couldn't possibly cut deeply enough to suit me.

That was when Mother's tears started to flow. "I never divorced him, Jakob. Thousands of miles, what difference would it make?"

"The difference, Frieda, is that you now have two husbands, and our children are bastards, do you understand what I'm saying? And one of your *husbands* happens to be an American, and now the Japanese say you're an American citizen, and they will lock you up in an internment camp, and then what's to become of us all?" Father shot to his feet. He needed space to stalk around in, walls to bang. He slid to the floor along one wall, with his knees jutting up, pulled a pillow to his lap, buried his face, and wept. Up to that moment, I believed that fathers never cried.

"Go to him, Mother!" I shouted.

She shook her head. I suppose nearly twenty years of marriage had taught her when to comfort him and when to let him be. After a few moments she hurried through the rest of the story.

"In the nineteen twenties Michael O'Halloran wrote me many letters begging me to come back. I never answered. And then I met you, Jakob."

Father refused to look up, so Mother turned to Erich and me. "It was different with your father, not so stormy as it was with Michael O'Halloran. I wrote to him when I married your father in nineteen twenty-five. He promised he would never interfere with my new life."

"And the letters and packages and money? Molly O'Toole—you let us invent a whole life for her. Oh, Mother," I moaned.

"What could I do, Ilse?"

"You could have been honest, Mother."

"Please," Mother begged. "Let me finish. Over the years we had very little contact, Michael and I. He didn't write for years, until Hitler. He was worried about our family. He knew about you two. He knew life would be difficult for us as Jews in Austria. I sent him a cable when we got here to Shanghai. I knew from the first moment off the ship that the day would come when we'd need his help, and he was willing. He sent what he could. But he never meant to cause me any trouble."

Father came back to the table. "And yet he has, hasn't he?"

"Tomorrow, first thing, Jakob, I will get this straightened out."

Father hurled the pillow across the room, knocking Mother's last remaining perfume bottle off a shelf. "You'll go to the Enemy Aliens Office, is what you'll do, Frieda, before you bring Japanese wrath down on my children."

"Jakob, listen. I will talk to U.S. officials, International Red Cross, *someone,* and see if we can all be repatriated. If I am a citizen, don't they have to get me out of China and safely to the United States?"

"Americans are powerless here, Frieda, don't you see that? The Japanese are at war with them, did you forget? Wake up."

Mother sank back in her chair. "I will try anyway. At least I can get us some extra rations, some relief supplies. At least." Her voice trailed off.

Father shook his head, smoothing his thinning hair over his scalp. I remembered in the old days when he'd lean into The Violin. During an arpeggio his wild red hair would fly about, and he'd toss it back with his raised shoulder so as not to miss a single note. Now? He had only wisps of hair left, gray and lifeless. He said, "Do whatever you wish, Frieda. Meanwhile, the children and I will have to learn to live without you, and you will have to prepare to live in an internment camp, like thousands of other enemy nationals. If you had divorced this man, we would be in a different position today. How could you hurt your family so? Tell me that, Frieda."

From our tiny window we watched Mother walk up the lane. One look at her face and I whispered to Erich, "Trouble, for sure."

We heard her footsteps slowly thumping up the stairs, then the key she kept on a string around her neck clicking against our door. I ran to open it, though I didn't greet her. She slid by me and flopped down on the bed with her back to us.

Erich sat beside her. How was it possible that he, angry at the world in general, seemed not to be mad at Mother? He asked, "What happened?"

Her back still turned, she said, "I must register. They made me sign a form saying I am an official enemy of the Japanese government."

"Those bastards," Erich barked.

Mother rolled over and raised her fist in the air, showing us a red armband with a capital *A* for American. "I must wear it all the time," she said, ripping it down her arm and tossing it across the room.

Part of me thought, *Good!* But soon I began to understand what this armband business actually meant for Mother, for all of us.

Father came home, spotted the thing on the floor, and stomped out again. I don't know where he slept that night, maybe on a park bench. Our neighbors shunned Mother, although the Kawashimas acted as if nothing had changed. They had American relatives in internment camps; they understood.

Everything was unfamiliar, as though we'd all been cast in a play without a script. The only normal thing was school, which was different from life in Hongkew. The grounds were lushly green, in the last days of spring. We laughed at school. The teachers never stopped us from laughing, because they knew that life in the ghetto was bleak. They had no idea how grim things had turned in my home.

The other thing about school was a half-decent lunch for a few weeks. It's a mystery how they came by food, when no one else could. The school was named for the Kadoories, a very rich family of Iraqi Jews who'd settled in China way before war refugees ever dreamed of being stuck there. So thanks to Mr. Kadoorie, for a short while we ate like pigs, carrying our trays back for seconds. Some of us hid food in our book bags to take home to our families. I didn't. I'm ashamed to say this, but I felt that Mother's betrayal entitled me to everything I could get my hands on, and I gorged myself at school until my stomach ached and I was left sluggish through the afternoon.

I told no one at school about Mother. Tanya might have sensed that something was wrong if she hadn't been head-over-heels in love and dreaming of a wedding. Once, I passed Shlomo and his study partner on the street. They were arguing Torah as usual and didn't notice me, so I had a chance to study Shlomo closely. His face was merry and animated, and I guessed that it wasn't just the Talmudic discussion that brought the color to his cheeks. It was the knowledge that each jaunty step down Chaufoong Road took him closer to the wedding chuppah where Tanya would join him.

All that bubbling joy just made me feel more miserable. I slogged around, sullen and cranky, and turned in half-finished assignments. My papers came back with gigantic question marks at the top. What a silly rebellion, but my heart felt pierced. Even the skin on my arms and legs felt bruised and tender.

It wasn't bad enough that the Japanese were taking Mother away from us at such a terrible time for our family. They also demanded that she provide her own bed and bedding, towels, cooking utensils, and a reading lamp. We sold everything we could spare to buy these things, which had to be shipped forty-eight hours before Mother was to report to the camp. She'd have to carry all other items—clothes, hygiene supplies, books, personal effects, food, photographs, medications, whatnots.

Mother met with other people who were being sent to internment camps. They became more her family than we were. No one knew which camp they'd be going to, what the conditions were, or how long they might be interned: A month? A year? No one knew when the Allies would win the war to set them free.

"*If* the Allies win," Father reminded us. "If they are defeated, your mother will become a prisoner of war." He made it sound like that was his wish. If my anger at Mother bubbled at a slow boil those two weeks, Father's must have been roiling. Anger seethed in sorrow—a deadly recipe.

He did only the minimum necessary to get Mother ready. He refused to meet with a man who'd been interned and was released to care for his dying parents. When the American, Mr. Henderson, arrived at our apartment, Father brushed past him and ran down the stairs.

I wanted to ask the man a thousand questions about life in America, but his time was short, and he had many stops to make.

"Mrs. Shpann, there are some things you should take that no one will tell you about who hasn't been there. Rope, for instance, for a clothesline. Seeds to plant, as large a Thermos as you can handle. Dried fruit; western peanut butter, if you can find some on the black market. Japanese peanut butter is not palatable. They mix it with soybean powder, but you will need protein, so eat it anyway. Also, take as much salt and sugar as you can get away with. Hard-milled soap that will last a long time. A musical instrument. Money, of course. A few valuables to trade or barter with, such as earrings or an extra wristwatch."

At this point, Mother took off her watch and handed it to me. "Yours," she murmured. "It belonged to your grandmother, you know."

Mr. Henderson didn't approve of such sentimentality. "I warn you, Mrs. Shpann, a watch is a necessity. Also, it'll be a long, hard walk to the barracks. Don't pack more than you can carry, but you can find ways to pin or tie items to your clothing so you can take more." He slipped some money into Mother's hand. "I know what it's like there, Mrs. Shpann, believe me." Despite her polite protests, Mr. Henderson closed her fist around the two bills. Wincing in pain, she nodded her thank-you. "Whatever is vital to your mind, body, and spirit, carry with you. God knows, you'll need it."

Mother was strong. Her body would survive, her mind also, but her spirit? We just didn't know, especially since Father barely spoke to her.

We had only days left to live together as a family, and we were at each other's throats. I wish I'd been kinder to Mother, but the hurt I felt at her betrayal sank into my soul like sand in the sea, and I had no heart for what she was feeling—her guilt, her loneliness, her fear of the frightening unknown that spread endlessly out in front of her.

Somewhere in the midnight thoughts that keep a person's eyes wide open in the dark, I felt a stab of grief that Mother was leaving us to care for ourselves. Dovid was always on my mind those weeks, fueling the realization that sooner or later, everyone I loved would leave me.

The week before Mother left, I asked Erich, "What's REACT doing about the internment camps?"

"Plenty. They've infiltrated some of them. REACTors smuggle in supplies and information. I'll find out more when we know which camp Mother's going to." That boosted my own sagging spirit, but of course, I couldn't tell Mother.

Before my sixteenth birthday she and two hundred others of various nationalities reported to the American Country Club on Great Western Road. From there, they'd be trucked to a bombed-out campus in Chaipei, just north of the International Settlement. All of them were bent with their loads. Chinese and Japanese people watched the parade, witnessing their disgrace, some taunting the internees.

"Now you're the same as us," one man called in a trembling voice, "poor and doubled over like a peasant."

Not all of them were heartless, though. One of the internees, a woman hobbling on swollen legs, dropped her water canteen. A Japanese man rushed forward to pick it up and tucked it into the crook of her arm, backing away and bowing in respect for her age. I watched all this through tears that were like a tattered veil.

Father, Erich, and I carried Mother's things as far as we were allowed to go, then settled them in her free arm, on her back, in her pockets, under her hat. She could barely lift the bulging suitcase an inch off the ground. Mother had never been demonstrative in public, and she wasn't about to create an emotional scene with so many people watching us. She brushed her dry lips across Erich's cheek, across mine, gave Father a lingering look, and marched forward, never glancing back.

Suddenly Father broke through the crowd despite a Japanese guard trying to prod him back with the butt of his rifle. Father pushed the guard away. *They'll shoot him!* I thought. We'll be left without either parent. Selfish. Mother had always reminded me how selfish I was. Dovid, too.

Father reached Mother just before she boarded the bus. I don't know what he said to her, but I was sure his words would sustain her in the loneliness and despair of the camp. I had to believe that. Otherwise she'd never come back to us.

If Mother thought she and I were alike in our impetuousness, she would be horrified to see how little of her Austrian sense of order I actually inherited. I never realized how much effort she'd given over to keeping our little box fit for living in. Within a week of her leaving us, we could barely walk across the floor, even with the mattresses rolled up. Laundry was a wretched burden, since the few clothes we had needed to be washed every two or three days. We had no hot water, and precious little soap. We hung wet clothes on a rope strung across our room, dodged drops, and stepped around puddles. The room smelled musty all the time.

"Do me a favor and don't get dirty," I warned Erich. He was gone more and more hours. Working with REACT? He wouldn't tell me. How he snuck past the ghetto guards in the black of night was a mystery. All I knew was that when I asked him about my next REACT assignment, he clamped his hand over my mouth and hissed, "Shhh. Too dangerous for you."

And so I scrubbed out my frustration on the laundry washboard. Father was no problem in the laundry department; he rarely changed his underthings. I think he was embarrassed to have me wash them. He began practicing again. The Kawashimas must have been going loony with the repetition and the unceasing music pounding the walls. I certainly was. But they never complained, bless their hearts.

The music didn't earn Father a fen.

"We can't live on the few coins I get from my deliveries," Erich growled. I remembered how even when things were lots better in our beautiful wedding cake room in the International Settlement, Erich used to joke, "You call this living?" *This*, in the ghetto, without Mother, definitely wasn't.

I realized how hard Mother had worked to make something out of nothing for our meals. Coal briquettes were scarce, cooking gas and electricity impossible to come by, so I began using briquettes molded of coal dust and sand and straw—a foul mishmash that nearly asphyxiated us with its acrid fumes. Matches were hard to find. Everything we desperately needed was in short supply. We even bought toilet paper by the square and used it sparingly. "Only for major productions," Erich said. He was a master of black humor tinged with white rage.

"Erich, remember the breakfast scones we used to eat? Dotted with bits of orange marmalade or loganberries? Oh, and eggs fried in fresh creamery butter until their golden suns barely jiggled on our plates, remember?"

"Don't, that's torture," Erich said.

"I know." Because for breakfast in the ghetto we ate *pao-fan*, which was nothing more than a runny cereal made from reheating and mashing last night's rice. If we had a pinch of sugar to add, we went ecstatic, or a splash of soybean milk, or a tangy pickle. We craved flavor, texture, any scant crumb of variety.

Hunger was the topic in every language. The Kadoorie School ran out of food to serve us for lunch, so in our Jewish studies, Mr. Rosen made a whole lesson out of the Hebrew proverb "Without bread, there is no Torah; without Torah, there is no bread." That reminded me of the Yiddish proverb Dovid had told me: "Love is good, but it's better with bread." And Mr. Hsu, the letter writer, had taught me to write the character *fu*, "happiness."

"You see, young lady? The character for happiness is formed around the idea of a full stomach. How can one be happy if one's stomach is as hollow as a gourd?"

Very good question. In the third week after Mother left, I announced to Father and Erich, "Starting tomorrow we go to the Ward Road Home for supper every night." They barely raised an eyebrow.

Tanya and Mrs. Mogelevsky and thousands of other starving people were already taking their evening meal at the homes. So as the chill and soggy winds returned, we bundled up in our tattered winter coats and mittens with half the fingers gone to slog through the slush.

"And for nothing," Erich complained. "What? For a bowl of hot vegetable stew with a few strands of stringy meat, all of it swimming in grease?"

In a rare burst of my old optimism, I told Erich and Father, "The grease is good. We need the fat." That earned me a pair of scowls.

At the home we filled up on hot tea and our slice of bread. I tore mine into at least twenty bites and let each one melt on my tongue, while Erich rolled his bread and violently stuffed the whole thing in his mouth. No more did he stash away half his meal for a midnight snack. "Who knows? I might not be alive by midnight." More black humor. His hunger, his anger, had no relief.

Father barely noticed how demeaning this miserable handout was. To him it was only a minor intermission in the violin concerto. The orchestra continued playing in his memory. We watched him counting, counting. Every so often his face snapped to attention at his cue to come in on the concerto. He'd sit up straighter and close his eyes and sway a bit with the music in his mind. How I wished I could be lost in something as thoroughly as he could, but I didn't have that privilege. I was the mother, the daughter, the sister, the cook, the housekeeper, the laundress, *and* the student.

Life was very unfair. We had heard that U.S. troops had landed in Normandy, France, that there was a Resistance uprising in Paris. Others in our ghetto dared to dream that the war would end soon; but for us, hope was lost. I thought of Erich's words, *"Lucky man, Dovid."* He was out of this misery, and I was deep in mine.

Mother was allowed a one-page letter per month, going each way. Erich and I worked on our letter to her a little every day, writing in the tiniest possible hand. I told her the homey details of my days—the stinky coal briquettes, my studies, Tanya's latest love-struck wedding plans, as if anybody could plan a future here. I wrote in my letter,

> Today I passed a bunch of the yeshiva boys on the street and winked at poor Shlomo until he blushed like a tomato. Do you still think I should have married him? Oh, and Mrs. Mogelev-sky is collecting scraps and patches to make Tanya's trousseau. She'll look like a ragamuffin on their wedding night!

All of this nonsense yammering helped to tame some of my anger, which I gave up a little morsel at a time. Too much, too fast, would have left me feeling exposed, like when ice hits a tender tooth.

I made my parts of the letter to Mother funny, suspecting

that her life in the camp and the agony of being separated from us weren't easy to bear. At least the three of us were together; she was alone.

We waited for her first letter so we'd know where to send ours. It came nine long weeks after she left, slipped under our door by some courageous soul:

Dear Ones, First, I am well, no need to worry. We are encamped in the Great China University, which hasn't been occupied since the bombings in 1932 and again in 1937. You can imagine the condition things are in. Ilse, remember what you said about Chinese toilets? There are 50 women in my barracks. We have formed quite a community. We've given our empty days some structure. Everyone has a job. There's not much need for an English teacher, as we are mostly Americans. (Are you laughing? I hope so.) I am a cook for the midday meal. So far we have enough food, although my first job of the day is to sort through the rice grain by grain. You never know what organic or inorganic substances might be in it. Use your imagination. Rats are everywhere. We bake with bean flour, which turns out a very ugly brownish bread difficult to digest. It's palatable if you leave it outside in the sun to toast. A smear of jam is welcome from time to time. Meat is scarce, and when we get it, we are never sure what animal it comes from. Some say it is the sad remains of the Japanese cavalry's stable. I am out of space on my allotted sheet of paper. Please write to me, dear ones. I miss you so. Jakob? Write to me.

Your devoted wife and mother, Frieda

We read the letter aloud to Father. He said little, but slipped it under his pillow until he thought we were fast asleep. I peeked from behind my curtain and found him reading the letter again and again by the sliver of moonlight our miserly window allowed.

Mother's next letter was odd. She left out spaces between some of the words:

Dearsshoemaker heretuesday. Waterfromoutside.
Sickneeds. Booksclockbulbs visit 1 permonthcome.
Familieshere, 3 babiesourhope. Youforgiveme? Needbadly.
Priestsmonksnuns. Manycountries, butfewjews. 2 ladyfriends
comfortlifesaver. Winterlongcold. Blanketcoatgloves?
IlseschoolKawashimas? Erichpeachesmaking $? Enoughtoeat?
    Jakob?
    Awaitingletter. Muchneeded. Lovetoall.
    WifemotherFrieda

For someone who loved language and careful diction, she'd made a mess of this.

"She's probably losing her mind in that camp," Erich said.

Swaddled in our blankets, our teeth chattering, we pored over this letter, trying to decipher it and read between the lines. We gave Father the gist of our translation. "Mother's doing okay, she's got some lady friends who are a comfort to her, plus three babies who provide hope for the future. But she's desperate to hear from us and worries about whether Erich's getting enough work so we're not starving to death."

I didn't mean for this to hurt Father, but I saw by the look on his gaunt face that it did. Quickly, I pointed to the second line of Mother's letter. "See this? We think this means we're allowed to visit her once a month. I'll go to the International Red Cross tomorrow to find out how. Oh, and Mother says there are things they need in the camp—medicines, blankets, books, lightbulbs, a clock. Maybe we can bring them when we visit."

"We will have to sell something to buy them," Father said, eyes closed. "What have we left to sell?"

Behind Father's back Erich mouthed, "A violin," but aloud he said, "People are there from a lot of countries, which means they must have gotten some new internees because the last letter said they were mostly Americans. A bunch of Catholics, but not many Jews."

"And she asks if we've forgiven her, Father." I pointed to his name in the letter.

Father ran his finger over the poignant extravagance of that one word, that whole lonely paragraph in the jungle of run-together fragments: "Jakob?"

"I don't get the first part, though," I said. "What does she mean by shoemakerheretuesday. Waterfromoutside?"

Erich scribbled out the jumble of words in the margin of a newspaper, moving the various parts around. I looked over his shoulder. The meaning kept eluding both of us. Suddenly I jumped up. "I see it now! She's telling us how to get something inside the camp. A shoemaker goes to the camp on Tuesdays, and Chinese water carriers go in, too. If we can get to them, we can send her things she needs, at least letters to lift her spirits. Sure. That's it. I'll get right on it."

"How?" Father asked, and Erich jumped in. "I have connections."

"I'm afraid to ask," Father murmured. He gathered up his coat and gloves. "I'm going for a walk." He glanced back to make sure The Violin would be safe alone with us.

As his footsteps echoed on the stairs I asked, "How come REACT hasn't given me a new assignment, Erich?"

"How should I know? You think they tell me anything?"

"Maybe I muddled the trip to Hangchow."

"No, no, Ilse. It went better than expected. Gerhardt just doesn't want to put you in any further danger." He looked away, avoiding my eyes.

"Erich Shpann! You've told them to leave me alone, haven't you? And you're still working for them. Why shouldn't I?"

"You've done too much already, Ilse. And the stakes are getting higher."

"You had no business speaking for me, Erich."

"For you? Nah. For me. I got you into this. I couldn't live with myself if you got caught. It's worse for women in those Japanese prisons, believe me. I've heard plenty. You're still not out of the woods, Ilse. Keep your eyes open."

"You, too," I murmured.

"I'm always careful, don't worry."

But I knew he was taking unimaginable risks every day.

The mystery of Mother's strange letter was solved. An International Red Cross worker told us that the Japanese imposed new rules, just in case they hadn't been quite inhospitable enough to their honored guests. Now a letter couldn't exceed twenty-five words, and each word was censored. Unbelievable—some fiend actually sat in a heated office and counted every word on every letter going in and out of that camp.

My face was burned by the wind, but the coat and hat and gloves staved off the freezing dampness as I waited for Mr. Hsu, the letter writer, to finish with his customer. The anxious man sat on the bamboo stool, twisting his hat and stamping his unstockinged feet against the threat of frostbite. I watched Mr. Hsu start the letter three different times, carefully laying each mistake into a bamboo basket tied to his table.

When the man left with his letter, calm and satisfied, I climbed onto Mr. Hsu's stool, enviously eyeing the sheets of clean newsprint with only two or three characters on each. I had a hundred purposes for that paper. I reached into the basket.

"Ah-ah. Not trash, young miss. See this sign?" He tapped the note on the basket, written in a flourish of Chinese characters I hadn't yet learned. "Please allow me to translate. 'You must respect paper with written words.'"

"Yes, yes, but are you going to let it go to waste?"

"Not to waste. My brother-in-law Chao goes all over the city collecting such papers. It is an ancient custom, a respect for scholarship. When he has a goodly pile, he burns them respectfully. We have a saying: 'He who rescues a thousand characters from being trodden under a heavy foot adds a year to his life.'"

"That's lovely, Mr. Hsu." Lovely or not, I couldn't help coveting that glorious, underused white paper that could become letters to Mother, sheet music for Father's compositions, kindling, or even stuffing for our holey shoes. He saw me eyeing the paper, and handed me a crisp, clean sheet to take home.

"Thank you, Mr. Hsu. You can't imagine what this means to me. May I ask you a question?"

Mr. Hsu waved behind me. "No one waiting. Please, ask."

"How can I contact the coolie who pushes the water cart into the Chaipei internment camp?"

Mr. Hsu carefully considered his spoken words as much as his written ones. He took a long time to answer. "Why must you know this?"

"My mother's there."

"I am so sorry, young miss, so sorry indeed."

"And she needs, well they all need, some medicines and food and books. You're a letter writer, Mr. Hsu. You can appreciate this. We are only allowed to send her one twenty-five-word letter a month. What can we possibly say in only twenty-five words?"

"Much, if the words are well chosen. But I understand." He scanned the gray sky in an arc. I noticed a few ice crystals on his beard, around his pink mouth. He stayed silent a long time, in the midst of the noise and confusion and clanging of the streets. I crawled into the tunnel of his silence, taking comfort there. Maybe shivering in the air heavy with the sleet of Shanghai, he was transported to Australia, where he told me he'd gone to university in the early 1900s. It was summer there while we shivered; maybe he warmed himself with the memory.

Finally completing his arc of the sky, his eyes settled on me again. "Come back in one week. Chao will have the answer."

There was so little in our apartment, and nothing of value to sell for Mother's supplies. Except books. I snatched up all of Mother's English textbooks, the atlas, and our German novels, including the one the underground had given me for my Hangchow trip. I'd read *The Magic Mountain* three times already; enough was enough.

The Lion Bookshop was empty when I slammed the bundle of books down on the counter. "You can have them all for ten dollars American."

Mr. Blau made a halfhearted effort to bargain with me, but Germans just don't have the stomach for haggling, and in the end, I left with a ten-dollar bill.

Next I wrote Mother a letter, covering every inch of Mr. Hsu's paper with breezy banter and jokes and poems and stick-figure cartoons and every scrap of news I could dredge up. I planned to smuggle it in with the supplies, pleased at the image of her taking an entire evening to read it. I hoped she'd believe I'd forgiven her for her deception. I hadn't, not entirely, but what did it matter at this point?

Then all I could do was wait, with the money and letter ready to go, until Mr. Hsu's brother-in-law had the information for me.

That night the apartment seemed darker than usual, and forbidding. The Kawashimas had gone to bed. God only knew where Erich was, and Father was probably propped up in a booth at a Viennese café, pouring the fifth cup of water over his lifeless tea leaves. I was utterly alone.

I huddled on my mattress, wrapped in a coat and three blankets—mine, Erich's, and Father's. My feet were jammed into two pairs of Molly O'Toole's wool socks that were thick and prickly with years' worth of darning thread in every which color. No, they were Michael O'Halloran's socks, not Molly O'Toole's.

And just as my head dropped to my shoulder I was jarred awake by the first relentless wail of air-raid sirens.

Father hurried home to me with the news: "American bombs have fallen."

"Oh, Father!"

He grabbed my bundled shoulders and danced me around the room. "No, no, Daughter, this is good news! Americans, our liberators!"

"Yes?"

"That is, if they don't kill us first."

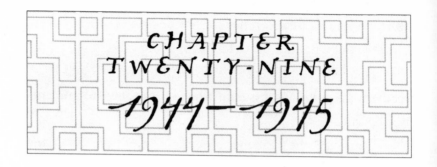

CHAPTER TWENTY-NINE
1944—1945

Chao, Mr. Hsu's brother-in-law, staked out the Chaipei camp so we'd know just when the water carrier would be there. Erich forged a letter to Miss Hartwich, the headmistress of my school, saying I had an appointment with an eye doctor. "Ilse does not see things clearly," Erich wrote, for his own amusement. He signed Father's name to the letter.

To leave the ghetto, I had to get permission from Ghoya, the King of the Jews. I dabbed a bit of Mother's old lipstick over my eyelid and rubbed it until it was puffy. In Ghoya's office, I squinted and winked piteously and said, "Pinkeye. It's very contagious, sir. I must get to an eye doctor, a specialist." That got his attention. He wrote a pass and dropped it on the floor so he wouldn't have to come close to my sickly eye.

With the pass in hand, I met up with Liu outside the Hongkew gates, and we hitchhiked to Chaipei. Liu whistled for a friend so we could ride part way, bouncing on bags of rice in his rickety wagon.

"Is he a relative?" I asked Liu.

"Uncle, cousin, brother." He pressed two fingers together. "We work like this." That meant Liu would be sharing a cut of his portion for this enterprise.

I'd converted the ten dollars from the sale of Mother's books into a five and five ones—seven dollars for Mother, and the rest for traveling, bartering, and bribery.

Liu negotiated with the water coolie in rapid-fire sparks of language. I didn't catch a single word between these two ace con men, but suddenly Liu snatched three dollars out of my hand and waved it under the nose of the coolie, then stuck the money in his own waistband next to the knife. The deal, as well as I could figure out, was that the waterman was to deliver my envelope with the name Molly O'Toole on it. Inside was my letter and seven American dollars. He'd get a dollar just for taking the envelope into the camp. If he succeeded in getting it to an American camp leader and it wasn't intercepted by a Japanese guard, he'd get the second dollar. It was all on the honor system. Liu trusted him—honor among thieves—so what choice did I have?

We waited behind some trees, Liu chattering away in Chinese. Whatever he was saying, the boy was a natural-born storyteller.

Twenty minutes later, the man came back with a grin on his face and his palm out for the second dollar.

Liu explained, "He gave to a Jesus man, missy. Good as gold."

On the way into the kitchen, the water carrier had wheeled his cart in front of the preacher, slipping the envelope into the man's pocket so smoothly that only a twinkle in the preacher's eye revealed that he'd received it. Liu's rendition of a twinkle looked like he had a cinder in his eye, but I got the general idea.

Now the water carrier pocketed the second dollar. Liu, of course, kept the last dollar. Success for all!

The night gathered around us, nearly warm and not as humid as usual, promising better times. There hadn't been streetlights for ages, and even the dim lights in the houses across the lane were gone because of blackout curtains for the air raids. American air strikes were stepping up and getting ever closer. The Allies aimed at crippling Japanese shipping lanes and supplies and arms. We shielded our eyes from blinding flashes in the night and woke to keening sirens. Buildings shook. If we were outside, we ran for shelter in a doorway. We lived at sea level, so no underground shelters protected us.

Inside our building, the impact propelled us across the room, and the bombs loosened ceiling plaster and shattered windows. Another reason to be grateful for our puny little window. It was too compact to break.

How strange—despite the constant fear, our lives were improving a bit because relief had begun to trickle into the ghetto. Laura Margolies, the American social worker, had pressured her country to use neutral Switzerland as a go-between. So finally, the Joint Distribution Committee could send money where we needed it desperately. Meat, of course, was still a distant memory, but Mr. Schmaltzer fired up his ovens on Tuesdays and Fridays to bake a few beautiful breads again. He hired me for two hours a week to replace Mother. There was still very little sugar or butter, so no cakes or sweet rolls appeared on our shelves; but the aroma of baking bread and the sight of those golden and mahogany loaves raised my spirits and mellowed my anger at Mother.

Some nights I lay awake waiting for the air-raid sirens and debated with myself. I pictured the debate as a boxing match.

Ilse the Reasonable would bound out of her corner spewing this argument: "Is it so terrible that Mother had a husband before Father? Lots of women marry twice. If I had the chance, I'd sure run off to America and wait for Dovid to find me on those golden streets. And if he never did, someday I'd meet a wonderful man, an American GI, maybe. Shouldn't we grab all the happiness we can?"

Ilse the Unforgiving would fire back: "The problem isn't that she had a husband before Father. The problem is she never divorced him! Why? Did she want to stay connected to him? Maybe, but the real problem is that she lied to all of us, even her parents. She let her whole life, *our* lives, be a masquerade. She made fools of us, especially Father. And look where those lies landed us today."

Hard blows fell, and I'd be convinced that Ilse the Unforgiving had won that round of the match. I'd press my eyes closed and await sleep. But Ilse the Reasonable would spring out of her corner and get in a few little punches as well: "Would you have been happier knowing all along that Mother was technically an American citizen, which put the whole family in danger? Better to know? Or is ignorance bliss, as the saying goes?"

Good point.

Night after night the matches raged, until one night, in the twilight between alert and asleep, Reasonable and Unforgiving met in the center of the ring and came to a startling agreement: "Yes, Mother should have divorced that man, but she didn't, and years passed, and maybe she thought it mattered less. But deep down, she must have been frightened that we'd learn her secret. She'd made her choice to hide the truth, both to protect herself from our disapproval, and to protect us from knowing something that would hurt us terribly. Maybe what we saw as deceit was also Mother's act of generosity."

Now that everything was out in the open, I realized what a terrible burden it must have been for her to carry the load all alone. We might have heard and healed and helped years ago.

Finally, the two warring camps in my mind shook hands and said together, "What else could Mother have done?" I suppose she could have, should have, divorced Michael

O'Halloran, but maybe in her shoes I'd have done the same thing she did—run away and leave it all behind.

Mr. and Mrs. Kawashima came by with a cake the size of Mother's compact. "Merry Chriss-a-muss," Mrs. K said. They were Shintos and wouldn't have known that we Jews didn't celebrate the Christian holiday. Father was about to set them straight, but I hugged Mrs. K and graciously accepted the cake and divided it geometrically so that each of us could have a sliver of precisely the same size when Erich came home.

That night he didn't come home at all, the first night he'd stayed away since Mother left. Father searched for him, but it was hopeless in the dark streets and crush of people in Hongkew. Besides, he'd probably fled the ghetto and could have been anywhere in the vast city.

We wrestled through sleepless nights. Father, Tanya, and I searched for Erich four full days. Our nerves were wound as tight as the strings of The Violin, and there was no sign of him *anywhere*.

Liu, yes, he'd find Erich for us!

Winter and summer, Liu was dressed just the same—in shorts and a knit shirt buttoned to the neck, no jacket—but now there was something new, a pair of combat boots at least three sizes too big. These he proudly displayed, showing me how he'd stuffed them with newspaper to take up the miles of space his feet didn't occupy. What drunken soldier had he stolen them from? I clucked over his boots the way we might have admired someone's new Mercedes in Vienna, and when I had him quite buttered up, I pulled out a photo of Erich. "Have you seen this one today?"

"Elder brother," he said. His intelligent eyes bored into the photo.

"Can you find him for me?"

Liu grinned at me. "Can do, missy, can do, can do, can do!"

But it was the one thing Liu *couldn't* do.

Not knowing where else to turn, we left the ghetto. Father and I talked Ghoya into a pass on the pretense of his playing a concert. We bent to the wind and walked all the way to the Beth Aharon shul to see the rebbe. Inside, it was blessedly warm and dark and velvety-quiet except for the muffled chanting of the students in the next room.

The old man listened patiently to our story, stroking his beard. His lively eyes reflected Father's worry. "Reb Shpann, my boys are free to walk the streets; they study as they walk. Each pound of the pavement drives deeper into their heads the words, they shouldn't forget a single one. You have maybe a picture of your son?"

Father handed him the photograph, already five years old but the best we had.

"My boys will look low and high, Reb Shpann. As the Holy Book says, 'If you save one life, it is as if you saved the world.'"

Three more days dragged by with no word.

A dozen times a day I asked at all the cafés, the homes,

the shops, the soccer fields. No one could remember seeing Erich in at least a week. Fear began to grow into a hard rope knot in my stomach.

Desperate, I took a giant risk and tapped the code at the door of the godown where REACT met. Gerhardt opened the door a crack, recognized me, and slammed it again. I banged ferociously until he gave up and grudgingly let me slip in the door rather than risk a ruckus that would bring Japanese soldiers to the godown.

"I know, I know, I shouldn't have come, but it's about Erich. He's gone missing."

Rolf came up behind Gerhardt. "Probably went under the bridge."

"Not drowned!" I cried.

"Nah. Just an expression. Means he got *out*. Without a pass. Just melted into the throng out there. *Pftt.*" He swirled his finger upward, implying that Erich had just billowed up like chimney smoke and vanished in the crystal air. "Or maybe they've got him in one of the jails. He'll turn up, one way or another."

Meaning alive, or dead.

Eight days passed. My nerves were unraveling like an old wool sweater, and it didn't help that The Violin screeched hour after hour. People down in the lane kept looking up to see where the suffering cats were being tortured. The urge was overwhelming to tear The Violin out of Father's arms and smash it against the windowsill. In desperation I turned to Mrs. Kawashima, the closest thing I had to a mother those days.

"It's Erich," I wailed, my hot tears soaking her blouse. "Nearly two weeks he's been missing. I don't know what to do!"

She listened and gently stroked my shoulder. "My husband has friend, very important person, from when Mr. Kawashima is translator. I will ask my husband if he can make careful question."

"Oh, would you?"

Her smile was warm, but her face was serious. "We must do in the Oriental way. Not march forward and ask too much, too soon, you understand? Very delicate."

And so we invited Mr. and Mrs. Kawashima to share our skimpy supper of half-rotten vegetables and potatoes cut so thin you could see daylight through them. Although the Kawashimas were just as poor as we were, somehow they managed to bring a fat orange—the only fresh fruit safe to eat because of its thick skin. We tore the orange into wedges. Mr. and Mrs. K ate their portions behind the cover of their hands, then daintily plucked the pulp out of their teeth with an ivory toothpick, in the Japanese style. Father and I just slurped and sucked, all the way to the bitter rinds.

After the formality of supper, Father bowed and got down to business. "Kawashima-san, forgive me for asking this of you, but is there anything you can do about my son, Erich? He's disappeared on the outside, with no pass and no papers."

My heart stopped, waiting for Mr. K's answer.

He picked a morsel of orange off his shirt. "Permit me to talk to the assistant deputy director of Sanitation."

"Oh, Mr. Kawashima, what on earth could Sanitation do?" I asked rudely. Father flashed me a disapproving look.

But this was man-to-man business, and Mr. K bowed toward Father. "My friend knows someone whose cousin is a regimental organizer in the Pao Chia, at the Hongkew gates. My friend's friend's cousin will study the situation, Shpann-san."

"We are enjoy your music," Mrs. K said. "So much prettier than noise outside."

Four more days crawled by, and finally Mr. K came with the news that his Sanitation friend's cousin had found Erich!

"Is he in danger, Kawashima-san?" Father asked.

"Little is known, Shpann-san. My sources are uncertain just where your son is. Maybe it is not good." His look suggested something far worse than his words did. "It is possible to get further information." Mr. K hesitated, and Mrs. K gravely nodded her encouragement. "I am grieved to tell you, Shpann-san, but there must be an exchange of money."

It seemed a bribe was necessary to oil the machinery if any progress was to be made.

"Please, Father," I begged, beyond all shame.

Father didn't even hesitate. He thrust The Violin into Mr. K's hands. "Take it. It is a worthless piece of lumber to me now, not enough wood even to burn for fuel."

Mr. K soberly cradled Father's Violin. Bowing deeply, he backed out of our apartment in silence.

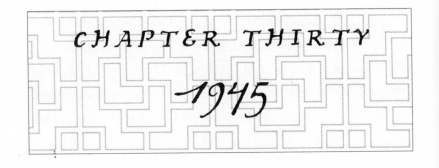

CHAPTER THIRTY
1945

Two days passed before we had any word.

"Shpann-san," Mr. Kawashima murmured, "I am sad to bring unhappy news."

Mrs. Kawashima clasped a paper-thin lilac handkerchief to her lips, signaling us to expect the worst.

"He is a political prisoner. Ward Road Jail," Mr. K said soberly.

I reeled, sinking into a chair. Everyone knew that two weeks in that dreadful place spelled death by typhus.

"What should we do, Kawashima-san?" Father asked, grasping my arm. His fingers were brittle and bony. I didn't think they could even hold a bow anymore.

"There is hope," Mr. K assured us. "On Wednesdays, sometimes the guards turn one eye away and allow family to bring food. Middle of the week, not many deliveries. Also, this saves money, you see. Very efficient." He glanced at Mrs. K, and she gazed off into the distance. "However, they will expect a small payment."

"But we have no money!" I cried, "and nothing left to sell."

"Ah, there is a solution. They know how it is with Shanghai people. Westerners, no money. Japanese, no money. Chinese, no money. But the day guard at Erich-san's cell-block has a . . . I believe American expression is sweet tooth."

Mrs. K snickered nervously behind her handkerchief.

"Sweet candy is very hard to find," Mr. K said. "He will bend rules for peppermints."

"And where are we to get peppermints in the middle of a war?" Father asked, his voice dripping with irony.

"I know, Father!"

Mr. K looked me over shrewdly, but kindly. "I see your daughter knows that the man Ghoya likes very much peppermints. He imports them from Harrod's, in London, somehow, I am told."

"I'll ask him for some," I said with confidence, remembering how he'd said, *I like redheaded girls.*"

Mr. K gave me another of his penetrating looks. "The man Ghoya does not welcome you to visit political prisoners. However, westerners can be very clever," Mr. K said, his mild voice full of craft.

After two hours of freezing in the stingy sunlight, I was finally next in line at Ghoya's office. Even outside the door it was clear that he was in a foul mood. His shouts came from all over the room while he circled his prey. When the door opened, a man staggered out, pale as parchment and no pass in hand.

"Next!" Ghoya shrieked. His secretary, one of our people, prodded me into the office with an apologetic sigh.

Ghoya was perched on the corner of his desk, with one bare foot tickling the floor. His odd, M-shaped mustache—like Hitler's, in fact—was also like a misplaced third eyebrow, and when he smiled, his eyes nearly disappeared. "A long time I haven't seen you, Redheaded Girl. Your eye is better?"

"Yes, sir."

The room was overheated, and Ghoya had two fans going to cool himself. Heating and cooling, both—what a greedy pig he was, with his hair fluttering in the wind of the fans as though he were lolling on a beach some windswept afternoon. The desk rocked on uneven legs when he shifted his weight, sending the fishbowl of peppermints tottering behind him. I was mesmerized by those candies and almost saw red and white stripes across Ghoya's homely face.

"What can the King of the Jews do for you today, ha? You want to go out? Meet a special boy, ha?"

I had my lies all planned out. "No, sir. It's my mother I want to see." This disappointed him, romantic lizard that he was. "She's in one of your excellent civil assembly centers, sir, the one in Chaipei."

"Yes, yes, we take good care."

"I'm sure, sir. And you generously allow one visit each month, too. I would dearly love to see my mother next Wednesday, sir."

"I can do this for you! What can you do for Ghoya?"

"Very little, I'm afraid, sir."

His eyes roved over me until bile rose in my throat. He hopped off the desk and circled my waist with his fat little hands. I might have been cast in bronze, so still I stood.

Ghoya said, "Skin and bone. Ghoya likes lotta meat on a girl." He dropped his hands in obvious revulsion, turned around, and stamped a pass for me. Red on white.

The peppermints. "You, you're too generous," I stammered, finally letting blood flow to my arms and legs again. "Oh, I'm ashamed to ask you one more favor. You see, my mother adores peppermints. She'd think so highly of you if she knew you'd sent two or three along with me. A special gift from you, I'd be sure to tell her."

"I import from London. Very expensive!" He wrapped his little arms around the fishbowl in a gesture that said, *Mine! You can't have any!* "We play a game, okay, Redheaded Girl?"

"Sir?"

"I shake candy bowl. Any fall out, you can take to your Jewish mama, okay?"

He tossed the bowl up above his head. Half a dozen wrapped candies sailed through the air before he caught the bowl. I scuttled to gather them all up, and while I was on the floor at his feet he dumped the entire bowl. Peppermint candy pelted me like hail.

"Ha-ha-ha!" His cackle was the sorriest excuse for laughter I'd ever heard.

I made sure to grab my pass before I left with a burglar's

booty of candies stuffed in my pockets, my shoes, my waist-band, even under my ponytail. All the way down the hall I heard his diabolical "Ha-ha-ha!" and pitied the next person in line.

At Ward Road Jail, in the cool of the morning on Wednesday, I clutched the meager bundle of food I'd scraped together by shamelessly distracting the Chinese owner of a sparse fruit stand on Housan Road. I'd pointed to the sky, wailing, "American bombers! Take cover!" and as the man tented his hand over his eyes to search the sky two puckered oranges sank into my pocket.

Oh, the glorious packages we used to get! Those American cigarettes would be such choice bribes for Japanese guards or a welcome diversion for the prisoners.

The concrete walls of Ward Road Jail loomed gray and forbidding, and made me feel like a hamster in a gigantic cage. At seven o'clock I waited inside the walls to be let into Erich's cellblock. I'd already been patted down for contraband by a guard whose lingering hands repulsed me. He and Ghoya were cut from the same slimy cloth.

He tore open the rag that bundled the food. His face lit up at the sight of the peppermints, which he handled with such tenderness you'd have thought he was caressing a newborn. Spittle formed at the corner of his mouth. "Not good for prisoners," he mewled, pocketing the candies.

Another guard led me past one cellblock after another, each cell crammed full of people. I gagged on the stench of air saturated with the rankest of human odors. The chill penetrated my bones.

In Erich's dark cell, about twenty Chinese and westerners hunched together on the concrete floor. My eyes pierced the darkness, and I made out a few women who occupied a back corner. On their knees in a circle, they formed a human curtain while one of them used a toilet built into the floor. The rest of the prisoners pretended not to notice, or no longer cared.

Nor did anyone seem to notice me standing there. It was as though they'd lost the will to move, since moving meant giving up their little plot of land—a wall to lean against, a clean patch of floor, a narrow swath to stretch out their legs, the broad back of a neighbor for support. Some of them could be dead already and still propped up. My head swam with the putrid odors and the sight of this desperate clinging to life that was less than life.

It took a while to spot Erich in the crowded cell. He and another foreigner, backed against one another, were rolling their shoulders in unison, in a pitiful attempt to exercise their stiff bodies.

"Erich," I whispered.

The suspicious eyes of a few men, trapped animals, darted about; but mostly people just ignored me. When Erich spotted me, he rolled to his knees, clearing a path toward me with his head. Someone else moved right into Erich's spot against his partner's back.

"Ilse? My God." His voice was little more than a wheeze.

I knelt to his level and thrust the oranges, the bread, a precious piece of crisp duck fat, between the narrow bars. Suddenly every starving dog picked up the scent, growled, and ripped the food out of Erich's hands. A man bit into one of the oranges, rind and all. The duck fat disappeared into the cave of an old man's mouth. I thought about Chinese fishermen who put rings around the necks of diving cormorants so the birds couldn't swallow the fish. I wanted to reach in and dig that duck fat out of the man's throat because he was old, his days were numbered. Erich desperately needed the nourishment.

I passed the Thermos of boiled water to him and stuffed a bag of tea leaves and three peppermints I'd hidden in my hair into his ragged pocket. "I'll get you out!" I hissed, squeezing his limp hand. "Please, Erich, don't lose hope. Promise me. Promise me!"

He nodded. His eyes were dark, sunken pools.

I wondered if the others would kill him for the peppermints.

Outside the prison walls, an old woman's tiny body shuddered with her dry, hacking cough as she pummeled a guard with a dead pigeon, dooming him and all his ancestors with vile Chinese curses. Whatever she was saying, I completely agreed.

U.S. air raids were getting more and more common. Sirens wailed, and we dashed for shelter wherever we could. Some ran to the Ward Road Jail and the protection of its high concrete walls, but I would rather have been blown to bits than take comfort in such a horrid place.

Tanya and my other school friends waved handkerchiefs and cheered at every B-17 bomber that soared overhead. Each plane convinced us that the war would be over soon and America would win. Americans had *always* won. But would Erich live to see it happen?

CHAPTER THIRTY-ONE

1945

"Redheaded Girl! So soon I see you again? You go out too much. Get in trouble too much. Where you want to go now?" Ghoya sat behind his gunmetal gray desk, which hadn't a single paper on it. Even the peppermint fishbowl was gone.

"Sir, please allow me to come right to the point. It's about my brother. He's in the Ward Road Jail."

"What he did?"

"Nothing, sir. It's a terrible mistake."

Ghoya jumped to his feet and pounded his desk. "No mistake! No mistake!"

"I understand, sir, but I beg you to listen to me." I stood at the foot of his desk, nearly choking on these words: "You are the King of the Jews. I implore you to be generous, like your own emperor, Hirohito. A monarch takes care of his people, sir."

He sat down again, leaning back in his swivel chair with his hands clasped behind his head and his feet propped up on the desk. He didn't look a bit regal. "What you want this time?"

"Please, sir, my brother is my family's only sustenance. As you know, my mother is gone to an internment camp."

"A *camp*? We don't have camp!"

"You're correct, as always, sir. I mean a civil assembly center, as a guest of the Japanese government. My father is a musician and isn't well. He can't find work. I only have two hours work a week. There are very few jobs in the ghetto."

"*Ghetto*? We don't have ghetto!"

"Forgive me. In Hongkew, sir. We've been taking one meal a day in a home. It's barely enough to keep some flesh on our bones. My brother has a job, sir. We all depend on his modest income. He's a delivery boy."

"Good. A boy with ambition. Like me, myself."

"Yes, sir. But my brother won't survive much longer in Ward Road. I saw him yesterday."

"Yesterday? Yesterday you visit your Jewish mama. She like peppermint from Harrods? Very expensive."

"Oh, yes, sir, more than you can imagine. After I left Chaipei, I went to see my brother, Erich, in Ward Road Jail. He's skin and bones, desperately in need of a bath and some meaty, hot soup. His spirit is nearly broken. I've heard that typhus spreads through the jail like fire."

"Ah, yes, typhus only in China. Dirty here. Not in Japan. Clean as a whistle in Japan."

Nowhere, I was getting nowhere with him.

"What your brother's name?"

I raised my head—still a chance?—and swallowed dry. "Erich Shpann, sir."

"Erich Shpann! Ghoya not like Erich Shpann!"

I felt the color drain from my face. Erich was the one who'd found and buried Mr. Shaum after Ghoya had placed him under house arrest. Word got around in the ghetto. Ghoya remembered, and now maybe I'd condemned my own brother to death.

I sighed so deeply that my spongy lungs whistled. "May I go, sir?"

Ghoya's arm shot out like Hitler's, pointing to the door. I knocked for the secretary to let me out.

In my whole life I had never felt so absolutely drained of hope as I did at that moment backing out of Ghoya's office.

I ran home to our empty apartment and buried my face in my pillow that had given up half its feathers and its linen cover years before. Hours passed. I suppose I slept, or else my daydreams were horribly vivid—all those prisoners, the dank and stench of Ward Road, Erich's raspy voice—when I awoke to a sound like fingernails or claws scraping on our door. Was Moishe back? I opened the door, expecting to shoo the cat away—and found Erich heaped on the floor.

"Erich! Good God, how did you get here?" No answer came from the ragged lump on my doorstep. *Dead?* I gently pushed his eyelids up and saw faint signs of blue-eyed movement. Not dead! "Soup, you need soup. We have some on the hot plate."

He nodded with barely a dipping of his jutted chin. I spoon-fed him a little watery potato soup, tilting his head back to pour it down his throat. It gurgled in his gullet, but after three spoonfuls, his eyes widened with gratitude.

It took every ounce of my energy to drag him down to the water closet and wrangle him into a few inches of cold water in the concrete tub. His rat-gnawed clothes peeled away like dead skin. Erich crouched in the tub, and I washed him with a sliver of soap I'd hidden just for this day. I think we were both embarrassed—Mother had always stressed modesty. But what could we do?

A neighbor ran to fetch Father at the café, and he returned just in time to help me lift Erich out of the washtub. Father burned Erich's lice-infested clothes in the tub and buried the ashes.

Back in our apartment, Erich lay curled on his mattress, wrapped in a sheet, face to the wall. How I missed Mother, who would know just what to do to bring Erich around.

Father said, "Let him be, Ilse. He needs to recover in his mind from that terrible place."

I awakened, thinking we were in an earthquake. I yanked the curtain away that separated Erich's bed from my own. His whole body was wracked with shivers.

"Father!"

He bolted up in his bed. "What! What!"

"Erich. Look at him."

Father came close, fear in his distant eyes. He touched Erich's forehead. "The boy's burning up."

Erich's eyes were small black buttons crying out to us

from deep within his red, swollen face. I ran for Mrs. Kawa-shima. One look at Erich, and her normally calm eyes blazed with fear also.

"We wash and wash him, make him cool," she whispered. "Nothing else to do."

I grabbed a basin and ran for water, sloshing it all the way back to our apartment. We began stroking Erich's arms, his neck, his face, his chest, with rags soaked in cold water and some alcohol that Mrs. Kawashima had hoarded from before the war. I placed aspirins far back in his throat and forced them down with a mouthful of water.

Erich thrashed around. Father held him down while I soothed him with memories of our childhood days in Vienna. "Remember the carousel, Erich, both of us on the same zebra? And I pushed you off when I reached out to catch the brass ring? You were so mad at me! Pookie, remember Pookie? The time she climbed inside Mother's piano? Oh, Erich! Think of peaches, how they ripped away from the pit when we bit into them. We used to see who could spit the peach pit the farthest, remember? You always won. Can you taste Mother's peach cobbler floating in cream?" Eventually I lulled him to sleep with our memories, and Mrs. K went on washing and washing him for hours. She hadn't slept more than an hour or two in days.

Then dark red eruptions appeared on Erich's chest, and the diagnosis was confirmed: typhus. Jail fever.

"Carried from one person in the cell to the next by lice," Doctor Stolz explained out in our hall. "Many do not survive, I'm afraid."

I staggered to the wall. Never before did I truly believe that either my brother or I would die before our parents.

Doctor Stolz gently clasped my arm, checked my pulse, probed the glands in my neck, then tried to reassure Father and me. "The boy is young, otherwise sturdy, and you are good caretakers. He has slightly better than a fifty-fifty chance."

"Those are terrible odds," I protested, and the doctor sadly nodded.

Father didn't like the odds any more than I did, but he said, "Pull yourself together, Daughter, for Erich's sake."

We composed ourselves and went back to the apartment to relieve Mrs. K.

Father said, "It'll take a couple of weeks, Son, but you'll be well after that, I promise you."

What good was such an empty promise?

Erich's fever dipped and spiked and dipped for two weeks. At its peak he ranted madly, yelling German gibberish, as though he'd gone back to baby talk, and those were the times that scared me most. I held his head and spooned rice gruel or potato soup into his mouth, or weak tea. His shoulders were sharp blades; I could count his ribs, which felt thin enough to snap like kindling. I slept for minutes at a time because I was sure that he needed me night and day.

I wasn't even seventeen? Impossible. I felt like an old woman. My only comfort was that Dovid would not see me like this—wispy-haired, staggering on swollen feet, plagued with tremors and headaches, and all hollowed out.

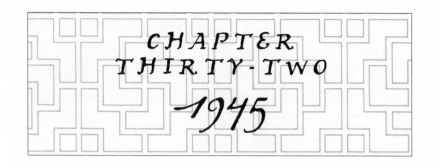

CHAPTER THIRTY-TWO

1945

Suddenly one morning, Erich sat up and announced, "The fever's broken."

I pressed my palm to his head, his ears, his arms. Gone the hot, clammy skin.

"I'm hungry," Erich said, surprising even himself.

"Well, aren't we all." I handed him a stale heel of bread I'd been saving for him, and he devoured it in seconds, licking the crumbs from his palm. He swung his legs off the mattress and tried to raise himself to a standing position.

Father rushed to his side. "Slowly, Son. You're not ready yet."

Erich flopped back down, sweating from the exertion. Tears of relief swelled in my eyes. He'd beaten the odds; he'd survived typhus. We'd *all* live to see the end of this war. Mother, too? Who knew?

After that, as Erich slowly recovered, he, Father, and I grew together, crowding one another like bulbs planted too close. Our lives gradually improved as a thin stream of foreign money reached the ghetto. Our bellies less hollow, I dared to believe the war would grind to an end soon and we could all go home. Not home, really. Enough news from Europe had seeped through the filter of the blockade to convince us that we Jews would not be returning to Austria. America was the home Erich and I allowed ourselves to dream about again.

Erich was still too weak to pedal Peaches to work, even though there was a demand for his services now that more food was reaching us in Hongkew. I'd been running his route. It was easy toting the fifty pound sacks of rice and flour because I'd been lifting my brother all the weeks of his illness.

We lived on nearly nothing. Father no longer showed even a twinge of guilt over bringing in no money. I wondered: When the war ends, will he be able to reclaim the life he's so carelessly shed? Will he even want to find another violin that fits him so perfectly as the one he's given up?

And then another question plagued me: When Mother comes home, and Father begins acting like a working father again, can I give up the power I've inherited from them and slip back down to being the dutiful daughter? Do I even want to?

We heard that an internment camp was hit by an errant U.S. bomb, rousing Father from his lethargy long enough to cry, "My God! Is your mother all right?" Frantic for news, we urged the Russian refugees on the outside to hound all the consulates for information. Word trickled down to us in Hongkew that it was Pootung Internment Camp that was hit, not Mother's.

So I was sick with relief, then ashamed at how low I'd sunk. I no longer cared if everyone in Pootung had been blown to bits so long as Mother's camp was spared.

The pass system loosened a little, and we visited Mother the first of every month. We told her we were plumping up, staying dry in the June deluge, cool in the heat of July. Stoic soldiers, each of us. We didn't tell her that Father sat for vacant hours staring at the wall, with The Violin's absence a *presence* that filled the room like fog. We didn't tell her that Erich had barely survived Ward Road Jail or about my humiliating visits to Ghoya's office. And especially, we did not tell her that she had left a deep crater in our lives; that we walked around its rim, afraid one of us would stumble and fall, and drag the other two down to the bottom of the canyon.

She lied to us, also: Life in the camp was easy, she said. So friendly everyone was, and they all had meaningful jobs, soft beds, plenty to eat. During our July visit she shooed Father and Erich away for a moment. "Go take a walk. Someone said there is licorice at the canteen today. You love licorice, Jakob," she said with a brittle smile. As soon as their backs were to us, she whispered, "The International Red Cross smuggled in a letter from America. Don't tell your father yet. Michael O'Halloran is trying to arrange for me to go to the United States after the war."

The buried anger flared, surprising me that its shallow grave in my soul was so close to the surface. *"You?* What about us?" I cried.

She seemed stunned by my question. "All of us, Ilse, all four. We are a family. Do you forget that? We will all go to America."

I expected Mother's news to fill me with joy. Well, it didn't. Long ago, feasting on American movies and magazines, I'd thought of that country as pure heaven. The one thing I knew for sure after struggling through nearly six years of war was that no nation—not America and not even our beloved Austria—was a perfect paradise.

I sensed Erich getting more and more restless as his strength came back. One morning he left the apartment with such iron determination that I just knew where he was heading, and I followed.

When Gerhardt opened the door for him, I pushed my way in as well.

Gerhardt shouted, "You two should never have come here!"

"I have to talk to you," Erich said.

"You're marked, Shpann. The Japs are onto your scent, and you're leading them right to our nest."

"I'll risk it."

"What gives you the right?" He turned angry eyes to me.

"Gerhardt, leave my sister alone and listen to me for a second. You think you and Rolf and the rest of you are the liberators of the Free World with REACT's mischief-making? Let me tell you, some of those men I knew in Ward Road Jail

247

were deeper into this than we ever were, Gerhardt. We're rank amateurs compared to them. Want to know what they told me?"

"No." But he listened.

"Germany surrendered. Hitler's defeated."

"Why are you the only one who knows this?" Gerhardt asked with a sneer.

"Believe me, I have this from people who are in a position to know."

"Jailbirds," Gerhardt muttered.

"Some of them did a lot of damage before they landed in Ward Road. Major damage. They say Japan's kept the news from us, but the fact is it's all over for Hitler, and the Japanese can't hold out much longer. They're hanging by a hair," Erich said. "They'll fall to the Allies in a month, six weeks at the most. But before that, they're going to come down hard on us as a last blast before it all ends."

I watched the fight drain out of Gerhardt. He rubbed his face with both hands, dragging his lower eyelids down to show bloodshot eyes. He needed sleep, and something else was bothering him while Erich talked.

"There will be tighter ghetto restrictions, no passes, more blackouts, mock food shortages, more political prisoners, brutal tortures, shootings—"

I nudged Erich in the middle of his tirade and flashed him a signal: *Look at him.*

Gerhardt sank to the bottom step and hung his hands

between his knees. "Word's filtering in from Europe about the camps."

"The concentration camps? Yeah, we know about that," Erich said impatiently.

Gerhardt's eyes blazed. "Extermination camps where people are gassed to death."

"You mean at Chelmno?" I remembered Dovid talking about that years earlier.

"Chelmno was a small operation. I'm talking about death on a huge scale. Mass graves. Ovens. Ashes floating out of the chimneys."

I grabbed Erich's arm. "Where is this happening?"

"All over," Gerhardt said gruffly. "Germany, Poland, the Sudetenland."

"How many have died this way?" Erich asked.

Gerhardt stared up at the ceiling two stories above. "Maybe a hundred thousand."

"A hundred thousand? Gerhardt, that's just impossible," I cried.

He turned his eyes to me, and what I read in them wasn't the gleam from the day he'd found me under the stone bench. No, this time it was grief, shock, horror, as he said, "Some reports from the West say a million. A million Jews exterminated like vermin."

We heard a rustling behind Gerhardt, and then a small figure materialized, still shrouded in shadows.

Madame Liang! Or at least the motorcycle girl I'd met in

Hangchow. She wore a blue sash across her chest, tied in a knot at her waist. I couldn't make out the Chinese characters on the sash.

"He's right," she said in her precise British English. "Far more dead than from the massacre at Nanking. A million, maybe more. Hitler had a most efficient killing machine, but he's through. Here, the Japanese are still pawing the dirt before they simper off when the rest of the world gets word of the atrocities."

I was swaying, reeling from shock upon shock. I braced myself on Erich's arm and stared at the girl until she said, "Your mouth is gaping open, Margaret Loeffler. Ah, you thought I was merely a figment of your imagination. I assure you, I'm real." As she came into the light, I saw a fresh wound across her cheek and the trek of tiny black stitches.

I stammered, "I thought you were in Hangchow."

"You've never seen me in Shanghai? Think. Remember the day you visited our dear Erich at Ward Road?"

"You were a prisoner in the cell with him?"

"Me? No, I'd swallow cyanide first! I was the cackling old woman in the courtyard, the one creating the distraction with the pigeon so you could get away without betraying all of us with your blithering sentimentality."

"It was my brother's life!"

Erich said, "Yeah, a month ago I thought I was dead. Surprise. I woke up alive one morning, and I like breathing in and out on a regular basis. It's habit-forming."

"Indeed, it is," the girl said. "We've all put our lives on

the line for years; we've done courageous work. Now we're too close to the finish to risk it all."

A strange look passed from her to Erich. Did they have some history between them? She said, "Now hear this, mates: Our work is through, and we're closing up shop."

Gerhardt's rage seemed to be reenergized, and he jumped to his feet, pumped with adrenaline. Turning to the girl, he said, "You, of all people, you're saying we should give up? Sit here and wait for the bombs to fall and the Yanks to lead the Japs away with their hands behind their heads? A million Jews dead in Europe, and we do *nothing*? That's Shpann's style, not mine."

"I'm not the hero you are, Gerhardt. Neither's my sister. We're out of this operation."

"Wait a minute!" I protested.

Erich clapped his hand over my mouth. "For once, Ilse, hold your tongue."

"Good advice," the girl said with a sardonic smile that obviously stretched and pained her wound. "Remember, I call the shots, and I say we rein in Rolf and the rest of them because in two months the war will be history, and I intend to be alive." She put her arm around Erich's waist and hooked her thumb into the back of his belt—a familiar gesture that obviously made him uncomfortable in front of me.

He slid away from her. "Yuming is right. We've got to stay out of jail. Another day at Ward Road, and I'd have been food for the rats. Is that what you want, you and Rolf and all of us dead before the war's over?"

Gerhardt was not giving in gently. He pounded the railing, which clanged and echoed through the empty warehouse. "I say we fight until the last Jap falls. Give them something to remember us by. Make their last days in China a fiery hell."

Erich yanked me toward him. "I'm out of it, and my sister's out of it, starting right now, and if you had any sense, you'd listen to Yuming." He pushed me toward the door, opening it a crack to make sure no one was watching us. I spotted Liu, who quickly rolled down the bank toward the river, out of sight. Erich looked back at Yuming, and we shut the door behind us.

Walking home, I leaned on my brother like a crutch and thought about Beehive day again. The man in the park, the heap of his broken bones. A beautiful sunset was wasted on me as I tried to imagine what a mountain of bones from a million corpses would look like.

In my dreams that night, I was smothered, crushed under an avalanche of those bloodless white bones fighting one another for breathing space.

CHAPTER THIRTY-THREE
1945

Gerhardt's wish came true. The last days of the occupation *were* a fiery hell, but no thanks to REACT. On July 17 American bombers missed a Japanese target. Some reports said they'd aimed at an airplane factory; others, that the Americans meant to destroy a radio transmitter that controlled Japanese shipping lanes. What difference did it really make? The bombs hit the fringe of our neighborhood instead. Home alone, I watched out the window as buildings burned to cinder or exploded into piles of wood and glass that flew everywhere.

It was stupid to go out into that flaming terror, but stupid to stay in as well. What if the fire leaped to our house? I couldn't risk being trapped in a burning building and charred alive. Rooted to the floor, I cried out, "Mother, what should I do?" and was answered by silence.

The Japanese made my dilemma easier by somehow sparing our lane, except for broken windows and wall cracks and cascading plaster.

When the barrage was over, I ventured out to help, though I wasn't sure just where I was needed.

Mr. Kawashima happened to be out for his daily stroll when the first bomb fell. He'd ducked into a store and escaped the worst injuries from the blast, but a dagger of glass from the store's shattered window impaled his cheek, a millimeter below his left eye.

I found him laid out in a vegetable garden amid dozens of other victims, a four-inch blade of glass sticking out of his face. He lay with his hands folded serenely over his chest, but the wound must have hurt terribly and frightened him even more.

"Oh, Mr. Kawashima! What can I do for you?"

He opened and closed his eyes, afraid to speak, afraid to move his face too much.

Erich showed up, along with Tanya. We did what little we could to help the doctors and nurses frantically treating five hundred wounded victims in courtyards and gardens without any catgut for sutures or sulfa for infection, and painkillers were a godsend we also didn't have.

What a daylight nightmare of scorched skin, severed limbs, pools of blood, the patient weeping of the wounded and the last gasps of the dying. It was way too much for a girl my age to see and hear. My head told me, *Run! Run away from this horror.* My heart whispered a different command, so I stayed, even after Tanya gave up and went home shaking. I kept my hands busy easing what little I could of the misery all around me.

The exhausted medics had no time for Mr. Kawashima's minor injury. Erich knelt beside Mr. K and started to pull the shard out, but a doctor zoomed by and shouted, "Don't touch. Nerve damage. Lose an eye."

"I'll bring Mrs. Kawashima to you," I murmured. Nothing else to do. That's what she'd told me when Erich was burning up with fever. "Nothing else to do."

Mr. Kawashima turned out to be one of the lucky ones. After two days of his lying in the garden, a doctor from the Japanese hospital was finally able to extract the glass properly. Mr. K.'s cheek drooped after that, as if he'd had a stroke, and he needed to keep wiping saliva from the corner of his lips, but at least he didn't end up with a dark hole where one eye should have been.

Thirty Jews were among the two hundred and fifty who'd died in the bombing. One funeral procession blended into the next. The streets, eerily still for Hongkew, echoed with the moans of victims still hanging on to life, the keening of Chinese mourners, and the Kaddish prayers of our people.

And yet, and yet, we clung to the belief that a hit this severe meant the war was coming to an end. Through the pain and grief we counted the days until there would be an Allied victory in the Pacific.

And it happened. Word sifted down to us: The war was over! Our six horrible years of exile from our own home, of being strangers in our new one, of isolation and starvation—finally it was coming to an end. We all poured out of our houses, wild with joy to find the streets clear of Japanese soldiers. We tore down Japanese flags from every public building, burned them or ripped them into strips as victory headbands, or rolled them into bandages. We replaced the dreaded rising sun banners with beautiful red, white, and blue American and British flags, rained down upon us from the Allied planes. Firecrackers turned the night sky into a brilliant kaleidoscope, and we danced up and down the Bund until dawn. Even Father danced, although I could swear that he'd lost his sense of rhythm.

Did Mother and the others in the camps have this glorious news? Surely they heard the riotous rejoicing in the streets, even behind their barbed-wire fences. They must have known that it was only a matter of hours until we stormed their gates and brought them all home to us. The war was over! We'd survived! Soon we'd all go home—wherever home was.

Mrs. Kawashima tapped lightly at our open door. "This is very happy time," she beamed. Her voice rose just a bit, apparently to signal Mr. K, and then we heard the Kawashimas' door click open on the other side of the plywood wall. "My husband," she announced proudly. "He has present for you, to celebrate."

Mr. K came into our apartment with The Violin in his hand, bowed deeply, and silently placed it in Father's outstretched arms.

I can't imagine what the Kawashimas sacrificed to save Father's violin. I fell into Mrs. K's arms, releasing tears I'd banked for days, weeks, and Father's grateful tears oiled The Violin's thirsty wood. He held it across his knees, the bow pointed toward the floor, as if waiting for his cue to come in on a concerto.

Later, describing the scene to Erich, Father said, "My children, it was like a soldier thinking he'd lost his best friend in the heat of battle, then finding him alive. *Alive!*"

"Best friend?" I asked. "What about Mother?"

Ashamed, Father quickly said, "The only reunion that will please me more is when we have your mother home with us. All of us together again, very soon."

And then we found out that the war *wasn't* over after all. What a cruel joke! In a final effort to subdue us, the Japanese streamed back into the city in full force, tightening restrictions and patrols in our bombed-out ghetto for another ten days. No one knew what horrors were going on in the last days of Bridge House and Ward Road Jail.

We gritted our teeth in fierce determination until, without fanfare, a notice was nailed to posts that the ghetto pass system had been canceled. Ghoya slithered away, and within two days we hardly saw a Japanese soldier anywhere in Shanghai.

In mid-August the internment camps were thrown open, and we brought Mother home.

CHAPTER THIRTY-FOUR
1945

"I've seen you every day of the last year, but when I opened my eyes, you were always gone," Mother said. "Now I can't get enough of your handsome faces." She reached gnarled hands toward Erich's cheek and mine, on either side of the table.

"It's good to have you home, Mother," Erich said. In time he'd have to tell her about Ward Road and typhus, but not this first day.

Her back was to Father, who refused to join us at the table. Though he'd sworn his happiness would be complete only when Mother came home, having her among us reminded him of how hurt he'd been by her betrayal. Those first strange hours he couldn't bring himself to welcome her home wholeheartedly, and so he lay on his bed, *their* bed, with his arm over his eyes, as if the ten-watt bulb might blind him.

Mother inspected every corner of the apartment from her throne at the head of the table. I'd tried to tidy up, but she must have noticed the corners of the room blackened with accumulated dirt that I'd never quite scraped clean and the light fixture above the table speckled with dead bugs. In Vienna, Father used to say, "Frieda Shpann was born with a dishrag in one hand and a mop in the other." Now she generously ignored the grime and disorder of our apartment. Nor did she mention all her beloved books, which I'd sold, or the way our room-divider sheets hung haphazardly, or the mattresses with cotton stuffing and straw poking through little holes I'd never gotten around to sewing up. She simply said, "Can you imagine how happy I am to be home? All we did, the other women and I, was talk about our families waiting for us on the outside." She paused, hoping Father would say something, but he didn't. Mother motioned toward him, as if to ask, *Is he always like this? What should I do?* Glances bounced among the three of us, but no one said a word about Father.

We heard the Kawashimas next door quietly padding around their room in their stockinged feet, their teacups tinkling and their companionable voices rainwater-soft. Since the bombing, Mr. K's speech was a bit slurred.

On our side of the plywood wall, the tension grew thick.

Mother and Father needed time together alone, that's all, I reassured myself. Look how much time I'd needed to stop crying about Dovid; how many sleepless nights, how many mental boxing matches, to give up my own hurt and anger, to forgive Mother.

She was so frail, a gust of wind could have blown her over. Her hair was nearly white with a few auburn streaks.

Making up for Father, I reached over and hugged her. "I'm so glad to have you home!" My eyes jumped to Father, back to Mother. We would have to leave them alone to talk to one another before the tension cracked our crumbling walls. I yanked Erich's arm and said, "We have deliveries to make, so we'll just take off and be back in an hour or two."

Mother's eyes widened in alarm: *Don't leave me alone with him*, she seemed to say, and Erich pointed to the second chair.

"Sit," he commanded.

Mother cleared her throat. "Jakob, come to the table. This is a family matter, and we must discuss it. Jakob? Can you hear me?"

"I can, Frieda."

"Come, then."

I jumped up to give Father the chair. It took monumental strength for Father to make the short trip from the bed to the table, but he managed it. He hadn't shaved in two days, and his eyes seemed to have sunk farther into their skeletal sockets.

"Jakob, it has been too long since I've heard a violin played with any artistry. Please, as a homecoming gift, will you play for us?"

Father glanced over at The Violin resting atop two rolled-up mattresses. Maybe he was conjuring it to leap across the room and tuck itself under his chin, since the divide between him and that corner of the room was so enormous. Mother sensed this and brought him The Violin, unsnapping its case and lifting it gently into his arms. She took a handkerchief from her pocket and placed it on the chin rest. I knew she would stand there for an hour, for a week, if necessary, until he raised The Violin to his chin and began to play.

His eyes were hauntingly sad. He drew the bow across the strings, frowning at the impure notes that forced him to tune the instrument. And then he played an adagio from a Brahms sonata, so sweet and melancholy that even Erich had tears in his eyes.

"That was sublime, Jakob," Mother said, pulling her chair over next to him. "Now we will talk, yes?"

Father rested The Violin on the floor between his knees, and we four began a heartbreaking conversation, the gist of it being this: Michael O'Halloran had arranged for all of us to go to America. Mother said, "There are certain privileges that go with this sad situation, just as there were conse-quences this past year I've been separated from you, my dear ones." He'd borrowed money, which he would wire to us by the end of September for our passage. Once we got to Amer-ica, to that place called Santa Rosa, he'd have official divorce papers ready, and Mother and Father would immediately marry according to the laws of California, America.

I watched Father trying to form the question that plagued us all. "And he still loves you, this Michael O'Halloran?"

Mother shook her head. "No, Jakob. He remembers the girl I used to be, but I am not that person anymore. He knows where my heart is."

"Then why is he doing this for us, Frieda? He is not a Jew. Tell me, why?"

"Michael O'Halloran understands what Hitler—may God curse him a thousand times—what this monster has done to Europe, to all of us Jews. Michael only wants to help."

"I do not understand such a man, such a saint," Father said gruffly.

"God knows, we've seen enough cruel people through these war years, haven't we, Jakob? Why should we question one who behaves like a decent human being? Now, first thing tomorrow, we must apply for proper papers so we can sail to America as soon as possible."

"I will not go to America."

Mother didn't respond for a long time. The Kawashimas next door grew as silent as snow so we'd forget they were there. Then Mother said firmly, "The children and I are going to America. There is no place else for us. I would like you to come with us." She touched Father's arm; he shrank away. "But if you cannot, Jakob, please understand this clearly: We are going anyway."

The shock of that statement was enough to propel Erich and me out of the apartment so our parents could have time to work all this through.

Our days passed in a fury of activity, and we were never sure how things rested with our parents. Who could think about it, with so much to do? We all needed to get our papers processed, book passage, and buy a few clothes with the newly released Hebrew Benevolent Society money so we wouldn't look like paupers when we landed in prosperous America. I wished I could step on American soil in loafers with shiny copper pennies on their tops; but instead, I'd be wearing the shoes I got for my harrowing Hangchow train trip in the autumn of 1943. Father nailed the heel back on crooked, so I looked a little drunk when I walked.

Also, we had to sell our few possessions to the even-poorer Chinese—our mattresses, our patched clothes and much-darned woolly socks, our rickety table and chairs and bookshelf, and one tin pot. The only thing left was Peaches.

"Erich, how much do you think you can get for a rusty, old, oil-guzzling bike like Peaches?"

He pretended to think hard. "It's got one good tire on it, not too patched. The bell works, if you like buzzers. I'd say, optimistically, it's worth about a bucket of stale sweat."

"I know where I can get that much for you."

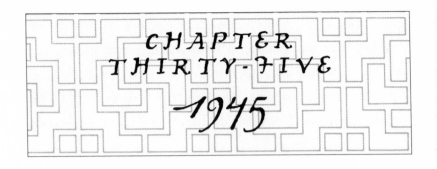

CHAPTER THIRTY-FIVE
1945

"Prepare yourself for the chickens and the spitting tobacco," I warned Mother and Father on their way to the train for an overnight in Hangchow.

They'd get to see the West Lake that I'd missed entirely when I made my odd little trip to that city for REACT. Erich and I hoped that twenty-four hours together would help Mother and Father work things out before our ship was to sail. Positive sign—Father actually left The Violin behind, which meant Mother would only have to compete with the music in his head, not in his hands.

As soon as they left for the depot, I packed our few remaining things while Erich fiddled some Viennese tunes, not too badly.

"Why, you *do* have some musical talent. You've done a terrific job of hiding it from Father all these years. I'm still hopeless, though."

"Maybe I'll take up the violin again in America," he teased. We were both giddy with freedom from our parents and with the limitless possibilities awaiting us in America. Still, we worried about Mother and Father.

"Oh, Erich, I can't bear to leave Father behind. Do you think he'll come with us?"

"Don't know. I haven't understood a single move he's made in years. Tell me I'm not like our father, Ilse."

"He can be very sweet." I remembered the times he saved me from Reb Chaim's clutches, and how readily he'd sacrificed The Violin, his most precious possession, for Erich's safety. "It wouldn't hurt you to be a little sweeter, you know."

"Ach, what for?" Erich said, dispelling the sappy thought.

"Because no American girl will want to marry such a serious grouch."

"Marry? Who said anything about marriage?"

"Erich, be honest. Are you in love with that—I don't know what to call her—Yuming person?"

His answer was one of those saucy American expressions we'd been practicing: "You've got rocks in your head!"

"Come on, I saw the two of you together that day. She likes you, and you looked at her, well, not the way you glare at Tanya."

"Tanya's a pain in the neck!" Erich glanced off in the distance, or maybe in the past, and said, "Yuming is an interesting girl, if you like tripping on the edge of a cliff. She won't live to see twenty. Not for me anymore." He pulled himself back to the present and waggled his eyebrows à la Groucho Marx. "I'll forget her when some busty American girl wraps her arms around my skinny body."

This lighthearted banter felt wonderful after so many years of urgency and growling bellies. I stacked our few dishes to give to Mrs. Kawashima. My wild curls were visible in the mirror of a dinner plate, gleaming again since Mother had come home. The relief of turning all the domestic responsibilities over to her made me feel almost like a carefree girl again. And I'd thought I might not want to give up the *power*? Ha!

I wondered, *Should I say anything to Erich?* I did: "Truth is, I'm a little bit scared to leave Shanghai. Aren't you?"

He shrugged, refusing to admit his own fears. Or had staring down the corridor of death in that jail cell scared away all his fears?

"Six years we've been here, Erich. A third of our lives."

"And, *jeepers creepers,* haven't they been a barrel of laughs?"

Outside, the brisk autumn breeze blew away the memory of the bitter cold and sizzling heat and moldy rain we'd lived through all those years. I pedaled Peaches, hearing her gears grind painfully. As usual, Liu materialized when I whistled. How many other people was he always on call for, or were there a half-dozen identical Lius scattered around Shanghai?

His impish little-boy grin of six years ago had given way to a slack-jawed lankiness. The sure-footed trot I used to have trouble keeping up with had turned into a swagger, and his face had finally grown to fit his huge eyes, but his teeth were still a mess. I suspected that he'd graduated from the knife to a gun, but I didn't want to know for sure.

Crooking my finger, I lured him over. During the years of our strange friendship I'd picked up some Chinese, and he'd picked up a lot more English, especially from American soldiers.

"Hallo, what's up, missy?"

"Liu, this week we leave Shanghai. Sunday, two o'clock our ship sails."

"Yeah, yeah, we go to America!"

"Not *we*. Me, with my family."

"What for do I stay here, missy?"

"This is where you belong. Your life's here."

"No ma, no pa, no whiskey, no soda!"

I inched Peaches toward him. "You want this?"

He circled the bike like a man about to buy a new automobile. He picked some gravel out of the tire, tugged at the grinding chain, spun the tired pedals. "Old bike. Not worth two cents."

"I'm not selling it. I'm giving it to you."

Liu slowly raised his head to stare at me, his mop of hair hanging in his eyes. "For no money?"

"Free. You almost stole it once. Now it's yours, if you want it."

He turned his back to me and stuffed his hands into his waistband. Crusty elbows jutted out. Suddenly I saw what was going on. No one had ever given him such a grand gift, and he didn't know how to handle it.

"Liu? Look at me." He turned his head like a suspicious cat, like Moishe used to, peering at me over his shoulder.

"You take the bike." I rolled it toward him, wrapped his hands around the handlebars. "Now, you say, '*xie xie*, thank you,' and you ride away. Here, climb on."

He shook his head, hair flying, and refused to get on the bike. We argued back and forth until I realized that this crook who knew his way around every swindle in Shanghai, and who'd probably left a body or two bloating in the Whangpoo, didn't know how to ride a bike!

I stabbed at his arm until he swung his leg over the bike and dropped down onto its ripped seat while I balanced the handlebars. One foot on each pedal, he began spinning them fiendishly.

"Goes nowhere!" he complained.

"That's because the kickstand's down. See?" I lifted it and continued to support the handlebars until he caught his balance. Well, I should have known—he was a born tightrope walker. Two tumbles, and he conquered the bicycle and rode off into the wind, yelling, "Bye-bye, missy, so long."

We searched Mother's and Father's faces for a clue as to how it had all gone in Hangchow.

"And?" I asked.

"So?" Erich asked.

Father cleared his throat for an announcement, and I braced myself for the worst—Father in China, us six thousand miles away in a new life.

Mother stood behind him, one hand on his shoulder, as if they were posing for a formal photograph. Father said,

"Your mother must teach me English before we arrive in Santa Rosa. I do not want to sound like a foreigner and embarrass all of you."

I rushed toward him and threw my arms around him. Erich, with his usual reserve, said, "Excellent."

Mother had tears in her eyes. "So, let us begin with the alphabet, Jakob. Say after me, *a, b, c, d, e . . .*"

Tanya's wedding had been scheduled for October, but she hurried the plans along so I wouldn't miss the big day. Mr. Bauman's entire café had to be made kosher under Reb Chaim's supervision. Tanya and I shrank from the blasting heat of the blowtorch as we helped the rebbe scorch Mr. Bauman's oven.

Proudly Tanya said, "Everything will be prepared according to strict Orthodox dietary laws. Also our home!"

Reb Chaim actually took his black coat off and rolled up his starched shirtsleeves to *kasher* the kitchen. His arms were covered in black hair, darker even than his beard.

Our job finished, Tanya ran to the butcher shop for a slab of brisket for the wedding dinner, and I stayed to clean up. The rebbe rolled his sleeves down over his furry arms, and I said, "Reb Chaim, something's on my mind. May I ask you a question?"

"Ah, the young lady with a mind of her own. Your father warned me! Yes, ask, ask."

"I'm happy that Tanya is Shlomo's *beshert*," *and I'm not*, but I didn't add this.

269

"So, if you are happy, why are you looking so sad?"

"I wondered, are we allowed to celebrate when so many of our people are dead in Europe? Their bodies are barely cold, Reb Chaim." My eyes filled with tears. To our horror more and more details were reaching us. Camps had been liberated: Dachau, . . . Auschwitz. We were seeing pictures of walking skeletons. The numbers of the dead were in the millions. All those bones.

Reb Chaim buttoned his sleeves and tugged at his beard before he looked me in the face sternly, his glasses lopsided on his nose. "The Holy One, blessed be He, commands that we rejoice with bride and groom, and so we rejoice."

I nodded, vowing to try.

"Even if our hearts are breaking," the rebbe added.

The magnificent red hat with the peacock feather was long gone from the milliner's window, so Tanya had to settle for my plain straw hat from the Hangchow trip, and also my yellow suit, which her mother altered to fit Tanya. She'd plumped up again on food Shlomo brought her from the yeshiva. Erich watched her duck-waddle and said, "She's got hips for bearing. They'll probably have fourteen snively little Shlomos."

The wedding! The day after my seventeenth birthday and two nights before we were to sail for America, everyone we knew jammed into Mr. Bauman's café, where Dovid and I had spent so many hours. How long ago? Two years.

Men on one side, women on the other, we flocked around the chuppah, the wedding canopy, behind Tanya and Shlomo, stepping back to allow room for Tanya to make the customary seven circles around her groom.

"May you soon bring many children into the shelter of your love," Reb Chaim said.

Tanya played the modest bride with fluttering eyelashes and hands clasped at her waist, but Shlomo strutted through his wedding as though he'd invented the role of bridegroom for a Hollywood movie. A klezmer trio played sweetly mournful tunes for the wedding ceremony, and raucous ones as soon as Reb Chaim officially pronounced Tanya and Shlomo husband and wife. Shlomo stomped the wedding glass to bits, and we all shouted, "Mazel tov! Mazel tov!" Mr. Bauman smiled generously, although I think it was his very last glass.

There was wild dancing, men with men, women with women, and a cake, which Mr. Schmaltzer baked in Mr. Bauman's kosher kitchen. Although the cake turned out smaller than Tanya's grand vision, it was the best we could do with our whole community's combined rations of eggs and flour and butter and sugar, and every guest had a bite.

Nothing so robust, so noisy, so messy, so purely joyful, so European, had happened in our Chinese ghetto for eons.

CHAPTER THIRTY-SIX
1945

The hardest thing about leaving Shanghai was saying good-bye to Tanya. She tore herself away from her new husband to spend the last hours with me. Well, he was already study-ing like a fiend, anyway, two days after their wedding. Tanya and I walked the streets of Shanghai with our arms locked. Me, a teenager on her way to America, and Tanya, already a married woman!

"Well?" I asked, curious about her wedding night. She wouldn't tell me a thing, when there was so much I needed to know. All I got out of her was, "My Shlomo, such a gentle-man he is," and she quickly changed the subject: "Oh, how I will miss you." She stopped to hug me again and again.

"You've been my dearest friend in the world." My voice sounded creamy with tears.

"Except for Dovid Ruzevich," she teased.

Him. I hadn't stopped thinking about him, but in my heart I knew our paths would never cross again. "Oh, he was only a childhood crush."

Tanya pushed me just far enough away so she could see my tear-streaked face. "Don't say that, Ilse. He was your first love, which makes him unforgettable. Look for his face in America. You'll meet again, you'll see, and so will *we*. Another two months, we'll be settled in Canada, Shlomo and I, so you'll come to visit us. Canada's just up the street from America."

We strolled along the Bund. The harbor was filling with merchant ships once again, no longer just the Japanese warships. My palm was tented to shade my eyes, and I glanced across the Whangpoo River over at Pootung, with its low, seedy warehouses and burned-out factories.

Tanya said, "We'll miss this awful place when our stomachs are full and we're sleeping on feather beds so high you need a stool to climb up."

"Miss China? No."

"Oh, admit it, Ilse."

"Never!"

But as we walked through the streets—both the grand concourse of the Bund and the dark back alleys—I thought a lot about what I was leaving. All the years I'd lived in Shanghai, six plus two months, I'd been a westerner in the East, a redheaded, pale-faced foreigner among millions of natives who belonged where I didn't. I'd always thought of China as a way station, a place to park our bodies until we could get *home*, wherever home turned out to be. And now . . .

If I should go back to China as an adult, I wondered,

would I find it frozen in time, just as it looked when I was leaving, just as it's looked for a hundred years, a thousand years?

The street markets with the eels and monkeys and frogs and wild, wing-flapping fowl and storm clouds of swarming flies.

The rickshaw pullers dripping sweat, napping between runs with their coolie hats pulled over their faces.

The Buddhist pagodas carving out long, thin swaths of the sky, and the old-fashioned buildings with their eaves curled upward like gigantic pixie toes.

The apothecaries promising cures in a thousand ginger jars, boxes, vials, tubes, and cellophane bags brimming with mysterious, dried brown herbs and powdered parts of exotic animals.

Street kitchens where live sea urchins and shrimp finally give up their fight in a giant pan sizzling over hot coals. Roasting gingko nuts. The sugary sweet potatoes. Clackety chopsticks.

And the people, millions and millions of them walking, bicycling, pulling and pushing weighted loads, all owning their space so surely that they never collided with one another. In six years I'd never learned that trick.

Ghoya. Hunger and cold. Bayoneted guards, passes, armbands, blackouts, bombs. Night soil. REACT.

Mr. Hsu, the letter writer. Reb Chaim and Mr. Bauman. The Kawashimas.

All of it, good and bad, a safe haven for the duration of the war. Otherwise we'd be dead.

"Yes, I'll miss China," I told Tanya with a deep sigh. We swung our arms and skipped down the Bund, and the Chinese stared at us carefree, show-offy foreigners, as they always had. "But I'm ready to go."

The dinky room suddenly looked huge with all our things gone. We gave Erich's mattress to Chang, so the beggar wouldn't have to sleep on the bare street any longer.

I made one last visit to Mr. Hsu's table.

"Have you come to visit your heart's song?" he asked.

"My heart's song is silent," I told him, thinking of Dovid.

"A young lady has many songs in her life. With patience you learn to sing them."

"Yes, but I'm afraid I've never quite gotten the knack of patience, Mr. Hsu."

"This does not surprise me." The old gentleman smiled warmly. "I will not see you again in this world, but we will remember one another, will we not? I give you something to take with you to America." He brushed some beautiful characters on a piece of yellowed paper. "It is an ancient proverb to remind you that we are not so far apart." He chanted it to me, moving my fingers over each character, and translated: "'The way is one, the winds blow together.'"

And then, after six endless years, it was suddenly time to leave China. Mrs. Kawashima soaked two handkerchiefs with tears. She clung to Mr. K's arm at the dock, both of them dwarfed by the giant ship that would glide us across the ocean. "Maybe someday we go to America," Mr. K said, giving us his new, lopsided smile.

Mother and Father thanked them for all their kindnesses. "For taking care of my children while I was away," Mother said, hugging Mrs. Kawashima.

Father bowed. "Kawashima-san, I cannot thank you properly for the gift of my violin."

Mr. K bowed toward Father and petted The Violin's case as if it were a patient dog waiting at Father's feet. "My honor to know you, Shpann-san." Both men bowed again, and Father quickly ushered Mother aboard the ship. They'd never been comfortable with farewells.

Erich was already aboard, waving to me from the deck and shouting into the wind, "Come on, you'll miss the boat, Ilse!"

Mrs. Kawashima tucked a round bundle under my arm, proud of her new prosperity to afford a whole loaf of crusty white bread. "Take for a bite if you get hungry," she said through her tears. "See? I tell you long time ago, *maskee!* Everything turn out all right."

"I'll never forget you, Mrs. Kawashima." I kissed both her cheeks and started up the gangplank. There were hordes of people everywhere, and the ship's whistle warning that we'd be pulling up anchor soon.

One familiar voice cut through the throng. "Wait, missy, wait for me!" I spun around, and there was Liu parting the crowd. He rode Peaches like a unicycle, with his arms straight up in the air, just as I'd seen once in a circus. He tried to pedal up the gangplank, but a white-uniformed crewman blocked Liu's path. I watched a ferocious argument between the two and made my way down to the dock to rescue the crewman from Liu's badgering and the loss of his wallet.

"Liu, what are you doing here?" The crewman backed away, clearly relieved.

"We go to America," Liu said merrily.

"I go. You don't have a ticket."

He waved an envelope. Did he have a ticket after all? Was he planning to go with us to set up his con artist enterprise in America! Was America ready for the likes of Liu?

The envelope was gray and crumpled and sweat-stained. "Somebody give this to me for you, missy. Long time ago."

"Who?"

Liu shrugged his shoulders, motioning someone tall, sad-eyed. What an actor! "He told me, when missy leave China, give her." Still straddling Peaches, the combat boots he'd finally grown into flat on the ground, Liu said, "Good trip to America, missy. I watch out for Shanghai till you come back home and whistle."

Home. This city was as much home as anywhere, yet never *home*.

"Bye-bye, missy, so long," Liu called to me, saluting like an American soldier as he stormed his way through the crowd on Peaches.

I scurried up the gangplank seconds before the crew pulled it up into the belly of the ship.

Most of the passengers were on the deck watching as we sailed out of port. The voices on the shore called out: "Bon voyage!" "Auf Wiedersehen!" "Sayonara!" "Zàijiàn!" But it was the silence and solitude I craved, not the farewell party, so I locked myself in my cabin. Beside my bed was a crystal pitcher of pure, cold water, so clear that I could read the clock on the other side of the room through the water and glass, even in the late-afternoon shadows.

Liu's envelope looked like something salvaged from the trash, which was Liu's home, of course. Clutching the envelope, I lay down on crisp white sheets that transported me to a distant memory of Vienna—sticky, wet starch and Mother's hot iron sizzling on a sheet still damp from the clothesline. Clean, everything in my cabin was clean and clear and quiet.

I turned the splotched envelope front and back. No writing on it. Liu said someone had given it to him for me, but the one thing I knew for sure about Liu was that you couldn't believe most of what he said. Maybe he was embarrassed to admit that it was really from himself. I tried to imagine what might be inside. Certainly not a farewell letter, since Liu couldn't read or write a word, not even his own name in his own language, and anyway, a good-bye letter would be too sentimental for hard-boiled Liu. And it wouldn't be money, since he had none, although I suspected he had a cache of booty stashed away under a pylon somewhere, and one day he'd be rich as a warlord, growing fat on sweetmeats and hundred-year-old eggs.

Liu, yes, I'd even miss the conniving bandit.

I opened the envelope, and out slid a rough sheet of sketch paper. Charcoal from the face side had bled through. My trembling hands unfolded the paper with my heart racing in anticipation. And there it was—a delicate sketch of a short bridge that dipped and rose gracefully like a harp. Smudges of black represented a Japanese couple strolling arm-in-arm across the bridge, suspended above gently rolling waters. In neat block letters the artist had captioned the sketch:

Kobe, Springtime

D.R. 1943

The motors churned, and the ship's whistle signaled that we were pulling out of port. Soon Shanghai would be a dot on the far horizon. So much behind. So much ahead. *Maskee!*

Author's Note

When I was five in 1947, I lived on a Caribbean island. The Dominican Republic—for its own self-serving reasons—was one of the few countries that opened its borders to Holocaust survivors without passports and without quotas or restrictions. My mother, then a young widow, worked for the American embassy as a translator for the Jewish refugees who poured into that country. She met a Polish man who had survived Hitler by escaping to Shanghai. Now he needed an American wife so he could immigrate to the United States. In an act of enormous generosity and faith, my mother married the man—and divorced him within weeks, according to their agreement. He never lived with us, and I have no idea what became of him once he settled in America.

Since then I've had a simmering curiosity about the Jewish experience in Shanghai. What was it like for European Jews to live in so alien a place as China? How did it feel to be stateless? To know that your homeland would never welcome you home again? To wonder where on earth *was* your home? And if the Japanese were aligned with Hitler, why did they shelter some twenty thousand Jews in their midst?

Years ago my husband and I went to Shanghai to capture details for this book. We visited a site dedicated to the "stateless Jews of Europe," in a lovely new park greening the ghetto of Hongkew (now spelled Hongkou). With tears running down our faces, we stood in front of that granite monument and read the words engraved in English, Hebrew, and Chinese. Around us stood a respectful half circle of elderly Chinese people who must have been puzzled by the reactions of such sentimental foreigners. This book, *Shanghai Shadows*, began to take form that day, and it has been with me every day since.

Two bits of information tie up the loose ends of this story. You have read about an entire Polish yeshiva (rabbinical seminary) of some four hundred students, teachers, and their families, all of whom were transported to Shanghai through the defiant courage of a Japanese diplomat named Chiune Sugihara. These men of the Mirrer Yeshiva continued their religious studies with barely an eyeblink of interruption. I've wondered where all those future rabbis ended up, and now I can account for one of them. My youngest son married a woman whose father grew up in Toronto. As a boy, he studied at a religious school—under the rigorous tutelage of one of those rabbis who survived Poland, moved through

Japan and China, and resettled in Canada. Many years passed, and now my husband and I share a beautiful grand-daughter with that Toronto man.

But that's still not the end of the story. In May 2002 I presented a paper on Jewish children's literature at an inter-national symposium in Nanjing, China. My novel sprang to life during that trip. And so with the publication of *Shanghai Shadows*, and the birth of Hannah Miriam, to whom this book is dedicated, the story begun more than a half century ago comes full circle.

Selected Bibliography

BOOKS

Barber, Noel. *The Fall of Shanghai: The Splendor and Squalor of the Imperial City of Trade, and the 1949 Revolution That Swept an Era Away*. New York: Coward, McCann & Geohagen, 1979.

Bloomfield, Sara J., ed. *Flight and Rescue*. Washington: United States Holocaust Memorial Museum, 2001.

Davidson-Houston, J. V. *Yellow Creek: The Story of Shanghai*. New York: Putnam, 1962.

Dong, Stella. *Shanghai: The Rise and Fall of a Decadent City*. New York: William Morrow, 2000.

Gilkey, Langdon. *Shantung Compound: The Story of Men and Women Under Pressure*. New York: Harper & Row, 1966.

Heppner, Ernest G. *Shanghai Refuge: A Memoir of the World War II Jewish Ghetto*. Lincoln: University of Nebraska Press, 1993.

Kranzler, David. *Japanese, Nazis & Jews: The Jewish Refugee Community of Shanghai, 1938–1945*. New York: Yeshiva University Press, 1976.

Lu, Hanchao. *Beyond the Neon Lights: Everyday Shanghai in the Early Twentieth Century*. Berkeley: University of California Press, 1999.

Mochizuki, Ken. *Passage to Freedom: The Sugihara Story*. New York: Lee & Low Books, 1997.

Pan, Guang, ed. *The Jews in Shanghai*. Shanghai: Shanghai Pictorial Publishing House, 1995.

Pan, Lynn. *Tracing it Home: A Chinese Journey*. New York and Tokyo: Kodansha International, 1993.

Patent, Gregory. *Shanghai Passage*. New York: Clarion Books, 1990.

Sergeant, Harriet. *Shanghai: Collision Point of Cultures, 1918–1939*. New York: Crown, 1990.

Tobias, Sigmund. *Strange Haven: A Jewish Childhood in Wartime Shanghai*. Chicago: University of Illinois Press, 1999.

Tokayer, Marvin, and Mary Swartz. *The Fugu Plan: The Untold Story of the Japanese and the Jews During World War II*. New York and London: Paddington Press, 1979.

Wei, Betty Peh-T'i. *Shanghai: Crucible of Modern China*. London: Oxford University Press, 1987.

PERIODICALS AND PAMPHLETS

Hannah, Norman B. "Strudel in Shanghai." *National Jewish Monthly* (October 1979): 35–47.

"Jews of Shanghai: The Story of Survival." Canadian China Society, March 21, 2002.

Kersey, Mary E. "Refugees Pour Into Shanghai." *Living Age* (October 1940): 159–163.

Kuhn, Irene Corbally. "Shanghai Revisited: A Postscript." *Gourmet* (April 1990): 102+.

"Ohel Moishe Synagogue." Jewish Refugee Memorial Hall of Shanghai, [1998?].